To Jackee
with love
mickie

terror by gaslight

terror by gaslight

more Victorian Tales of Terror

Edited by

HUGH LAMB

Taplinger Publishing Company
New York

First published in the United States in 1976 by
TAPLINGER PUBLISHING CO., INC.
New York, New York

Library of Congress Catalog Card Number: 75-27980

ISBN 0-8008-7559-1

For Christopher

Contents

Editor's Foreword

In 1891, obviously weary of the Victorian passion for spirit-ualism and the supernatural, Lionel A. Weatherly and the famous magician, J. N. Maskelyne, collaborated on a now-forgotten work explaining the inexplicable. They called their book quite simply *The Supernatural?* with great emphasis on that question mark.

Dr Weatherly was quite straightforward in his views. 'Why should we fly to the spirit world?' he asked, 'why should we hug mysticism to our bosom and, revelling in its degrading influence, ascribe to something supernatural what can so well be explained as the result of natural causation?

'The faulty and weak reasoning of the ignorant, uneducated and superstitious folk must, of course, be answerable for their implicit belief in ghosts, vampires, dream prophecy and all kinds of evil omens.'

All of which is very interesting (and insulting) but even the redoubtable Dr Weatherly could not overlook one important factor.

'That there are many educated persons who still believe in the absolute reality of all the wildest stories of magic, witch-craft and the supernatural can readily be gathered from news-paper reports and books which from time to time make their appearance.'

For the rest of the book, despite his avowed intent to lead the reader 'through the ford of scientific truth ... safely to the firm land of common sense and right judgement,' Dr Weatherly never quite got round that particular problem. And it is a problem which still defies explanation. To borrow Dr Weatherly's prejudice and argument, the backward clod who

stands on the village green expounding his belief in the hereafter can easily be explained away by those 'of common sense
and right judgement' as being merely backward and therefore
suspect. But what of the many learned men, neither fools nor
charlatans, who express just the same belief but choose the
lecture rostrum instead of the village green?

Dr Weatherly could not manage to explain it; I would not
dare to try. What is important is that for centuries clod and
sage have equally enjoyed the thought of ghosts and demons
and it is intriguing that the era that saw the massive surge forward in science and knowledge also saw an equivalent increase
in reports of the supernatural. I refer of course to the
Victorian era, time of discovery and exploration, of science
and philosophy, and of superstition and spiritualism.

Not content with their real-life horrors (Jack the Ripper,
cholera, poverty, etc.) the Victorians invented a galaxy of
fictional terrors. This was the time of the Penny Dreadful, when
'orrible murders were enjoyed in stage re-enactments at the
music hall, and a time when authors excelled themselves at
producing a string of literary horrors.

In *Victorian Tales of Terror*, I brought together some of the
best and most neglected stories from this splendid era. *Terror
by Gaslight* is a further selection from the days of the Victorian
tale of terror and I trust it will prove as entertaining as its
predecessor.

Of the authors included in this volume, three appeared in
the first book but still deserve a second showing through the
quality of their stories. Grant Allen contributes an early tale
of voodoo, Dick Donovan a splendid tale of the sea and
Erckmann-Chatrian a chilling tale of the evil eye.

Some names may be familiar: Fitz James O'Brien is still
fairly well known but *The Wondersmith* is one of his least
reprinted tales. Andrew Lang, again, is not unfamiliar but his
short stories are certainly among the most unobtainable in the
genre. I have been fortunate in finding one for this anthology.
Rhoda Broughton enjoyed a faint revival in the 1940s when
her volume of ghost stories was reprinted but she is still very
much neglected, despite being a relative of the great Sheridan
le Fanu. It has been my privilege to introduce R. Murray

Gilchrist in one of my anthologies this year and he is probably the most unusual contributor to this particular collection.

Of the rest, I am confident that connoisseur and casual reader will find many new names in the contents list. In fact, of the fourteen stories in this anthology only three have ever appeared in a similar work and the rest have been out of print since their original publication before the turn of the century.

There is real vintage terror in this book. Though separated from us by two wars and a world changed beyond recognition, Victorian terror still retains its unique potency. And despite Dr Weatherly, can still be enjoyed for what it was—one of the finest periods in the history of the tale of terror.

HUGH LAMB
Sutton, Surrey.

Purification

by

ROBERT BARR

As the first story in this second collection of Victorian tales of terror, Purification *is ideal, set as it is in the salon atmosphere of nineteenth-century Paris.*

Robert Barr (1850-1912) is now almost forgotten, though he was one of the most popular magazine contributors of his day. Born in Glasgow, he emigrated to Canada, where he worked as the headmaster of a public school, then went on to Detroit as a reporter on the Free Press. In 1881 he returned to England and started work as a journalist. This culminated in his partnership with Jerome K. Jerome on The Idler, *a magazine which ran from 1892 to 1897 and produced much good material.*

Though he was a prolific writer of fiction, Barr was better known in his lifetime for his journalism, much of which he wrote under the name of Luke Sharp. However, his short stories have stood the test of time and, in particular, those in his collection Revenge! *(1896) from which 'Purification' is taken. They deal with human passions and greed, and the basic element in them all is revenge. For the time they were written, they have a realism and lack of literary pretence that shows the journalistic background of their writer. I hope you will enjoy this particular story; it is one of the best of the tales in Barr's book, and certainly one of the best in this collection.*

Eugène Caspilier sat at one of the metal tables of the Café Égalité, allowing the water from the carafe to filter slowly through a lump of sugar and a perforated spoon into his glass

of absinthe. It was not an expression of discontent that was to
be seen on the face of Caspilier, but rather a fleeting shade of
unhappiness which showed he was a man to whom the world
was being unkind. On the opposite side of the little round table
sat his friend and sympathizing companion, Henri Lacour. He
sipped his absinthe slowly, as absinthe should be sipped, and it
was evident that he was deeply concerned with the problem
that confronted his comrade.

'Why, in Heaven's name, did you marry her? That, surely,
was not necessary.'

Eugène shrugged his shoulders. The shrug said plainly, 'Why,
indeed? Ask me an easier one.'

For some moments there was silence between the two. Henri
did not seem to expect any other reply than the expressive
shrug, and each man consumed his beverage dreamily.

'A man must live,' said Caspilier at last; 'and the profession
of decadent poet is not a lucrative one. Of course there is un-
dying fame in the future, but then we must have our absinthe
in the present. Why did I marry her, you ask? I was the victim
of my environment. I must write poetry; to write poetry, I
must live; to live, I must have money; to get money, I was
forced to marry. Valdorême is one of the best pastry-cooks in
Paris; is it my fault, then, that the Parisians have a greater love
for pastry than for poetry? Am I to blame that her wares are
more sought for at her shop than are mine at the booksellers'?
I would willingly have shared the income of the shop with her
without the folly of marriage, but Valdorême has strange, barbaric notions which were not overturnable by civilized reason.
Still my action was not wholly mercenary, nor indeed mainly
so. There was a rhythm about her name that pleased me. Then
she is a Russian, and my country and hers were at that moment
in each other's arms, so I proposed to Valdorême that we
follow the national example. But, alas! Henri, my friend, I
find that even ten years' residence in Paris will not eliminate
the savage from the nature of a Russian. In spite of the name
that sounds like the soft flow of a rich mellow wine, my wife
is little better than a barbarian. When I told her about Denise,
she acted like a mad woman—drove me into the streets.'

'But why did you tell her about Denise?'

'*Pourquoi?* How I hate that word! Why! Why!! Why!!! It dogs one's actions like a bloodhound, eternally yelping for a reason. It seems to me that all my life I have had to account to an inquiring why. I don't know why I told her; it did not appear to be a matter requiring any thought or consideration. I spoke merely because Denise came into my mind at the moment. But after that, the deluge; I shudder when I think of it.'

'Again the why?' said the poet's friend. 'Why not cease to think of conciliating your wife? Russians are unreasoning aborigines. Why not take up life in a simple poetic way with Denise, and avoid the Rue de Russie altogether?'

Caspilier sighed gently. Here fate struck him hard. 'Alas! my friend, it is impossible. Denise is an artist's model, and those brutes of painters who get such prices for their daubs, pay her so little each week that her wages would hardly keep me in food and drink. My paper, pens, and ink I can get at the cafés, but how am I to clothe myself? If Valdorême would but make us a small allowance, we could be so happy. Valdorême is madame, as I have so often told her, and she owes me something for that; but she actually thinks that because a man is married he should come dutifully home like a bourgeois grocer. She has no poetry, no sense of the needs of a literary man, in her nature.'

Lacour sorrowfully admitted that the situation had its embarrassments. The first glass of absinthe did not show clearly how they were to be met, but the second brought bravery with it, and he nobly offered to beard the Russian lioness in her den, explain the view Paris took of her unjustifiable conduct, and, if possible, bring her to reason.

Caspilier's emotion overcame him, and he wept silently, while his friend, in eloquent language, told how famous authors, whose names were France's proudest possession, had been forgiven by their wives for slight lapses from strict domesticity, and these instances, he said, he would recount to Madame Valdorême, and so induce her to follow such illustrious examples.

The two comrades embraced and separated; the friend to use his influence and powers of persuasion with Valdorême; the

husband to tell Denise how blessed they were in having such a
friend to intercede for them; for Denise, bright little Parisienne
that she was, bore no malice against the unreasonable wife
of her lover.

Henri Lacour paused opposite the pastry-shop on the Rue de
Russie that bore the name of 'Valdorême' over the temptingly
filled windows. Madame Caspilier had not changed the title of
her well-known shop when she gave up her own name. Lacour
caught sight of her serving her customers, and he thought she
looked more like a Russian princess than a shopkeeper. He
wondered now at the preference of his friend for the petite
black-haired model. Valdorême did not seem more than twenty;
she was large, and strikingly handsome, with abundant auburn
hair that was almost red. Her beautifully moulded chin denoted
perhaps too much firmness, and was in striking contrast to
the weakness of her husband's lower face. Lacour almost
trembled as she seemed to flash one look directly at him, and,
for a moment, he feared she had seen him loitering before the
window. Her eyes were large, of a limpid amber colour, but
deep within them smouldered a fire that Lacour felt he would
not care to see blaze up. His task now wore a different aspect
from what it had worn in front of the Café Égalité. Hesitating
a moment, he passed the shop, and, stopping at a neighbouring
café, ordered another glass of absinthe.

Fortified once again, he resolved to act before his courage
had time to evaporate, and so, goading himself on with the
thought that no man should be afraid to meet any woman, be
she Russian or civilized, he entered the shop, making his most
polite bow to Madame Caspilier.

'I have come, madame,' he began, 'as the friend of your
husband, to talk with you regarding his affairs.'

'Ah!' said Valdorême; and Henri saw with dismay the fires
deep down in her eyes rekindle. But she merely gave some
instructions to an assistant, and, turning to Lacour, asked him
to be so good as to follow her.

She led him through the shop and up a stair at the back,
throwing open a door on the first floor. Lacour entered a
neat drawing-room, with windows opening out upon the street.
Madame Caspilier seated herself at a table, resting her elbow

upon it, shading her eyes with her hand, and yet Lacour felt them searching his very soul.

'Sit down,' she said. 'You are my husband's friend. What have you to say?'

Now, it is a difficult thing for a man to tell a beautiful woman that her husband—for the moment—prefers some one else, so Lacour began on generalities. He said a poet might be likened to a butterfly, or perhaps to the more industrious bee, who sipped honey from every flower, and so enriched the world. A poet was a law unto himself, and should not be judged harshly from what might be termed a shopkeeping point of view. Then Lacour, warming to his work, gave many instances where the wives of great men had condoned and even encouraged their husbands' little idiosyncrasies, to the great augmenting of our most valued literature.

Now and then, as this eloquent man talked, Valdorême's eyes seemed to flame dangerously in the shadow, but the woman neither moved nor interrupted him while he spoke. When he had finished, her voice sounded cold and unimpassioned, and he felt with relief that the outbreak he had feared was at least postponed.

'You would advise me then,' she began, 'to do as the wife of that great novelist did, and invite my husband and the woman he admires to my table?'

'Oh, I don't say I could ask you to go so far as that,' said Lacour; 'but—'

'I'm no half-way woman. It is all or nothing with me. If I invited my husband to dine with me, I would also invite this creature— What is her name? Denise, you say. Well, I would invite her too. Does she know he is a married man?'

'Yes,' cried Lacour eagerly; 'but I assure you, madame, she has nothing but the kindliest feelings towards you. There is no jealousy about Denise.'

'How good of her! How very good of her!' said the Russian woman, with such bitterness that Lacour fancied uneasily that he had somehow made an injudicious remark, whereas all his efforts were concentrated in a desire to conciliate and please.

'Very well,' said Valdorême, rising. 'You may tell my husband that you have been successful in your mission. Tell him

that I will provide for them both. Ask them to honour me
with their presence at breakfast tomorrow morning at twelve
o'clock. If he wants money, as you say, here are two hundred
francs, which will perhaps be sufficient for his wants until
midday tomorrow.'

Lacour thanked her with a profuse graciousness that would
have delighted any ordinary giver, but Valdorême stood impas-
sive like a tragedy queen, and seemed only anxious that he
should speedily take his departure, now that his errand was
done.

The heart of the poet was filled with joy when he heard
from his friend that at last Valdorême had come to regard
his union with Denise in the light of reason. Caspilier, as he
embraced Lacour, admitted that perhaps there was something
to be said for his wife after all.

The poet dressed himself with more than usual care on the
day of the feast, and Denise, who accompanied him, put on
some of the finery that had been bought with Valdorême's
donation. She confessed that she thought Eugène's wife had
acted with consideration towards them, but maintained that
she did not wish to meet her, for, judging from Caspilier's
account, his wife must be a somewhat formidable and terrifying person; still she went with him, she said, solely through
good nature, and a desire to heal family differences. Denise
would do anything in the cause of domestic peace.

The shop assistant told the pair, when they had dismissed
the cab, that madame was waiting for them upstairs. In the
drawing-room Valdorême was standing with her back to the
window like a low-browed goddess, her tawny hair loose over
her shoulders, and the pallor of her face made more conspicuous
by her costume of unrelieved black. Caspilier, with the grace
characteristic of him, swept off his hat, and made a low,
deferential bow; but when he straightened himself up, and
began to say the complimentary things and poetical phrases he
had put together for the occasion at the café the night before,
the lurid look of the Russian made his tongue falter; and Denise,
who had never seen a woman of this sort before, laughed a
nervous, half-frightened little laugh, and clung closer to her
lover than before. The wife was even more forbidding than

she had imagined. Valdorême shuddered slightly when she saw this intimate movement on the part of her rival, and her hand clenched and unclenched convulsively.

'Come,' she said, cutting short her husband's halting harangue, and sweeping past them, drawing her skirts aside on nearing Denise, she led the way up to the dining-room a floor higher.

'I'm afraid of her,' whimpered Denise, holding back. 'She will poison us.'

'Nonsense,' said Caspilier, in a whisper. 'Come along. She is too fond of me to attempt anything of that kind, and you are safe when I am here.'

Valdorême sat at the head of the table, with her husband at her right hand and Denise on her left. The breakfast was the best either of them had ever tasted. The hostess sat silent, but no second talker was needed when the poet was present. Denise laughed merrily now and then at his bright sayings, for the excellence of the meal had banished her fears of poison.

'What penetrating smell is this that fills the room? Better open the window,' said Caspilier.

'It is nothing,' replied Valdorême, speaking for the first time since they had sat down. 'It is only naphtha. I have had this room cleaned with it. The window won't open, and if it would, we could not hear you talk with the noise from the street.'

The poet would suffer anything rather than have his eloquence interfered with, so he said no more about the fumes of naphtha. When the coffee was brought in, Valdorême dismissed the trim little maid who had waited on them.

'I have some of your favourite cigarettes here. I will get them.'

She arose, and, as she went to the table on which the boxes lay, she quietly and deftly locked the door, and, pulling out the key, slipped it into her pocket.

'Do you smoke, mademoiselle?' she asked, speaking to Denise. She had not recognized her presence before.

'Sometimes, madame,' answered the girl, with a titter.

'You will find these cigarettes excellent. My husband's taste in cigarettes is better than in many things. He prefers the Russian to the French.'

Caspilier laughed loudly.

'That's a slap at you, Denise,' he said.

'At me? Not so; she speaks of cigarettes, and I myself prefer the Russian, only they are so expensive.'

A look of strange eagerness came into Valdorême's expressive face, softened by a touch of supplication. Her eyes were on her husband, but she said rapidly to the girl—

'Stop a moment, mademoiselle. Do not light your cigarette until I give the word.'

Then to her husband she spoke beseechingly in Russian, a language she had taught him in the early months of their marriage.

'Yevgenii, Yevgenii! Don't you see the girl's a fool? How can you care for her? She would be as happy with the first man she met in the street. I—I think only of you. Come back to me, Yevgenii!'

She leaned over the table towards him, and in her vehemence clasped his wrist. The girl watched them both with a smile. It reminded her of a scene in an opera she had heard once in a strange language. The prima donna had looked and pleaded like Valdorême.

Caspilier shrugged his shoulders, but did not withdraw his wrist from her firm grasp.

'Why go over the whole weary ground again?' he said. 'If it were not Denise, it would be somebody else. I was never meant for a constant husband, Val. I understood from Lacour that we were to have no more of this nonsense.'

She slowly relaxed her hold on his unresisting wrist. The old, hard, tragic look came into her face as she drew a deep breath. The fire in the depths of her amber eyes rekindled, as the softness went out of them.

'You may light your cigarette now, mademoiselle,' she said almost in a whisper to Denise.

'I swear I could light mine in your eyes, Val,' cried her husband. 'You would make a name for yourself on the stage. I will write a tragedy for you, and we will—'

Denise struck the match. A simultaneous flash of lightning and clap of thunder filled the room. The glass in the window fell clattering into the street. Valdorême was standing with her back against the door. Denise, fluttering her helpless little hands before her, tottered shrieking to the broken window. Caspilier, staggering panting to his feet, gasped—

'You Russian devil! The key, the key!'

He tried to clutch her throat, but she pushed him back.

'Go to your Frenchwoman. She's calling for help.'

Denise sank by the window, one burning arm over the sill, and was silent. Caspilier, mechanically beating back the fire from his shaking head, whimpering and sobbing, fell against the table, and then went headlong on the floor.

Valdorême, a pillar of fire, swaying gently to and fro before the door, whispered in a voice of agony—

'Oh, Eugène, Eugène!' and flung herself like a flaming angel —or fiend—on the prostrate form of the man.

The Beckoning Hand

by

GRANT ALLEN

Canadian-born Grant Allen (1848-1899) graduated from Oxford after education in America and France. He followed a scientific and teaching career, and his first published writings were scientific articles. Once, in order to promote a particular scientific argument, he cast it in the form of a story, which was so successful that he was asked to write more fiction. These first stories were published under a pseudonym but eventually Allen published his first collection of tales under his own name, Strange Stories (1884) and that same year saw publication of his first novel Philistia. From then on, he produced equal quantities of short story collections and novels. Few of his philosophical essays and scientific articles have survived but a brief selection appeared posthumously in The Hand of God (1909).

'The Beckoning Hand' was the title story of his second volume of tales, published in 1887. It deals with voodoo, a subject then almost unknown in literary works (note the original French spelling of the word in the story). Early in his career Grant Allen spent three years teaching in the West Indies and this experience undoubtedly enabled Allen to give this tale its most authentic background.

I

I first met Césarine Vivian in the stalls at the Ambiguities Theatre.

I had promised to take Mrs Latham and Irene to see a

French play. I wasn't at the time exactly engaged to poor Irene, though I knew Irene herself considered it practically equivalent to an understood engagement. We had known one another intimately from childhood for the Lathams were sort of second cousins of ours, three times removed : and we had always called one another by our Christian names, and been very fond of one another in a simple girlish and boyish fashion as long as we could either of us remember. Still, I maintain, there was no definite understanding between us; and if Mrs Latham thought I had been paying Irene attentions, she must have known that a young man of 22 with a decent fortune and a nice estate in Devonshire, was likely to look about him for a while before he thought of settling down and marrying quietly.

I had brought the yacht up to London Bridge, and was living on board and running about town casually, when I took Irene and her mother to see *Faustine*, at the Ambiguities. As soon as we had got in and taken our places, Irene whispered to me, 'Just look at the very dark girl on the other side of you, Harry! Did you ever in your life see anybody so perfectly beautiful?'

It has always been a great comfort to me that Irene herself was the first person to call my attention to Césarine Vivian's extraordinary beauty.

I turned round, as if by accident, and gave a passing glance, where Irene waved her fan, at the girl beside me. She was beautiful, certainly, in a terrible, grand, statuesque style of beauty; and I saw at a glimpse that she had Southern blood in her veins, perhaps Negro, perhaps Moorish, perhaps only Spanish, or Italian, or Provençal. Her features were proud and somewhat Jewish-looking; her eyes large, dark, and haughty; her black hair waved slightly in sinuous undulations as it passed across her high, broad forehead; her complexion, though a dusky olive in tone, was clear and rich, and daintily transparent; and her lips were thin and very slightly curled at the delicate corners, with a peculiarly imperious and almost scornful expression of fixed disdain. I had never before beheld anywhere such a magnificently repellent specimen of womanhood. For a second or so, as I looked, her eyes met mine with a defiant

inquiry, and I was conscious that moment of some strange and
weird fascination in her glance that seemed to draw me irresistibly towards her, at the same time that I hardly dared to fix
my gaze steadily upon the piercing eyes that looked through
and through me with their keen penetration.

'She's very beautiful, no doubt,' I whispered back to Irene,
'though I must confess I don't exactly like the look of her. She's
a trifle too much of a tragedy queen for my taste: a Lady
Macbeth, or a Beatrice Cenci. I prefer our simple little English
prettiness to this southern splendour. Besides, I fancy the girl
looks as if she had a drop or two of black blood somewhere
about her.'

'Oh, no,' Irene cried warmly. 'Impossible, Harry. She's exquisite: exquisite. Italian, you know, or something of that sort.
Italian girls have always got that peculiar gipsy-like type of
beauty.'

Low as we spoke, the girl seemed to know by instinct we
were talking about her; for she drew away the ends of her light
wrap coldly, in a significant fashion, and turned with her
opera-glass in the opposite direction, as if on purpose to avoid
looking towards us.

A minute later the curtain rose, and the first act of *Faustine*
distracted my attention for the moment from the beautiful
stranger.

Marie Leroux took the part of the great empress. She was
grand, stately, imposing, no doubt, but somehow it seemed to
me she didn't come up quite so well as usual that evening to
one's ideal picture of the terrible, audacious, superb Roman
woman. I leant over and murmured so to Irene. 'Don't you
know why?' Irene whispered back to me with a faint movement of the play-bill towards the beautiful stranger.

'No,' I answered; 'I haven't really the slightest conception.'

'Why,' she whispered, smiling; 'just look beside you. Could
anybody bear comparison for a moment as a Faustine with
that splendid creature in the stall next to you?'

I stole a glance sideways as she spoke. It was quite true. The
girl by my side was the real Faustine, the exact embodiment of
the dramatist's creation; and Marie Leroux, with her stagey
effects and her actress's pretences, could not in any way stand

the contrast with the genuine empress who sat there eagerly watching her.

The girl saw me glance quickly from her towards the actress and from the actress back to her, and shrank aside, not with coquettish timidity, but half angrily and half as if flattered and pleased at the implied compliment. 'Papa,' she said to the very English-looking gentleman who sat beyond her, 'ce monsieur-ci ...' I couldn't catch the end of the sentence.

She was French, then, not Italian or Spanish; yet a more perfect Englishman than the man she called 'papa' it would be difficult to discover.

'My dear,' her father whispered back in English, 'if I were you ...' and the rest of that sentence also was quite inaudible to me.

My interest was now fully roused in the beautiful stranger, who sat evidently with her father and sister, and drank in every word of the play as it proceeded with the greatest interest. As for me, I hardly cared to look at the actors, so absorbed was I in my queenly neighbour. I made a bare pretence of watching the stage every five minutes, and saying a few words now and again to Irene or her mother; but my real attention was all the time furtively directed to the girl beside me. Not that I was taken with her; quite the contrary; she distinctly repelled me; but she seemed to exercise over me for all that the same strange and indescribable fascination which is often possessed by some horrible sight that you would give worlds to avoid, and yet cannot for your life help intently gazing upon.

Between the third and fourth acts Irene whispered to me again, 'I can't keep my eyes off her, Harry. She's wonderfully beautiful. Confess now: aren't you over head and ears in love with her?'

I looked at Irene's sweet little peaceful English face, and I answered truthfully, 'No, Irene. If I wanted to fall in love, I should find somebody—'

'Nonsense, Harry,' Irene cried, blushing a little, and holding up her fan before her nervously. 'She's a thousand times prettier and handsomer in every way—'

'Prettier?'

'Than I am.'

At that moment the curtain rose, and Marie Leroux came forward once more with her imperial diadem, in the very act of defying and bearding the enraged emperor.

It was a great scene. The whole theatre hung upon her words for twenty minutes. The effect was sublime. Even I myself felt my interest aroused at last in the consummate spectacle. I glanced round to observe my neighbour. She sat there, straining her gaze upon the stage, and heaving her bosom with suppressed emotion. In a second, the spell was broken again. Beside that tall, dark southern girl, in her queenly beauty, with her flashing eyes and quivering nostrils, intensely moved by the passion of the play, the mere actress who mouthed and gesticulated before us by the footlights was as sounding brass and a tinkling cymbal. My companion in the stalls was the genuine Faustine: the player on the stage was but a false pretender.

As I looked a cry arose from the wings: a hushed cry at first, rising louder and ever louder still, as a red glare burst upon the scene from the background. Then a voice from the side boxes rang out suddenly above the confused murmur and the ranting of the actors—'Fire! Fire!'

Almost before I knew what had happened, the mob in the stalls was surging and swaying wildly towards the exits, in a general struggle for life. Dense clouds of smoke rolled from the stage and filled the length and breadth of the auditorium; tongues of flame licked up the pasteboard scenes and hangings, like so much paper; women screamed, and fought, and fainted; men pushed one another aside and hustled and elbowed, in one wild effort to make for the doors at all hazards to the lives of their neighbours. Never before had I so vividly realized how near the savage lies to the surface in our best and highest civilized society. I was to realize it still more vividly and more terribly afterwards.

One person alone I observed calm and erect, resisting quietly all pushes and thrusts, and moving with slow deliberateness to the door, as if wholly unconcerned at the universal tumult around her. It was the dark girl from the stalls beside me.

For myself, my one thought was for poor Irene and Mrs Latham. Keeping the two women in front of me, and thrusting hard with my elbows on either side to keep off the crush, I managed to make a tolerably clear road for them down the central row of stalls and out on to the big external staircase. The dark girl, now separated from her father and sister by the rush, was close in front of me. By a careful side movement, I managed to include her also in our party. She looked up to me gratefully with her big eyes, and her mouth broke into a charming smile as she turned and said in perfect English, 'I am much obliged to you for your kind assistance.' Irene's cheek was pale as death; but through the strange young lady's olive skin the bright blood still burned and glowed amid that frantic panic as calmly as ever.

We had reached the bottom of the steps, and were out into the front, when suddenly the strange lady turned around and gave a little cry of disappointment. 'Mes lorgnettes! Mes lorgnettes!' she said. Then glancing round carelessly to me she went on in English : 'I have left my opera-glasses inside on the vacant seat. I think, if you will excuse me, I'll go back and fetch them.'

'It's impossible,' I cried, 'my dear madam. Utterly impossible. They'll crush you underfoot. They'll tear you to pieces.'

She smiled a strange haughty smile, as if amused at the idea, but merely answered, 'I think not,' and tried to pass lightly by me.

I held her arm. I didn't know then she was as strong as I was. 'Don't go,' I said imploringly. 'They will certainly kill you. It would be impossible to stem a mob like this one.'

She smiled again, and darted back in silence before I could stop her.

Irene and Mrs Latham were now fairly out of all danger. 'Go on, Irene,' I said loosing her arm. 'Policeman, get these ladies safely out. I must go back and take care of that mad woman.'

'Go, go quick,' Irene cried. 'If you don't go, she'll be killed, Harry.'

I rushed back wildly after her, battling as well as I was able against the frantic rush of panic-stricken fugitives, and found my companion struggling still upon the main staircase. I helped her to make her way back into the burning theatre, and she ran lightly through the dense smoke to the stall she had occupied, and took the opera-glasses from the vacant place. Then she turned to me once more with a smile of triumph. 'People lose their heads so,' she said, 'in all these crushes. I came back on purpose to show papa I wasn't going to be frightened into leaving my opera-glasses. I should have been eternally ashamed of myself if I had come away and left them in the theatre.'

'Quick,' I answered, gasping for breath. 'If you don't make haste, we shall be choked to death, or the roof itself will fall in upon us and crush us!'

She looked up where I pointed with a hasty glance, and then made her way back again quickly to the staircase. As we hurried out, the timbers of the stage were beginning to fall in. I took her hand and almost dragged her out into the open. When we reached the Strand, we were both blackened with smoke and ashes. Pushing our way through the dense crowd, I called a hansom. She jumped in lightly. 'Thank you so much,' she said, quite carelessly. 'Will you kindly tell him where to drive? Twenty-seven, Seymour Crescent.'

'I'll see you home, if you'll allow me,' I answered. 'Under these circumstances, I trust I may be permitted.'

'As you like,' she said, smiling enchantingly. 'You are very good. My name is Césarine Vivian. Papa will be very much obliged to you for your kind assistance.'

I drove round to the Lathams' after dropping Miss Vivian at her father's door, to assure myself of Irene's safety, and to let them know of my own return unhurt from my perilous adventure. Irene met me on the doorstep, pale as death still. 'Thank heaven,' she cried, 'Harry, you're safe back again! And that poor girl? What has become of her?'

'I left her,' I said, 'at home.'

Irene burst into a flood of tears. 'Oh, Harry,' she cried, 'I thought she would have been killed there. It was brave of you, indeed, to help her through with it.'

II

Next day, Mr Vivian called on me at my club the address on the card I had given his daughter. I was in when he called, and I found him a pleasant, good-natured Cornishman, with very little that was strange or romantic in any way about him. He thanked me heartily, but not too effusively, for the care I had taken of Miss Vivian over-night. We got on very well together, and I soon gathered from what my new acquaintance said that, though he belonged to one of the best families in Cornwall, he had been an English merchant in Haiti, and had made his money chiefly in the coffee trade. He was a widower, I learned incidentally, and his daughters had been brought up for some years in England, though at their mother's request they had also passed part of their lives in convent schools in Paris and Rouen. 'Mrs Vivian was a Haitian, you know,' he said casually : 'Catholic of course. The girls are Catholics. They're good girls, though they're my own daughters; and Césarine, your friend of last night, is supposed to be clever. I'm no judge myself. Oh, by the way, Césarine said she hadn't thanked you half enough herself yesterday, and I was to be sure and bring you round this afternoon to a cup of tea with us at Seymour Crescent.'

In spite of the impression Mlle Césarine had made upon me the night before, I somehow didn't feel at all desirous of meeting her again. I was impressed, it is true, but not favourably. There seemed to me something uncanny and weird about her which made me shrink from seeing anything more of her if I could possibly avoid it. And as it happened, I was luckily engaged that very afternoon to tea at Irene's. I made the excuse, and added somewhat pointedly—on purpose that it might be repeated to Mlle Césarine—'Miss Latham is a very old and particular friend of mine—a friend whom I couldn't for worlds think of disappointing.'

Mr Vivian laughed the matter off. 'I shall catch it from Césarine,' he said good-humouredly, 'for not bringing her cavalier to receive her formal thanks in person. Our West-Indian born girls, you know, are very imperious. But if you can't, you can't.'

I can't say why, but at that moment, in spite of my intense desire not to meet Césarine again, I felt I would have given whole worlds if he would have pressed me to come in spite of myself. But, as it happened, he didn't.

At five o'clock, I drove round to Irene's, having almost made up my mind, if I found her alone, to come to a definite understanding with her and call it an engagement. She wasn't alone, however. As I entered the drawing-room, I saw a tall and graceful lady sitting opposite her, with her back towards me. The lady rose, moved round, and bowed. To my immense surprise, I found it was Césarine.

I noted to myself at the moment, too, that in my heart, though I had seen her but once before, I thought of her already simply as Césarine. And I was pleased to see her: fascinated: spell-bound.

Césarine smiled at my evident surprise. 'Papa and I met Miss Latham this afternoon in Bond Street,' she said gaily, in answer to my mute inquiry, 'and we stopped and spoke to one another, of course, about last night; and papa said you couldn't come round to tea with us in the Crescent, because you were engaged already to Miss Latham. And Miss Latham very kindly asked me to drive over and take tea with her, as I was so anxious to thank you once more for your great kindness to me yesterday.'

'And Miss Vivian was good enough to waive all ceremony,' Irene put in, 'and come round to us as you see, without further introduction.'

I stopped and talked all the time I was there to Irene; but, somehow, whatever I said, Césarine managed to intercept it, and I caught myself quite guiltily looking at her from time to time, with an inexpressible attraction that I could not account for.

By-and-by, Mr Vivian's carriage called for Césarine, and I was left a few minutes alone with Irene.

'Well, what do you think of her?' Irene asked me simply.

I turned my eyes away: I dare not meet hers. 'I think she's very handsome,' I replied evasively.

'Handsome! I should think so. She's wonderful. She's splendid. And doesn't she talk magnificently, too, Harry?'

'She's clever, certainly,' I answered shuffling. 'But I don't know why, I mistrust her, Irene.'

I rose and stood by the door with my hat in my hand, hesitating and trembling. I felt as if I had something to say to

Irene, and yet I was half afraid to venture upon saying it. My fingers quivered, a thing very unusual with me. At last I came closer to her, after a long pause, and said, 'Irene.'

Irene started, and the colour flushed suddenly into her cheeks. 'Yes, Harry,' she answered tremulously.

I don't know why, but I couldn't utter it. It was but to say 'I love you,' yet I hadn't the courage. I stood there like a fool, looking at her irresolutely, and then—

The door opened suddenly, and Mrs Latham entered and interrupted us.

III

I didn't speak again to Irene. The reason was that three days later I received a little note of invitation to lunch at Seymour Crescent from Césarine Vivian.

I didn't want to accept it, and yet I didn't know how to help myself. I went, determined beforehand as soon as lunch was over to take away the yacht to the Scottish islands, and leave Césarine and all her enchantments for ever behind me. I was afraid of her, positively afraid of her. I couldn't look her in the face without feeling at once that she exerted a terrible influence over me.

The lunch went off quietly enough, however. We talked about Haiti and the West Indies; about the beautiful foliage and the lovely flowers; about the moonlight nights and the tropical sunsets; and Césarine grew quite enthusiastic over them all. 'You should take your yacht out there some day, Mr Tristram,' she said softly. 'There is no place on earth so wild and glorious as our own beautiful neglected Haiti.'

She lifted her eyes full upon me as she spoke. I stammered out, like one spellbound, 'I must certainly go, on your recommendation, Mlle Césarine.'

'Why Mademoiselle?' she asked quickly. Then, perceiving I misunderstood her by the start I gave, she added with a blush, 'I mean, why not "Miss Vivian" in plain English?'

'Because you aren't English,' I said confusedly. 'You're Haitian, in reality. Nobody could ever for a moment take you for a mere Englishwoman.'

I meant it for a compliment, but Césarine frowned. I saw I had hurt her, and why; but I did not apologize. Yet I was conscious of having done something very wrong, and I knew I must try my best at once to regain my lost favour with her.

'You will take some coffee after lunch?' Césarine said, as the dishes were removed.

'Oh, certainly, my dear,' her father put in. 'You must show Mr Tristram how we make coffee in the West Indian fashion.'

Césarine smiled, and poured it out—black coffee, very strong, and into each cup she poured a little glass of excellent pale neat cognac. It seemed to me that she poured the cognac like a conjuror's trick; but everything about her was so strange and lurid that I took very little notice of the matter at that particular moment. It certainly was delicious coffee: I never tasted anything like it.

After lunch, we went into the drawing-room, and thence Césarine took me alone into the pretty conservatory. She wanted to show me some of her beautiful orchids, she said; she had brought the orchids herself years ago from Haiti. How long we stood there I could never tell. I seemed as if intoxicated with her presence. I had forgotten now all about my distrust of her: I had forgotten all about Irene and what I wished to say to her: I was conscious only of Césarine's great dark eyes, looking through and through me with their piercing glance, and Césarine's figure, tall and stately, but very voluptuous, standing close beside me. She talked to me in a low and dreamy voice; and whether the wine at lunch had got into my head, or whatever it might be, I felt only dimly and faintly aware of what was passing around me. I was unmanned with love, I suppose: but, however it may have been, I certainly moved and spoke that afternoon like a man in a trance from which he cannot by any effort of his own possibly awake himself.

'Yes, yes,' I overheard Césarine saying at last, as through a mist of emotion, 'you must go some day and see our beautiful mountainous Haiti. I must go myself. I long to go again. I don't care for this gloomy, dull, sunless England. A hand seems always to be beckoning me there. I shall obey it some day, for Haiti—our lovely Haiti, is too beautiful.'

Her voice was low and marvellously musical. 'Mademoiselle Césarine,' I began timidly.

She pouted and looked at me. 'Mademoiselle again,' she said in a pettish way. 'I told you not to call me so, didn't I?'

'Well, then, Césarine,' I went on boldly. She laughed low, a little laugh of triumph, but did not correct or check me in any way.

'Césarine,' I continued, lingering I know not why over the syllables of the name, 'I will go, as you say. I shall see Haiti. Why should we not both go together?'

She looked up at me eagerly with a sudden look of hushed inquiry. 'You mean it?' she asked, trembling visibly. 'You mean it, Mr Tristram? You know what you are saying?'

'Césarine,' I answered, 'I mean it. I know it. I cannot go away from you and leave you. Something seems to tie me. I am not my own master.... Césarine, I love you.'

My head whirled as I said the words, but I meant them at the time, and heaven knows I tried ever after to live up to them.

She clutched my arm convulsively for a moment. Her face was aglow with a wonderful light, and her eyes burned like a pair of diamonds. 'But the other girl!' she cried. 'Her! Miss Latham! The one you call Irene! You are ... in love with her! Are you not? Tell me!'

'I have never proposed to Irene,' I replied slowly. 'I have never asked any other woman but you to marry me, Césarine.'

She answered me nothing, but my face was very near hers, and I bent forward and kissed her suddenly. To my immense surprise, instead of struggling or drawing away, she kissed me back a fervent kiss, with lips hard pressed to mine, and the tears trickled slowly down her cheeks in a strange fashion. 'You are mine,' she cried. 'Mine for ever. I have won you. She shall not have you. I knew you were mine the moment I looked upon you. The hand beckoned me. I knew I should get you.'

'Come up into my den, Mr Tristram, and have a smoke,' my host interrupted in his bluff voice, putting his head in unexpectedly at the conservatory door. 'I think I can offer you a capital Manilla.'

The sound woke me as if from some terrible dream, and I followed him still in a sort of stupor up to the smoking room.

IV

That very evening I went to see Irene. My brain was whirling even yet, and I hardly knew what I was doing; but the cool air revived me a little, and by the time I reached the Lathams' I almost felt myself again.

Irene came down to the drawing-room to see me alone. I saw what she expected, and the shame of my duplicity overcame me utterly.

I took both her hands in mine and stood opposite her, ashamed to look her in the face, and with the terrible confession weighing me down like a burden of guilt. 'Irene,' I blurted out, without preface or comment, 'I have just proposed to Césarine Vivian.'

Irene drew back a moment and took a long breath. Then she said, with a tremor in her voice, but without a tear or a cry, 'I expected it, Harry. I thought you meant it. I saw you were terribly, horribly in love with her.'

'Irene,' I cried, flinging myself upon the sofa in an agony of repentance, 'I do not love her. I'm afraid of her, fascinated by her! I love you, Irene. The moment I'm away from her, I hate her. For heaven's sake, tell me what am I to do! I do not love her. I hate her, Irene.'

Irene came up to me and soothed my hair tenderly with her hand. 'Don't, Harry,' she said, with sisterly kindliness. 'Don't speak so. I know what you feel. But I am not angry with you. You mustn't talk like that. If she has accepted you, you must go and marry her. I have nothing to reproach you with. Never say such words to me again. Let us be as we have always been, friends only.'

'Irene,' I cried, lifting up my head and looking at her wildly, 'it is the truth : I do not love her, except when I am with her : and then, some strange enchantment seems to come over me. I don't know what it is, but I can't escape it. In my heart, Irene, I love you, and you only. I can never love her. My darling, tell me how to get myself away from her.'

'Hush,' Irene said, laying her hand on mine persuasively. 'You're excited tonight, Harry. You are flushed and feverish. You don't know what you're saying. You mustn't talk so. If you do, you'll make me hate you and despise you. You must keep your word now, and marry Miss Vivian.'

V

The next six weeks seem to me still like a vague dream : everything happened so hastily and strangely. I got a note next day from Irene. It was very short. 'Dearest Harry,—Mamma and I think, under the circumstances, it would be best for us to leave London for a few weeks. I am not angry with you. With best love, ever yours affectionately, Irene.'

I was wild when I received it. I couldn't bear to part so with Irene. I would find out where they were going and follow them immediately. I would write a note and break off my mad engagement with Césarine. I must have been drunk or insane when I made it. I couldn't imagine what I could have been doing.

On my way round to inquire at the Lathams's, a carriage came suddenly upon me at a sharp corner. A lady bowed to me from it. It was Césarine with her father. They pulled up and spoke to me. From that moment my doom was sealed. The old fascination came back at once, and I followed Césarine blindly to her house to luncheon, her accepted lover.

In six weeks more we were really married.

The first seven or eight months of our married life passed away happily enough. As soon as I was actually married to Césarine, that strange feeling I had at first experienced about her slowly wore off in the closer, commonplace, daily intercourse of married life. I almost smiled at myself for ever having felt it. Césarine was so beautiful and so queenly that when I took her home to Devonshire, and introduced her to the old manor, I really found myself immensely proud of her. Everybody at Teignbury was delighted and struck with her; and, what was a great deal more to the point, I began to discover that I was positively in love with her myself. She

softened and melted immensely on nearer acquaintance; the
Faustina air faded slowly away, when one saw her in her own
home among her own occupations; and I came to look on her
as a beautiful, simple, innocent girl, delighted with country
pleasures, fond of a breezy canter on the slopes of Dartmoor,
and taking an affectionate interest in the ducks and chickens,
which I could hardly ever have conceived possible when I first
saw her. The imperious, mysterious, terrible Césarine disappeared entirely, and I found in her place, to my immense
relief, that I had married a graceful, gentle, tender-hearted
English girl, with just a pleasant occasional touch of southern
fire and impetuosity.

As winter came round again, however, Césarine's cheeks
began to look a little thinner than usual, and she had such a
constant, troublesome cough, that I began to be a trifle alarmed
at her strange symptoms. Césarine herself laughed off my fears.
'It's nothing, Harry,' she would say; 'nothing at all, I assure
you, dear. A few good rides on the moor will set me right
again. It's all the result of that horrid London. I'm a country-
born girl, and I hate big towns. I never want to live in town
again, Harry.'

I called in our best Exeter doctor, and he largely confirmed
Césarine's own simple view of the situation. 'There's nothing
organically wrong with Mrs Tristram's constitution,' he said
confidently. 'No weakness of the lungs or heart in any way.
She has merely run down—outlived her strength a little. A
winter in some warm genial climate would set her up again.'

'Let us go to Algeria with the yacht, Reeney,' I suggested,
much reassured.

'Why Algeria?' Césarine replied, with brightening eyes. 'Oh,
Harry, why not dear old Haiti? You said once you would go
there with me—you remember when, darling; why not keep
your promise now, and go there? I want to go there, Harry:
I'm longing to go there.' And she held out her delicately
moulded hand in front of her, as if beckoning me, and drawing
me on to Haiti after her.

'Ah, yes; why not the West Indies?' the Exeter doctor
answered meditatively. 'I think I understood you that Mrs
Tristram is West Indian born. Quite so. Her native air. Depend

upon it, that's the best place for her. By all means, I should say, try Haiti.'

I don't know why, but the notion for some reason displeased me immensely. There was something about Césarine's eyes when she beckoned with her hand in that strange fashion, which reminded me exactly of the weird, uncanny, indescribable impression she had made upon me when I first knew her. Still I was very fond of Césarine, and if she and the doctor were both agreed that Haiti would be the best place for her, it would be foolish and wrong for me to interfere with their joint wisdom.

The end of it all was, that in less than a month from that day, we were out in the yacht on the broad Atlantic, with the cliffs of Falmouth fading slowly behind us in the distance, and the white spray dashing in front of us, like fingers beckoning us on to Haiti.

VI

The bay of Port-au-Prince is hot and simmering, a deep basin enclosed in a ringing semicircle of mountains, with scarce a breath blowing on the harbour, and with tall cocoa-nut palms rising unmoved into the still air above on the low sand-spits that close it in to seaward. The town itself is wretched, squalid, and hopelessly ramshackle, a despondent collection of tumble-down wooden houses, interspersed with indescribable negro huts, mere human rabbit-hutches, where parents and children herd together, in one higgledy-piggledy, tropical confusion. I had never in my days seen anything more painfully desolate and dreary, and I feared that Césarine, who had not been here since she was a girl of fourteen, would be somewhat depressed at the horrid actuality, after her exalted fanciful ideals of the remembered Haiti. But, to my immense surprise, Césarine did not appear at all shocked or taken aback at the squalor and wretchedness all around her. On the contrary, the very air of the place seemed to inspire her from the first with fresh vigour; her cough disappeared at once as if by magic; and the colour returned forthwith to her cheeks, almost as soon as we had cast anchor in Haitian waters.

The very first day we arrived at Port-au-Prince, Césarine said to me, with more shyness than I had ever yet seen her exhibit, 'If you wouldn't mind it, Harry, I should like to go at once, this morning—and see my grandmother.'

I started with astonishment. 'Your grandmother, Césarine!' I cried incredulously. 'My darling! I didn't know you had a grandmother living.'

'Yes, I have,' she answered, with some slight hesitation, 'and I think if you wouldn't object to it, Harry, I'd rather go and see her alone, the first time at least, please dearest.'

In a moment, the obvious truth, which I had always known in a vague sort of fashion, but never thoroughly realized, flashed across my mind in its full vividness, and I merely bowed my head in silence. It was natural she should not wish me to see her meeting with her Haitian grandmother.

She went alone through the streets of Port-au-Prince, without inquiry, like one who knew them of old, and I dogged her footsteps at a distance unperceived. After a few hundred yards, she turned out of the main road and down a tumbledown alley of scattered negro cottages, till she came at last to a rather better house that stood by itself in a little dusty garden of guava-trees and cocoa-nuts. I slipped into the next compound before Césarine observed me, beckoned the lazy negro from the door of the hut, with one finger placed as a token of silence upon my lips, dropped a dollar into his open palm, and stood behind the paling, looking out into the garden beside me through a hole.

Césarine knocked at the door, and in a moment was answered by an old negress, tall and bony, dressed in a loose sack-like gown of coarse cotton print, with a big red bandanna tied around her short grey hair, and a huge silver cross dangling carelessly upon her bare and wrinkled black neck. She wore no sleeves, and bracelets of strange beads hung loosely around her shrunken and skinny wrists. A more hideous old hag I had never in my life beheld; and yet I saw that she had Césarine's great dark eyes and even white teeth, and something of Césarine's figure lingered still in her lithe and sinuous yet erect carriage.

'Grand'mère!' Césarine said convulsively, flinging her arms with wild delight around that grim and withered black woman,

It seemed to me she had never since our marriage embraced me with half the fervour she bestowed upon this hideous old African witch.

'Hé, Césarine, it is thee, then, my little one,' the old negress cried out suddenly, 'I did not expect thee so soon, my cabbage. Thou hast come early. Be the welcome one, my granddaughter.'

I reeled with horror as I saw the wrinkled and haggard African kissing once more my beautiful Césarine. It seemed to me a horrible desecration. I had always known, of course, since Césarine was a quadroon, that her grandmother on one side must necessarily have been a full-blooded negress, but I had never yet suspected the reality could be so hideous, so terrible as this.

I crouched down speechless against the paling in my disgust and astonishment, and motioned with my hand to the negro in the hut to remain perfectly quiet. The door of the house closed, and Césarine disappeared : but I waited there, as if chained to the spot, under a hot and burning tropical sun, for fully an hour, unconscious of anything in heaven or earth, save the shock and surprise of that unexpected disclosure.

At last the door opened again, and Césarine apparently came out once more into the neighbouring garden. The gaunt negress followed her close, with one arm thrown caressingly about her beautiful neck and shoulders.

They came close up to the spot where I was crouching in the dust behind the fence, and then I heard rather than saw that Césarine had flung herself passionately down upon her knees on the ground, and was pouring forth a muttered prayer, in a tongue unknown to me, full of harsh and uncouth gutturals. It was not Latin; it was not even the coarse Creole French, the negro *patois* in which I heard the people jabbering in the streets around me : it was some still more hideous and barbaric language, a mass of clicks and inarticulate noises, such as I could never have believed might possibly proceed from Césarine's lips.

At last she finished, and I heard her speaking again to her grandmother in the Creole dialect. 'Grandmother, you will pray and get me one. You will not forget me. A boy. A pretty one; an heir to my husband!' It was said wistfully, with infinite longing. I knew then why she had grown so pale and thin and haggard before we sailed away from England.

The old hag answered in the same tongue, but in her shrill withered note, 'You will bring him up to the religion, my little one, will you?'

Césarine seemed to bow her head. 'I will,' she said. 'He shall follow the religion. Mr Tristram shall never know anything about it.'

They went back once more into the house, and I crept away, afraid of being discovered, and returned to the yacht, sick at heart, not knowing how I should ever venture again to meet Césarine.

But when I got back, and had helped myself to a glass of sherry to steady my nerves, from the little flask on Césarine's dressing-table, I thought to myself, hideous as it all seemed, it was natural Césarine should wish to see her grandmother. After all, was it not better, that proud and haughty as she was, she should not disown her own flesh and blood? And yet, the memory of my beautiful Césarine wrapped in that hideous old black woman's arms made the blood curdle in my very veins.

As soon as Césarine returned, however, gayer and brighter than I had ever seen her, the old fascination overcame me once more, and I determined in my heart to stifle the horror I could not possibly help feeling. And that evening, as I sat alone in the cabin with my wife, I said to her, 'Césarine, we have never spoken about the religious question before: but if it should be ordained we are to have any little ones of our own, I should wish them to be brought up in their mother's creed. You could make them better Catholics, I take it, than I could ever make them Christians of any sort.'

Césarine answered never a word, but to my intense surprise she burst suddenly into a flood of tears, and flung herself sobbing on the cabin floor at my feet in an agony of tempestuous cries and writhings.

VII

A few days later, when we had settled down for a three

months' stay at a little bungalow on the green hills behind Port-au-Prince, Césarine said to me early in the day, 'I want to go away today, Harry, up into the mountains, to the chapel of Notre Dame de Bon Secours.'

I bowed my head in acquiescence. 'I can guess why you want to go, Reeney,' I answered gently. 'You want to pray there about something that's troubling you. And if I'm not mistaken, it's the same thing that made you cry the other evening when I spoke to you in the cabin.'

The tears rose hastily once more into Césarine's eyes, and she cried in a low distressed voice, 'Harry, Harry, don't talk to me so. You are too good to me. You will kill me. You will kill me.'

I lifted her head from the table, where she had buried it in her arms, and kissed her tenderly. 'Reeney,' I said, 'I know how you feel, and I hope Notre Dame will listen to your prayers, and send you what you ask of her. But if not, you need never be afraid that I shall love you any the less than I do at present.'

Césarine burst into a fresh flood of tears. 'No, Harry,' she said, 'you don't know about it. You can't imagine it. To us, you know, who have the blood of Africa running in our veins, it is not a mere matter of fancy. It is an eternal disgrace for any woman of our race and descent not to be a mother. I cannot help it. It is the instinct of my people. We are all born so: we cannot feel otherwise.'

It was the only time either of us ever alluded in speaking with one another to the sinister half of Césarine's pedigree.

'You will let me go with you to the mountains, Reeney?' I asked, ignoring her remark. 'You mustn't go so far by yourself, darling.'

'No, Harry, you can't come with me. It would make my prayers ineffectual, dearest. You are a heretic, you know, Harry. You are not Catholic. Notre Dame won't listen to my prayer if I take you with me.'

I saw her mind was set upon it, and I didn't interfere. She would be away all night, she said. There was a rest-house for pilgrims attached to the chapel, and she would be back again at our bungalow the morning after.

That afternoon she started on her way on a mountain pony accompanied only by a negro maid. I couldn't let her go quite unattended through those lawless paths, beset by cottages of half savage Africans; so I followed at a distance, aided by a black groom, and tracked her road along the endless hill-sides up to a fork in the way where the narrow bridle-path divided into two, one of which bore away to leftward, leading, my guide told me, to the chapel of Notre Dame de Bon Secours.

At that point the guide halted. He peered with hand across his eyebrows among the tangled brake of tree-ferns with a terrified look; then he shook his woolly-black head ominously. 'I can't go on, Monsieur,' he said, turning to me with an unfeigned shudder. 'Madame has not taken the path of Our Lady. She has gone to the left along the other road, which leads at last to the Vaudoux temple.'

I looked at him incredulously. I had heard before of Vaudoux. It is the hideous African cannibalistic witchcraft of the relapsing half-heathen Haitian negroes. But Césarine a Vaudoux worshipper! It was too ridiculous. The man must be mistaken: or else Césarine had taken the wrong road by accident.

Next moment, a horrible unspeakable doubt seized upon me irresistibly. What was the unknown shrine in her grandmother's garden at which Césarine had prayed in those awful gutturals? Whatever it was, I would probe this mystery to the very bottom. I would know the truth, come what might of it.

'Go, you coward!' I said to the negro. 'I have no further need of you. I will make my way alone to the Vaudoux temple.'

'Monsieur,' the man cried, trembling visibly in every limb, 'they will tear you to pieces. If they ever discover you near the temple, they will offer you up as a victim to the Vaudoux.'

'Pooh,' I answered, contemptuous of the fellow's slavish terror. 'Where Madame, a woman, dares to go, I, her husband, am certainly not afraid to follow her.'

'Monsieur,' he replied, throwing himself on the path before me, 'Madame is Creole; she has the blood of the Vaudoux worshippers flowing in her veins. Nobody will hurt her. She is free of the craft. But Monsieur is a pure white and uninitiated.... If the Vaudoux people catch him at their rites, they

will rend him in pieces, and offer his blood as an expiation to
the Unspeakable One.'

'Go,' I said, with a smile, turning my horse's head up the
right-hand path towards the Vaudoux temple. 'I am not afraid.
I will come back again tomorrow.'

I followed the path through a tortuous maze, till I came at
last to a spur of the hill, where a white wooden building
gleamed in front of me, in the full slanting rays of tropical
sunset. A skull was fastened to the lintel of the door. I knew
at once it was the Vaudoux temple.

I dismounted at once, and led my horse aside into the
brake, and tying him by the bridle to a mountain cabbage palm,
in a spot where the thick underbrush completely hid us from
view, I lay down and waited patiently for the shades of evening.

It was a moonless night, according to the Vaudoux fashion;
and I knew from what I had already read in West Indian
books that the orgies would not commence till midnight.

From time to time, I rubbed a match against my hand
without lighting it, and by the faint glimmer of the phosphorus
on my palm, I was able to read the figures of my watch without
exciting the attention of the neighbouring Vaudoux worshippers.

Hour after hour went slowly by, and I crouched there still
unseen among the agave thicket. At last, as the hands of the
watch reached together the point of twelve, I heard a deep
rumbling noise coming ominously from the Vaudoux temple.
I recognized at once the familiar sound. It was the note of the
bull-roarer, that mystic instrument of pointed wood, whirled
by a string round the head of the hierophant, by whose aid
savages in their secret rites summon to their shrines their gods
and spirits.

I crept out through the tangled brake, and cautiously
approached the back of the building. A sentinel was standing
by the door in front, a powerful negro, armed with revolver
and cutlass. I skulked round noiselessly to the rear, and lifting
myself by my hands to the level of the one tiny window, I
peered in through a slight scratch on the white paint, with
which the glass was covered internally.

I only saw the sight within for a second. Then my brain

reeled, and my fingers refused any longer to hold me. But in that second, I had read the whole terrible, incredible truth : I knew what sort of a woman she really was whom I had blindly taken as the wife of my bosom.

Before a rude stone altar covered with stuffed alligator skins, human bones, live snakes, and hideous relics of African superstition, a tall and withered black woman stood erect, naked as she came from her mother's womb, one skinny arm raised aloft, and the other holding below some dark object, that writhed and struggled awfully in her hand on the slab of the altar. I saw in a flash of the torches behind it was the black hag I had seen at the Port-au-Prince cottage.

Beside her, whiter of skin, and faultless of figure, stood a younger woman, beautiful to behold, imperious and haughty still, like a Greek statue, unmoved before that surging horrid background of naked black and cringing savages. Her head was bent, and her hand pressed convulsively against the swollen veins in her throbbing brow; and I saw at once it was my own wife—a Vaudoux worshipper—Césarine Tristram.

In another flash, I knew the black woman had a sharp flint knife in her uplifted hand; and the dark object in the other hand I recognized with a thrill of unspeakable horror as a negro girl of four years old or thereabouts, gagged and bound, and lying on the altar.

Before I could see the sharp flint descend upon the naked breast of the writhing victim, my fingers refused to bear me, and I fell half fainting on the ground, too shocked even to crawl away out of reach of the awful unrealizable horror.

But by the sounds within, I knew they had completed their hideous sacrifice, and that they were smearing Césarine—my own wife—the woman of my choice—with the warm blood of the human victim.

Sick and faint, I crept away slowly through the tangled underbrush, tearing my skin as I went with the piercing cactus spines; untied my horse and rode him down without drawing rein, cantering round sharp angles and down horrible ledges, till he stood at last, white with foam, by the grey dawn, in front of the little piazza of our bungalow.

VIII

That night, the thunder roared and the lightning played round the tall hilltops in the direction of the Vaudoux temple. The rain came down in fearful sheets, and the torrents roared and foamed in cataracts, and tore away great gaps in the rough paths on the steep hill-sides. But at eight o'clock in the morning Césarine returned, soaked to the skin and with a strange frown upon her haughty forehead.

I did not know how to look at her or how to meet her.

'My prayers are useless,' she muttered angrily as she entered. 'Some heretic must have followed me unseen to the chapel of Notre Dame de Bon Secours. The pilgrimage is a failure.'

'You are wet,' I said, trembling. 'Change your things, Césarine.' I could not pretend to speak gently to her.

She turned upon me with a fierce look in her big black eyes. Her instinct showed her at once I had discovered her secret. 'Tell them, and hang me,' she cried fiercely.

It was what the law required me to do. I was otherwise the accomplice of murder and cannibalism. But I could not do it. Profoundly as I loathed her and hated her presence, now, I couldn't find it in my heart to give her up to justice, as I knew I ought to do.

I turned away and answered nothing.

Presently, she came out again from her bedroom, with her wet things still dripping around her. 'Smoke that,' she said, handing me a tiny cigarette rolled round in a leaf of fresh tobacco.

'I will not,' I answered with a vague surmise, taking it from her fingers. 'I know the smell. It is manchineal. You cannot any longer deceive me.'

She went back to her bedroom once more. I sat, dazed and stupefied, on the front piazza. What to do, I knew not, and cared not. I was tied to her for life, and there was no help for it, save by denouncing her to the rude Haitian justice.

In an hour or more, our English maid came out to speak to me. 'I'm afraid, sir,' she said. 'Mrs Tristram is getting delirious. She seems to be in a high fever. Shall I ask one of these poor black bodies to go out and get the English doctor?'

I went into my wife's bedroom. Césarine lay moaning piteously on the bed, in her wet clothes still; her cheeks were hot, and her pulse was high and thin and feverish. I knew without asking what was the matter with her. It was yellow fever.

The night's exposure in that terrible climate, and the ghastly scene she had gone through had broken down even Césarine's iron constitution.

I sent for the doctor and had her put to bed immediately. The black nurse and I undressed her between us. We found next to her bosom, tied by a small red silken thread, a tiny bone, fresh and ruddy-looking. I knew what it was, and so did the negress. It was a human finger-bone—the last joint of a small child's fourth finger. The negress shuddered and hid her head. 'It is Vaudoux, Monsieur!' she said. 'I have seen it on others. Madame has been paying a visit, I suppose, to her grandmother.'

For six long days and nights I watched and nursed that doomed criminal, doing everything for her that skill could direct or care could suggest to me: yet all the time fearing and dreading that she might yet recover, and not knowing in my heart what either of our lives could ever be like if she did live through it.

A merciful Providence willed it otherwise.

On the sixth day, the fatal *vomito negro* set in—the symptom of the last incurable stage of yellow fever—and I knew for certain that Césarine would die. She had brought her own punishment upon her. At midnight that evening she died delirious.

Thank God, she had left no child of mine behind her to inherit the curse of her mother's blood!

Nothing but the Truth

by

RHODA BROUGHTON

Victorian London was the scene of many haunted house stories, both in fact and fiction. The enormous popularity of spiritualism and interest in the occult which was imported from America at this time provoked many arguments and led to many residences being cited as examples of haunted houses, though often without foundation. Zealous teams of investigators, both amateur and professional (and nearly all previously prejudiced one way or the other) delved into the mysteries of these extremely undesirable residences. These investigations were not only confined to London, of course; one of the most entertaining was recorded in Annie Goodrich-Freer's The Alleged Haunting Of Ballechin House *(1899), a most intriguing case set in Scotland where the ratio of ghosts seemed to increase in proportion to the number of investigators.*

But it was undoubtedly London that held the crown of the most haunted city. One of the most famous cases of all was No. 50 Berkeley Square, where all kinds of horrors were reputed to occur. The premises still stand, now occupied by a highly reputable antiquarian bookseller. Anyone who has read of that house will instantly recognize from where this story received its inspiration.

Rhoda Broughton (1840-1920) had an honourable ghost-story writing pedigree; her uncle was J. Sheridan le Fanu. Miss Broughton was born in Denbigh and lived in Wales until the death of her parents, when she moved to Headington, Oxford. Her most famous works were her novels of country-house life, but as she became more famous and could write much as she pleased, she tended towards the short story. Le Fanu himself serialized her first novel in his Dublin University Magazine *and was instrumental in helping her find a publisher.* Twilight Stories (*1879), from which comes this tale, was her only collection of ghost stories. It was undoubtedly a collection of which her uncle would have approved, as this story will show you.*

MRS DE WYNT TO MRS MONTRESOR.

'18, Eccleston Square,
'May 5th.

'My Dearest Cecilia,

'I had no idea till yesterday how closely we were packed in this great smoky beehive, as tightly as herrings in a barrel. Don't be frightened, however. By dint of squeezing and crowding, we have managed to make room for two more herrings in our barrel, and those two are yourself and your husband. Let me begin at the beginning. After having looked over, I verily believe, every undesirable residence in West London; after having seen nothing intermediate between what was suited to the means of a duke, and what was suited to the needs of a chimney-sweep; after having felt bed-ticking, and explored kitchen-ranges till my brain reeled under my accumulated experience, I arrived at about half-past five yesterday afternoon at 32, —— Street, Mayfair.

' "Failure No. 253, I don't doubt," I said to myself, as I toiled up the steps, feeling as ill-tempered as you please. So much for my spirit of prophecy. Once inside, I thought I had got into a small compartment of Heaven by mistake. Fresh as a daisy, clean as a cherry, bright as a seraph's face, it is all these, and a hundred more. Two drawing-rooms, marvellously, *immorally* becoming, my dear, as I ascertained entirely for your benefit, Persian mats, easy chairs, and lounges suited to every possible physical conformation, and a thousand of the important trivialities that make up the sum of a woman's life: peacock fans, Japanese screens, naked boys and *décolletée* shepherdesses; not to speak of a family of china pugs, with blue ribbons round their necks, which ought of themselves to have added fifty pounds a year to the rent. Apropos, I asked, in fear and trembling, what the rent might be—"Three hundred pounds a year." A feather would have knocked me down. I could hardly believe my ears, and made the woman repeat it several times, that there might be no mistake. To this hour it is a mystery to me.

'With that suspiciousness which is so characteristic of you, you will immediately begin to think that there must be some terrible unaccountable smell, or some odious inexplicable noise haunting the reception-rooms. Nothing of the kind, the woman assured me, and she did not look as if she were telling stories. Its last occupant was an elderly and unexceptionable Indian officer, with a most lawful wife. They did not stay long, it is true, but then, as the housekeeper told me, he was a deplorable old hypochondriac, who never could bear to stay a fortnight in any one place. So lay aside that scepticism, which is your besetting sin, and give unfeigned thanks to your tutelar saint, for having provided you with a palace at the cost of a hovel, and for having sent you such an invaluable friend as

'Your attached
'ELIZABETH DE WYNT.

'P.S.—I am so sorry I shall not be in town to witness your first raptures, but dear Artie looks so pale and thin and tall after hooping-cough, that I am sending him off at once to the sea, and as I cannot bear the child out of my sight, I am going into banishment likewise.'

MRS MONTRESOR TO MRS DE WYNT.

'32, —— STREET, MAYFAIR,
'May 14th.

'DEAREST BESSY,

'Why did not dear little Artie defer his hooping-cough convalescence &c., till August? It is very odd, to me, the perverse way in which children always fix upon the most inconvenient times and seasons for their diseases. Here we are installed in our Paradise, and have searched high and low, in every hole and corner, for the serpent, without succeeding in catching a glimpse of his spotted tail. Most things in this world are disappointing, but 32, —— Street, Mayfair, is not. The mystery of the rent is still a mystery. I have been for my first ride in the Row this morning; my horse was a little fidgety; I am half afraid that my nerve is not what it was. Adela comes to us next week; I am so glad. It is dull driving by oneself of an afternoon; and I always think that one young woman alone in a brougham, or with only a dog beside her, does not look *good*. We sent round our cards a fortnight before we came up, and have been already deluged with callers. Considering that we have been two years exiled from civilized life, and that London memories are not generally of the longest, we shall do pretty well, I think. Ralph Gordon came to see me on Sunday; he is in the Hussars now. He has grown up such a *dear* fellow, and so good-looking! Just my style, large and fair and whiskerless! I intend to be quite a *mother* to him. I hear a knock at the door! Peace is a word that might as well be expunged from one's London dictionary.

'Yours affectionately,
'CECILIA MONTRESOR.'

——

MRS DE WYNT TO MRS MONTRESOR.
'THE LORD WARDEN, DOVER,
'*May* 18th.

'DEAREST CECILIA,

'You will perceive that I am about to devote only one small sheet of note-paper to you. This is from no dearth of time, Heaven knows! time is a drug in the market here, but from a total dearth of ideas. My life here is not an eminently suggestive one. It is spent in digging with a wooden spade, and eating prawns. Those are my employments at least; my relaxation is going down to the Pier, to see the Calais boat come in. When one is miserable oneself, it is decidedly consolatory to see someone more miserable still; and wretched and bored, and reluctant vegetable as I am, I am not *sea-sick*. I always feel my spirits rise after having seen that peevish, draggled procession of blue, green and yellow fellow-Christians file past me. There is a wind here *always*. There are heights to climb which require more daring perseverance than ever Wolfe displayed, with his paltry heights of Abraham. There are glaring white houses, glaring white roads, glaring white cliffs. If any one knew how unpatriotically I detest the chalk-cliffs of Albion! Having grumbled through my two little pages—I have actually been reduced to writing very large in order to fill even them—I will send off my dreary little billet. How I wish I could get into the envelope myself too, and whirl up with it to dear, beautiful, filthy London. Not more heavily could Madame de Staël have sighed for Paris from among the shades of Coppet.

'Your disconsolate,
'BESSY.'

———

MRS MONTRESOR TO MRS DE WYNT.

'32, —— STREET, Mayfair,
'May 27th.

'Oh, my dearest Bessy, how I wish we were out of this dreadful, dreadful house! Please don't think me very ungrateful for saying this, after your taking such pains to provide us with a Heaven upon earth, as you thought.

'What has happened could, of course, have been neither foretold, nor guarded against, by any human being. About ten days ago, Benson (my maid) came to me with a very long face, and said, "If you please, ma'am, did you know that this house was *haunted*?" I was *so* startled: you know what a coward I am. I said, "Good Heavens! No! is it?" "Well, I'm pretty nigh sure it is," she said, and the expression of her countenance was about as lively as an undertaker's; and then she told me that cook had been that morning to order in groceries from a shop in the neighbourhood, and on her giving the man the direction where to send the things to, he had said, with a very peculiar smile, "No. 32, —— Street, eh? h'm? I wonder how long *you*'ll stand it; last lot held out just a fortnight." He looked so odd that she asked him what he meant, but he only said, "Oh! nothing! only that parties never *do* stay long at 32." He had known parties go in one day, and out the next, and during the last four years he had never known any remain

over the month. Feeling a good deal alarmed by this information, she naturally inquired the reason; but he declined to give
it, saying that if she had not found it out for herself, she had
much better leave it alone, as it would only frighten her out
of her wits; and on her insisting and urging him, she could
only extract from him, that the house had such a villainously
bad name, that the owners were glad to let it for a mere song.
You know how firmly I believe in apparitions, and what an
unutterable fear I have of them; anything material, tangible,
that I can lay hold of—anything of the same fibre, blood, and
bone as myself, I could, I think, confront bravely enough; but
the mere thought of being brought face to face with the "bodi-
less dead", makes my brain unsteady. The moment Henry
came in, I ran to him, and told him; but he pooh-poohed the
whole story, laughed at me, and asked whether we should turn
out of the prettiest house in London, at the very height of the
season, because a grocer said it had a bad name. He derided
my "babyish fears", as he called them, to such an extent that
I felt half ashamed, and yet not quite comfortable, either; and
then came the usual rush of London engagements, during which
one has no time to think of anything. Adela was to arrive
yesterday, and in the morning our weekly hamper of flowers,
fruit, and vegetables arrived from home. I always dress the
flower vases myself, servants are so tasteless, and as I was
arranging them, it occurred to me—you know Adela's passion
for flowers—to carry up one particular cornucopia of roses
and mignonette and set it on her toilet-table, as a pleasant
surprise for her. As I came downstairs, I had seen the housemaid—a fresh, round-faced country girl—go into the room,
which was being prepared for Adela, with a pair of sheets that
she had been airing over her arm. I went upstairs very slowly,
as my cornucopia was full of water, and I was afraid of spilling
some. I turned the handle of the bedroom-door and entered,
keeping my eyes fixed on my flowers, to see whether any of
them had fallen out. Suddenly a sort of shiver passed over me;
and feeling frightened—I did not know why—I looked up
quickly. The girl was standing by the bed, leaning forward a
little with her hands clenched rigid, every nerve tense; her
eyes, wide open, starting out of her head, and a look of unut-

terable horror in them; her cheeks and mouth livid as those of one that died awhile ago in mortal pain. As I looked at her, her lips moved a little, and an awful hoarse voice, not like hers in the least, said, "Oh! my God, I have seen it!" and then she fell down suddenly, like a log, with a heavy noise. Hearing the noise audible all through the thin walls and floors of a London house, Benson came running in, and between us we managed to lift her on to the bed, and tried to bring her to herself by rubbing her feet and hands, and holding strong salts to her nostrils. And all the while we kept glancing over our shoulders, in a vague cold terror of seeing some awful, shapeless apparition. Two long hours she lay in a state of utter unconsciousness. Meanwhile Harry, who had been down to his club, returned. At the end of two hours we succeeded in bringing her back to sensation and life, but only to make the awful discovery that she was raving mad. She became so violent that it required all the combined strength of Harry and Phillips (our butler) to hold her down in the bed. Of course, we sent instantly for a doctor, who, as she grew a little calmer towards evening, removed her in a cab to his own house. He has just been here to tell me that she is now pretty quiet, not from any return to sanity, but from sheer exhaustion. We are, of course, utterly in the dark as to *what* she saw, and her ravings are far too disconnected and unintelligible to afford us the slightest clue. I feel so completely shattered and upset by this awful occurrence, that you will excuse me, dear, I'm sure, if I write incoherently. One thing I need hardly tell you, and that is, that no earthly consideration would induce me to allow Adela to occupy that terrible room. I shudder and run by quickly as I pass the door.

'Yours, in great agitation,
'CECILIA.'

———

MRS DE WYNT TO MRS MONTRESOR.
'THE LORD WARDEN, DOVER,
'May 28th.

'DEAREST CECILIA
'Yours just come; how very dreadful! But I am still uncon-

vinced as to the house being in fault. You know I feel a sort of godmother to it, and responsible for its good behaviour. Don't you think that what the girl had might have been a fit? Why not? I myself have a cousin who is subject to seizures of the kind, and immediately on being attacked his whole body becomes rigid, his eyes glassy and staring, his complexion livid, exactly as in the case you describe. Or, if not a fit, are you sure that she has not been subject to fits of madness? *Please* be sure and ascertain whether there is not insanity in her family. You know my utter disbelief in ghosts. I am convinced that most of them, if run to earth, would turn out about as genuine as the famed Cock Lane one. But even allowing the possibility, nay, the actual unquestioned existence of ghosts in the abstract, is it likely that there should be anything to be seen so horribly fear-inspiring, as to send a perfectly sane person *in one instant* raving mad, which you, after three weeks' residence in the house, have never caught a glimpse of? According to your hypothesis, your whole household ought, by this time, to be stark staring mad. Let me implore you not to give way to a panic which may, possibly, probably prove utterly groundless. Oh, how I wish I were with you, to make you listen to reason! Artie ought to be the best prop ever woman's old age was furnished with, to indemnify me for all he and his hooping-cough have made me suffer. Write immediately, please, and tell me how the poor patient progresses. Oh, had I the wings of a dove! I shall be on wires till I hear again.

'Yours,

'BESSY.'

———

MRS MONTRESOR TO MRS DE WYNT.

'No 5, BOLTON STREET, PICCADILLY,

'*June* 12th.

'DEAREST BESSY,

'You will see that we have left that terrible house. How I wish we had escaped from it sooner! Oh, my dear Bessy, I shall never be the same again. Let me try to be coherent, and to tell you what has happened. And first, as to the housemaid, she has been removed to a lunatic asylum, where she remains in much the same state. She has had several lucid intervals, and during them has been closely, pressingly questioned as to what it was she saw; but she has maintained an absolute, hopeless silence, and only shudders, moans, and hides her face in her hands when the subject is broached. Three days ago I went to see her, and on my return was sitting resting in the drawing-room, before going to dress for dinner, talking to Adela about my visit, when Ralph Gordon walked in. He has always been walking in the last ten days, and Adela has always flushed up and looked happy whenever he made his appearance. He looked very handsome, dear fellow, just come in from the park; seemed in tremendous spirits, and was as sceptical as even you could be, as to the ghostly origin of Sarah's seizure. "Let me come here to-night and sleep in that room; *do*, Mrs Montresor," he said, looking very eager and excited. "With the gas lit and a poker, I'll engage to exorcise every demon that shows his ugly nose."

' "You don't mean really?" I asked, incredulously. "Don't I? that's all," he answered emphatically. "I should like nothing better. Well, is it a bargain?" Adela turned quite pale. "Oh, don't," she said, hurriedly, "*please*, don't! why should you run such a risk? How do you know that you might not be sent mad too?" He laughed very heartily, and coloured a little with pleasure at seeing the interest she took in his safety. "Never fear," he said, "it would take more than a whole squadron of ghosts with the devil at their head, to send me crazy." He was so eager, so persistent, so thoroughly in earnest, that I yielded at last, though with a certain strong reluctance, to his entreaties. Adela's blue eyes filled with tears, and she walked away hastily to the conservatory. Nevertheless, Ralph got his own way; it was so difficult to refuse him anything. We gave up all our engagements for the evening, and he did the same. At about ten o'clock he arrived, accompanied by a friend and brother officer, Captain Burton, who was anxious to see the result of the experiment. "Let me go up at once," he said, looking very happy and animated. "I don't know when I have felt in such good tune; a new sensation is a luxury not to be had every day of one's life; turn the gas up as high as it will go; provide a good stout poker, and leave the issue to

Providence and me." We did as he bid. "It's all ready now,"
Henry said, coming downstairs after having obeyed his orders;
"the room is nearly as light as day. Well, good luck to you,
old fellow!" "Good-bye, Miss Bruce," Ralph said, going over
to Adela, and taking her hand with a look, half laughing, half
sentimental—

> ' " 'Fare thee well, and if for ever,
>   Then for ever, fare thee well.'

that is my last dying speech and confession. Now mind," he
went on, standing by the table, and addressing us all; "if I ring
once, *don't* come. I may be flurried, and lay hold of the bell
without thinking; if I ring twice, *come*." Then he went, jumping up the stairs three steps at a time, and humming a tune. As
for us, we sat in different attitudes of expectation and listening
about the drawing-room. At first we tried to talk a little, but
it would not do; our whole souls seemed to have passed into
our ears. The clock's ticking sounded as loud as a church bell.
Addy lay on the sofa, with her white face hidden in the
cushions. So we sat for exactly an hour; but it seemed like
two years, and just as the clock began to strike eleven, a
sharp *ting*, *ting*, *ting*, rang clear and shrill through the house.
"Let us go," said Addy, starting up and running to the door.
"Let us go," I cried too, following her. But Captain Burton
stood in the way, and intercepted our progress. "No," he said,
decisively, "you must not go; remember Gordon told us distinctly, if he rang once *not* to come. I know the sort of fellow
he is, and that nothing would annoy him more than having his
directions disregarded."

' "Oh, nonsense!" Addy cried, passionately, "he would never
have rung if he had not seen something dreadful; let us go!"
she ended, clasping her hands. But she was overruled, and we
all went back to our seats. Ten minutes more of suspense,
unendurable; I felt a lump in my throat, a gasping for breath;
—ten minutes on the clock, but a thousand centuries on our
hearts. Then again, loud, sudden, violent, the bell rang! We
made a simultaneous rush to the door. I don't think we were
one second flying upstairs. Addy was first. Almost simultane-

ously she and I burst into the room. There he was, standing in the middle of the floor, rigid, petrified, with that same look— that look that is burnt into my heart—of awful, unspeakable fear on his brave young face. For one instant he stood thus; then stretching out his arms stiffly before him, he groaned in a terrible, husky voice, "Oh, my God! I have seen it!" and fell down *dead*. Not in a swoon or in a fit, but *dead*. Vainly we tried to bring back the life to that strong young heart; it will never come back again till that day when the earth and the sea give up the dead that are therein. I cannot see the page for the tears that are blinding me; he was such a dear fellow! I can't write any more today.

'Your broken-hearted
'CECILIA.'

The Haunted House of Paddington

CHARLES OLLIER

The second of our haunted house tales is 'The Haunted House of Paddington' by Charles Ollier (1788-1859).

Ollier and his brother James established their own publishing house in London and among the many famous authors of their day they published were Leigh Hunt, Shelley and Keats. Charles Ollier was also responsible for publishing the collected works of Charles Lamb.

Many of Ollier's own stories belong properly in the Gothic era, if not in date then certainly in style. Montague Summers researched Ollier thoroughly and uncovered many of his short stories. Among his novels were Altham and His Wife *(1818) and* Ferrers *(1824). This particular tale probably dates from near the middle of the century and despite the theatrical style in which it is written, still maintains a high level of suspense which culminates in some effective supernatural terror.*

The old manor-house was now a gloomy ruin. It was surrounded by an old-fashioned, spacious garden, overgrown with weeds, but, in the drowsy and half-veiled light of an April dawn, looking almost as beautiful as if it had been kept in trim order. The gravel-walks were green with moss and grass, and the fruit-trees, trained against the wall, shot out a plenteous overgrowth of wild branches which hung unprofitably over the borders. A rank crop of thistles, bind-weed, and groundsel, choked the beds, over which the slimy trace of slugs and snails shone in the horizontal gleam of the uprising sun. The noble elms, which stood about the lawn in groups, were the only objects that did not bear the melancholy evidence of neglect. All was silent, deserted, desolate.

Two men stood, in the silence of an April morning, contemplating the deserted scene. One of them appeared to know something of its history, and, yielding to the entreaty of his companion, related the following story:—

'Ten years ago,' said he, 'there dwelt in this house a man of high repute for virtue and piety. He had no wife nor children, but he lived with much liberality, and kept many servants. He was constant in his attendance at church, and gladdened the heart of the neighbouring poor by the frequency of his almsgiving.

'His fame among his neighbours was increased by his great hospitality. Scarcely a day passed without his entertaining some of them with feasts at his house, when his conversation was admired, his judgment appealed to as something more than ordinarily wise, his decisions considered final, and his jokes received with hearty laughter, according to the time-hallowed and dutiful practice of guests at the tables of rich men.

'Nothing could exceed the costliness and rarity of this man's wines, the lavish profusion of his plate, nor the splendour of his rooms which were decorated with the richest furniture, the most costly specimens of the Italian and Flemish schools of painting, and resounded nightly with the harmony of dainty madrigals.

'One summer evening, after a sumptuous dinner had been enjoyed by himself and a numerous party, the weather being very sultry, a proposal was made by the host that the wine and dessert should be taken to the lawn, and that the revelry should be prolonged under the shade of the leafy elms which stood about the garden in groups, as now you see them. The company accordingly adjourned thither, and great was the merriment beneath the green boughs which hung over the table in heavy masses, and loud the songs in the sweet air of evening.

'Twilight came on; but still the happy revellers were loath to leave the spot, which seemed sacred to wine and music, and indolent enjoyment. The leaves which canopied them were motionless; even those which hung on the extreme point of the tenderest sprays, quivered not. One shining star, poised in the

clear ether, seemed to look down with curious gaze on the
jocund scene; and the soft west wind had breathed its last
drowsy evening hymn. The calm, indeed, was so perfect that
the master of the house ordered lights to be brought there
where they sat, that the out-of-door carouse might be still
enjoyed.

'"Hang care!" exclaimed he. "This is a delicious evening;
the wine has a finer relish here than in the house, and the song
is more exciting and melodious under the tranquil sky than in
the close room, where sound is stifled. Come, let us have a
bacchanalian chant—let us, with old Sir Toby, make the welkin
dance, and rouse the night-owl with a catch. I am right merry.
Pass the bottle, and tune your voices—a catch, a catch! The
lights will be here anon."

'Thus he spoke; but his merriment seemed forced and unnatural. A grievous change awaited him.

'As one of the servants was proceeding from the house with
a flambeau in his hand, to light the tapers already placed on
the table, he saw, in the walk leading from the outer gate, a
matron of lofty bearing, in widow's weeds, whose skin, as the
rays of the torch fell on it, looked white as a monumental effigy,
and made a ghastly contrast with her black robe. Her face was
like that of the grisly phantom, Death-in-Life; it was rigid and
sunken; but her eyes glanced about from their hollow sockets
with a restless motion, and her brow was knit as if in anger.
A corpse-like infant was in her arms; and she paced with proud
and stately tread towards the spot where the master of the
house was sitting amongst his jovial friends.

'The servant shuddered as he beheld the strange intruder;
but he, too, had partaken of the good cheer, and felt bolder than
usual. Mustering up his courage, he faced the awful woman,
and demanded her errand.

'"I seek your master," said she.

'"He is engaged, and cannot be interrupted," replied the man.
"Ugh! turn your face from me—I like not your looks. You
are enough to freeze one's very blood."

'"Fool!" returned the woman. "Your master *must* see me."
And she pushed the servant aside.

'The menial shivered at the touch of her hand, which was

heavy and cold, like marble. He felt as if rooted to the spot; he could not move to follow her as she walked on to the scene of the banquet.

'On arriving at the spot, she drew herself up beside the host, and stood there without uttering a word. He saw her, and shook in every joint. The song ceased; the guests were speechless with amazement, and sat like statues bending their gaze towards the strange and solemn figure which confronted them.

'"Why comest thou here?" at length demanded the rich man in low and gasping accents. "Vanish! Who opened the vault to let thee forth? Thou shouldst be a hundred miles away. Sink again into the earth! Hence, horrible thing!—delusion of hell!—dead creature!—ghost!—hence! What seekest thou? What can I do to keep thee in the grave? I will resign thy lands; to whom shall they be given? Thy child is dead. Who is now thy heir? Speak! and be invisible!"

'The pale woman stooped and whispered something in his ear, which made him tremble still more violently. Then beckoning him, she passed through the deepening twilight towards the house, while he, with bristling hair and faltering gait, followed her. The terror-stricken man, the gaunt woman, and white child, looked like three corpses moving in the heavy and uncertain shades of evening.

'After waiting an hour for their friend's return, the guests, who had now recovered from their first panic, became impatient to solve the mystery, and determined to seek the owner of the house, and offer such comfort as his evident trepidation required. They accordingly directed their steps towards the room into which they were informed the woman and child, and their host had entered.

'On approaching the door, piteous groans, and incoherent exclamations were heard; above which these words were plainly audible in a female voice: "Remember what I have said! Think of my slaughtered husband! A more terrible intruder will some night come to thy house! Thou shalt perish here and hereafter!"

'Hearing these groans and these menaces, the party instantly burst into the room, followed by a servant with a light. The man, whose face was buried in his hands, was standing alone.

But, as his friends gazed around in amazement, a shadow of the woman with the infant in her arms was seen to flicker on the wall, as if moved by a faint wind. By degrees it faded entirely away. No one knew how the stately widow herself had disappeared, nor by what means she had obtained admittance through the outer gate.

'To the earnest inquiries of his friends the host would give no answer; and the party left the place perplexed with fearful thoughts. From that time no feasts were given in the manor house. The apartment where the secret interview took place, and which is to this day called 'The Room of the Shadow', was closed, and, it is said, has never since been opened. It is the chamber immediately above this, and is now the haunt of bats.

'After having lived here several years in comparative solitude, a mortal sickness came upon the owner of the house. But, if his bodily sufferings were grievous to behold, the agony of his mind seemed tenfold greater. He felt that he must shortly appear before the Supreme Judge; and the anticipated terrors of the judgment were already upon his spirit. His countenance underwent many ghastly changes, and the sweat of dismal suffering poured in heavy beads from his face and breast.

'The throes of his conscience were too strong to be any longer endured and hidden; and, summoning one or two of his neighbours to his bedside, he confessed many sins of which he had been guilty in another part of England; he had, he said, enriched himself by the ruin of widows and orphans; and, he added, that the accursed lust for gold had made him a murderer.

'It was in vain that the pastor of the parish, who saw his bitter agony, strove to absolve him of his manifold crimes. He could not be comforted. "His works, and alms, and all the good endeavour" of the latter years of his life were of no avail. They were as chaff, and flew off from the weight of his transgressions. The vengeance of eternal fire haunted him while living, and he did not dare even to pray. "Alas! my friends," said he, to those who besought him to lift up his voice in supplication to the Most High, "I have no heart to pray, for I am already condemned! Hell is even now in my soul, there to burn for ever. Resign me, I pray you, to my lost condition, and to the fiends hovering around to seize me."

'The menace of the strange woman was now about to be fulfilled.

'On the last night of this person's miserable life, one of his neighbours sat with the expiring wretch by his bedside. He had for some time fallen into a state of stupor, being afraid to look any human being in the face, or even to open his eyes. He slept or seemed to sleep for a while; then suddenly arousing himself, he appeared to be in intolerable agitation of body and mind, and with an indescribable expression of countenance, shrieked out, "Oh the intolerable horrors of damnation!"

'Midnight had now arrived. The servants were in bed, and no one was stirring in the house but the old nurse, and the friend who watched the last moments of the sufferer. All was in quiet profound as that of the sepulchre, when suddenly the sound of loud and impatient footsteps was heard in the room adjoining the forlorn man's bedchamber.

'"What can that be?" said the nurse under her breath, and with an expression of ghastly alarm. "Hark! the noise continues!"

'"Is any one up in the house?" inquired the friend.

'"No; besides, would a servant dare to tramp with such violence about the next room to that of his dying master?"

'The gentleman snatched up a lamp, and went forth into the next chamber. It was empty! but still the footsteps sounded loudly as those of a person waiting in angry impatience.

'Bewildered and aghast, the friend returned to the bedside of the wretch, and could not find utterance to tell the nurse what had been the result of his examination of the adjoining room.

'"For the love of Heaven!" exclaimed the woman, "speak! —tell me what you have seen in the next chamber. Who is there? Why do you look so pale? What has made you dumb? Hark! The noise of the footsteps grows louder and louder. Oh! how I wish I had never entered this accursed house—this house abhorred of God and man!"

'Meanwhile the sound of the horrid footsteps grew not only louder, but quicker and more impatient.

'The scene of their tramping was, after a time, changed. They approached the sick man's room, and were plainly heard close by the bedside of the dying wretch, whose nurse and friend stared with speechless terror upon the floor, which sounded and shook as the invisible foot-falls passed over it.

' "Something is here—something terrible—in this very room, and close to us, though we cannot see it!" whispered the gentleman in panting accents to his companion. "Go upstairs —and call the servants—and let all in the house assemble here."

' "I dare not move," exclaimed the trembling woman. "I shall go mad! Let us fly from this place—the fiend is here. Help! help! in the name of the Almighty."

' "Be composed, I beseech you," said the gentleman in a voice scarcely audible. "Recall your scattered senses. I too should be scared to death, did I not with a strong effort keep down the mad throbbings that torment me. Recollect our duty. We are Christians, and must not abandon the expiring man. God will protect us. Merciful Heaven!" he continued, with a frenzied glance into the shadowy recesses of the chamber— "listen! the noise is stronger than ever—those iron footsteps! —and still we cannot discern the cause! Go and bring some companions—some human faces!"

'The nurse, thus adjured, left the demon-haunted apartment with a visage white as snow; and the benevolent friend, whose spirits had been subdued by long watching in the chamber of death, and by witnessing the sick man's agony and remorse, became, now that he was left alone, wild and frantic. Assuming a courage from the very intensity of fear, he shrieked out in a voice which scarcely sounded like his own, "What art thou, execrable thing! that comest at this dead hour? Speak, if thou canst; show thyself, if thou darest!"

'These cries roused the dying man from the miserable slumber into which he had fallen. He opened his glassy eyes— gasped for utterance, and seemed as though he would now have prayed—prayed in mortal anguish; but the words died in his throat. His lips quivered and seemed parched, as if by fire; they stood apart, and his clenched teeth grinned horribly. It was evident that he heard the footsteps; for an agony, fearful to behold, came over him. He arose in his bed—held out his arms, as if to keep off the approach of some hateful thing; and, having sat thus for a few moments, fell back, and with a dismal groan expired!

'From that very instant the sound of the footsteps was heard no more! Silence fell upon the room. When the nurse re-entered, followed by the servants, they found the sick man dead, with a face of horrible contortion, and his friend stretched on the floor in a swoon.

'The mortal part of the wretch was soon buried; and after that time (the dismal story becoming generally known) no one would dare to inhabit the house, which gradually fell into decay, and got the fatal reputation of being haunted.'

A Dreadful Night

by

EDWIN LESTER ARNOLD

One of the most remarkable books to be published in the 1890s was Edwin Lester Arnold's The Story of Ulla (1895). While not much is known about the author, the stories themselves were really ahead of their time. Among the subjects Arnold handled were the psychological effects of terror, reincarnation, the dehumanizing effects of violence, and other themes most uncommon in the literature of the day. He dealt with a bloody invasion of Ireland by the Vikings in one tale, with a detailed description of the horrors involved that makes many of today's writers of blood and thunder novels look like amateurs. It would be interesting to find out exactly what the reaction was to Arnold's book in its day; I regret I have been unable to do so. Judge for yourself what it might have been from this tale of pure terror, taken from Arnold's book, which tells of a hunter's adventure in the Colorado mountains. It is fascinating how, despite the wealth of adjectives and at times theatrical descriptions Arnold employs, he never, for one sentence, loses his grip on the tight reins by which he guides the reader through this terrifying little tale.

Only he who has been haunted by a dream, a black horror of the night so real and terrible that many days of repugnance and effort are needed to purge the mind of its ugly details, can understand how a dream that was a fact—a horrible waking fantasy, grotesque and weird, a repetition in hard actuality of the ingenious terrors of sleep—clings to him who, with his faculties about him, and all his senses on the alert, has experienced it.

Some five years ago I was hunting in the southwest corner of Colorado, where the great mountain-spurs slope down in rocky ravines and gullies from the inland ranges towards the green plains along the course of the Rio San Juan. I had left my camp, late one afternoon, in charge of my trusty comrade, Will Hartland and had wandered off alone into the scrub. Some five or six miles from the tents I stalked and wounded a buck. He was so hard hit that I already smelt venison in the supper-pot, and followed the broad trail he had left with the utmost eagerness. He crossed a couple of stony ridges with their deep intervening hollows, and came at last into a wild desolate gorge, full of loose rocks and bushes, and ribboned with game tracks, but otherwise a most desolate and Godforsaken place, where no man had been, or might come for fifty years. Here I sighted my venison staggering down the glen, and dashed after him as fast as I could, through the bushy tangled, and the dry, slippery, summer grass. In a few hundred yards the valley became a pass, and in a score more the steep, bare sides had drawn in until they were walls on either hand, and the way trailed along the bottom of what was little better than a knife-cleft in the hills.

I was a good runner, and the hunter blood was hot within me; my moccasins flashed through the yellow herbage; my cheeks burnt with excitement; I dropped my gun to be the freer—the quarry was plunging along only ten yards ahead, and seemed a certain victim! In front was the outing of that narrow ravine —long reaches of the silver San Juan twining in countless threads through interminable leagues of green pasture and forest—I saw it all like a beautiful picture in the narrow black frame of the rocks; the evening wind was blowing softly up the cañon, and the sky was already gorgeous and livid with the streaks of sunset. Another ten yards and we were flying down the narrowest part of the defile, the beast-path under our feet hardly a foot wide, and almost hidden by long, wiry, dead grass.

Suddenly the wounded buck, now within my grasp, staggered up on to its hind legs, in a mad fit of terror, just as, with a shout of triumph, I leapt up to it, and in half a breathing space I and the stag were reeling on the very brink of a horrible funnel,—a slippery yellow slope that had opened suddenly before us, leading down to a cavernous mouth gaping dark and dreadful in the heart of the earth. With a scream louder than my shout of triumph I threw up my hands and tried to stop; it was too late; I felt my feet slip from under me, and in a second, shouting and plunging, and clutching at the rotten herbage, I was flying downwards. I caught a last glimpse of the San Juan and the blaze of the sky overhead and then I was spinning into darkness, horrible stygian darkness, through which I fell for a giddy, senseless moment or two, and then landed with a thud which ought to have killed me, bruised and nearly senseless, on a soft quaggy mound of something that seemed to sink under me like a feather bed. I passed out.

My first sensation on recovering consciousness was that of an overpowering smell, a sickly, deadly taint in the air that there was no growing accustomed to, and which, after a few gasps, seemed to have run its deadly venom into every corner of my frame, and, turning my blood yellow, to have transformed my constitution into keeping with its own accursed nature. It was a damp, musty, charnel-house smell, sickly and wicked, with the breath of the slaughter-pit in it—an aroma of blood and corruption. I sat up and glared, gasped about in the gloom, and then I carefully felt my limbs up and down. All were safe and sound, and I was unhurt, though as sore and bruised as if my body had stood a long day's pummelling. Then I groped about me in the pitch dark, and soon touched the still warm body of the dead buck I had shot, and on which indeed I was sitting. Still feeling about, I found on the other side something soft and furry too. I touched and patted it, and in a minute recognized with a start that my fingers were deep in the curly mane of a bull bison. I pulled, and the curly mane came off in stinking tufts. That bull bison had been lying there six months or more. All about me, wherever I felt, was cold, clammy fur and hair and hoofs and bare ribs and bones mixed in wild confusion, and as that wilderness of death unfolded itself in the darkness to me, and the foetid, close atmosphere mounted to my head, my nerves began to tremble like harp-strings in a storm, and my heart, that I had always thought terror-proof, to patter like a girl's.

Plunging and slipping I got upon my feet, and then became conscious of a dim circle of twilight far above, representing the hole through which I had fallen. The twilight was fading outside every moment, and it was already so faintly luminous that my hand, held in front of me, looked ghostly and scarcely discernible. I began to explore slowly round the walls of my prison. With a heart that grew sicker and sicker, and sensations that you can imagine better than I can describe, I traced the jagged but unbroken circle of a great chamber in the underground, a hundred feet long, perhaps, by fifty across, with cruel, remorseless walls that rose sloping gently inwards from an uneven horrible floor of hides and bones to that narrow neck far overhead, where the stars were already twinkling in a cloudless sky. By this time I was fairly frightened, and the cold perspiration of dread began to stand in beads upon my forehead.

A fancy then seized me that some one might be within hearing distance above. I shouted again and again, and listening acutely each time as the echoes of my shout died away, I could have sworn something like the clash of ghostly teeth on teeth, something like the rattle of jaws in an ague fit, fell on the silence behind. With beating heart, and an unfamiliar dread creeping over me, I crouched down in the gloom and listened. There was water dripping out in the dark, monotonous and dismal, and something like the breath from a husky throat away in the distance of the cavern came fitfully to my ears, though so uncertain that at first I thought it might have been only the rustle of the wind in the grass far overhead.

Again mastering all my resolution, I shouted until the darkness rang, then listened eagerly with every faculty on stretch; and again from the dimness came that tremulous gnashing of teeth, and that wavering, long-drawn breath. Then my hair literally stood on end, and my eyes were fixed with breathless wonder in front of me, for out of the remotest gloom, where the corruption of the floor was already beginning to glow with pale blue wavering phosphorescent light as the night fell, rose glimmering itself with that ghastly lustre, something slim and

tall and tremulous. It was full of life and yet was not quite of
human form, and reared itself against the dark wall, all agleam,
until its top, set with hollow eyes, was nine or ten feet from
the ground, and oscillated and wavered, and seemed to feel
about, as I had done, for an opening—and then on a sudden
collapsed in a writhing heap upon the ground, and I distinctly
heard the fall of its heavy body as it disappeared into the blue
inferno that burnt below.

Again that spectral thing rose laboriously, this time many
paces nearer to me, to twice the height of a man, and wavered
and felt about, and then sank down with a fall like the fall
of heavy draperies, as though the energy that had lifted it
suddenly expired. Nearer and nearer it came, travelling round
the circuit of the walls in that strange way, and awed and
bewildered I crept out into the open to let that dreadful thing
go by. And presently, to my infinite relief, it travelled away,
still wavering and writhing and I breathed again.

As that luminous shadow faded into the remote corners of
the cave, I shouted once more, for the pleasure, it must have
been, of hearing my own voice,—again there was that gnashing
of teeth—and the instant afterwards such a hideous chorus of
yells from the other side of the cavern, such a commingled
howl of lost spirits, such an infernal moan of sorrow and shame
and misery, that rose and fell on the stillness of the night, that,
for an instant, lost to everything but that dreadful sound, I
leapt to my feet, with the stagnant blood cold as ice within
me, my body pulseless for the moment, and mingled my mad
shouting with the voices of those unseen devils in a hideous
chorus. Then my manhood came back with a rush upon me,
and judgment and sense, and I recognised in the trembling
echoes a cry that I had often listened to in happier circumstances. That uproar came from the throats of wolves that
had been trapped like myself. But, were they alive? I thought
in fascinated wonder,—how could they be in this horrible pit?
and if they were not, picture oneself cornered in such a trap
with a pack of wolfish spirits—it would not bear thinking of;
already my fancy saw constellations of fierce yellow eyes
everywhere, and herds of wicked grey backs racing to and fro
in the shadows. With a tremulous hand I felt in my pocket for

a match, and found I had two—and two only!

By this time the moon was up and a great band of silver light, broad and bright, was creeping down the walls of our prison, but I would not wait for it. I struck the match with feverish eagerness, and held it overhead. It burnt brightly for a moment, and I saw I was in a great natural crypt, with no outlet anywhere but by the narrow neck above, and all chance of reaching that was impossible, as the walls sloped inwards everywhere as they rose to it. All the floor was piled thigh-deep with a ghastly tangle of animal remains, in every state of return to their native earth, from the bare bones, that would have crumbled at a touch, to the hide, still glossy and sleek, of the stag that had fallen in only a week or two before. Such a carnage place I never saw,—such furs, such trophies, such heads and horns there were all round, as raised the envy of my hunter spirit, even in that emergency.

But what held me spell-bound and rooted my eyes into the shadows was—twenty paces off, lying full stretch along the glossy, undulating path which the incessant feet of new victims had worn, month after month, over the hill and valley of dead bodies under the walls—a splendid eighteen-foot python. It was this creature's ghostly rambles and ineffectual attempts to scale the walls that had first scared me in that place of horrors. I turned round, for the match was short, and scarcely noticing a score or two of dejected rats, who squeaked and scrambled amongst lesser snakes and strange reptiles, looked hard across the cave.

There, on their haunches, in a huddle against the far wall, staring at me with dull cold eyes, were five of the biggest, ugliest wolves ever mortal saw. I had often seen wolves, but never any like those. All the pluck, grace and savage vigour of their kind had gone from them; their bodies, gorged with carrion, were vast, swollen, and hideous; their shaggy fur was hanging in tatters from their red and mangy skins, the saliva streamed from their jaws in yellow ribbons, their bleary eyes were drowsy and dull, their great throats, as they opened them to howl in sad chorus at the handful of purple night above, were dry and yellow, and there was about them such an air of disgusting misery and woebegoneness, that, with a shudder and a cry I could not suppress, I let the last embers of the burning match fall to the ground.

How long I crouched in the darkness against the wall, with those hideous serenaders grinding their foam-flecked teeth and bemoaning our common fate in hideous unison, I do not know. Nor have I space to tell the wild horrible visions which filled my mind for the next hour or two, but presently the moonlight had come down off the wall, and was spread at my feet in a silver carpet, and as I sullenly watched the completion of that arena of light, I was aware that the wolves were moving. Very slowly they came forward out of the darkness, led by the biggest and ugliest, until they were all in the silver circle, gaunt, spectral, and vile, every mangy tuft of loose hair upon their sore-speckled backs clear as daylight. Then those pot-bellied phosphorescent undertakers began the strangest movements, and after watching them for a moment or two in fascinated wonder, I saw they had come to me in their despair to solicit my companionship and countenance. I could not have believed it possible that dumb brutes could have made their meaning so clear, as those poor shaggy scoundrels did. They halted ten yards off, and with humble heads sagged down, and averted eyes, slowly wagged their mud-locked tails. Then they came a few steps further and whined and fawned, and then another pace, and lay down upon their stomachs, putting their noses between their paws like dogs who watch and doze, while they regarded me steadfastly with sad, great eyes, forlorn and terrible.

Foot by foot, grey and silver in the moonlight, they advanced with the offer of their dreadful friendship, until at last I was fairly bewitched, and when the big wolf came forward till he was at my knees, a horrible epitome of corruption, and licked my hand with his great burning tongue, I submitted to the caress as readily as though he were my favourite hound. Henceforth the pack seemed to think the compact was sealed, and thrust their odious company upon me, trotting at my heels, howling when I shouted, and muzzling down to me, putting their heavy paws upon my feet, and their great steaming jaws upon my chest whenever, in despair and weariness, I tried to snatch a moment's sleep.

But it would be impossible to go step by step through the infinitely painful hours of that night. Not only was the place full of spectral forms and strange cries, but presently legions of unclean things of a hundred kinds, that had lived on those dead beasts when they too were living, swarmed in thousands and assailed us, adding a new terror to the inferno, ravaging us who still kept body and soul together, till our flesh seemed burning on our bones.

There was no rest for man or brute; the light was a mockery and the silence hideous. Round and round we pattered, I and the gaunt wolves, over the dim tracks worn by the feet of disappointment and suffering; we waded knee-deep through a wavering sea of steamy blue flame, that rose from the remains and bespattered us from head to heel, stumbling and tripping and groping, and cursing our fates, each in his separate tongue, while the night waned, the dew fell clammy and cold into our prison, and the stars, who looked down upon us from the free purple sky overhead, made a dim twilight in our cell.

I was blundering and staggering round the walls for the hundredth time, feeling about with my hands in a hopeless search for some cleft or opening, when the grimmest thing of the whole evening happened. In a lonely corner of the den, in a little recess not searched before, pattering about in the dark, I suddenly touched with my hand—think with what a shock it thrilled me—the cloth-clad shoulder of a man! With a gasp and a cry I leapt back, and stood trembling and staring into the shadows, scarcely daring to breathe. Much as I had suffered in that hideous place, nothing affected me half so much as dropping my hand upon that dreadful shoulder. Heaven knows we were all cowards down there, but for a minute I was the biggest coward of us, and felt full of those strange throes of superstitious terror that I had often wondered before to hear weaker men describe.

Then I mustered my wavering spirit, and with the gaunt wolves squatting in a luminous circle around me, went into the recess again, and put my hand once more upon my grim companion. The coat upon him was dry and rough with age, and beneath it—I could tell by the touch—there was nothing but bare, rattling bones! I stood still, grimly waiting for the flutter of my physical cowardice to subside, and then I thought of that second match, and in a moment of keen intensity, with such care as you may imagine, struck it against the wall. It lit, and at my feet, in ragged miner's garb, sitting against the wall with his knees drawn up and his chin upon them, was the skeleton of a man so bleached and dry, that it must have been there for fifty years at least. At his side lay his miner's pick and pannikin, an old dusty pocket-Bible, the fragments of a felt hat, and a pair of heavy boots, still neatly side by side, just as the luckless fellow had placed the well-worn things when, for some reason, he last took them off.

And overhead something scratched upon a flat face of the rock. Hastily I snatched a scrap of paper from my pocket and, lighting it at the expiring match, read on the stone,—

> 'Monday,'
> 'Tuesday,'
> 'Wednesd—'

—there was nothing but that, and even the 'Wednesday' was unfinished, dying away in a shaky, uncertain scratch, that spoke infinitely more plainly than many words would have done, of the growing feebleness of the hand that traced it,—and then all was darkness again.

I crept back to my distant corner, and crouched like the dead man against the wall, with my chin upon my knees, and kept repeating to myself the horrible simplicity of that diary— 'Monday, Tuesday, Wednesday!' 'Poor nameless Monday, Tuesday, Wednesday! And was this to be my fate?' I laughed bitterly,—I would begin such another record with the first streak of dawn, and in the meantime I would sleep, whatever befell, and sleep I did, with those restless blue wolves cantering round the well-worn paths of the charnel-house, to their own hideous music, the silent unknown away in the distance, and the opal eyes of the great serpent staring at me like baleful planets, cold, sullen, and cruel, from between the dead man's feet.

It was a shout that woke me next morning, a clear ringing

shout, that jerked me from dreadful dreams. I scrambled to my feet and saw from the bright light about me that it was day above, and while I still staggered and wandered stupidly, again came that shout. I stared up overhead where the sunlight was making the neck of the trap a disc of intolerable brightness and there, when my eyes grew accustomed to that shining, was a round something that presently resolved itself into the blessed face of my steadfast chum, Will Hartland.

There is little need to say more. With the help of his strong cow-rope, at his saddle-bow, and a round point of earth-embedded rock as purchase, he had me out of that accursed hole in an incredibly, ridiculously short space of time. And there I was, leaning on his shoulder, free again, in the first flush of as glorious a morning as you could wish for, with the San Juan away in the distance, winding in a sapphire streak through miles of emerald forests, a sweet blue sky above, and underfoot the earth wet with morning mist, smelling like a wine cooler, and every bent and twig underfoot gemmed with glittering prismatic dewdrops. I sat down on a stone, and after a long pull at Will's flask, told him something like the narrative I have just given. And when the tale was done I paused a minute, and then said somewhat shyly, 'And now I am going back, Will, old man! back for those poor devils down yonder, who haven't a chance for their lives unless I do.' Will, who had listened to my narrative with horror and wonder flitting across his honest brown face, started up at this as though he thought the night's adventure had fairly turned my head. But he was a good fellow, chivalrous and tender of heart under his Mexican jacket, and speedily acknowledging that I was right, set to work to help me.

Down I went back into the pit, the very sight and shadow of which now made me sick, and with the noose end of Will's lasso (he holding the other end above) set to work to secure those poor beasts, who whined and crowded round my legs in hideous glee to have me back again amongst them. 'Twas easy work; they were stupid and heavy, and seemed to have time, and when a wolf was fast, shouted to Will, who hauled some idea of my intentions, and thus I noosed them one at a away with scant ceremony, and up the grey ghoul went into that sunshine he had not seen for many weeks, until he and all his comrades were free once more, spinning, and struggling, and yelping—truly a wonderful sight.

But nothing would move the python. I followed him round and round, trying all I knew to get his cruel, cynical head through the noose, and then, when he had refused it a dozen times, I grew angry and cursed him and gathering up all the tortoises, lizards, and lesser beasts I could find into my waistband, ascended into the sweet outer air once more.

A very few hours afterwards a heavy blasting-charge, fetched from a neighbouring mine, was dangling by a string just inside the mouth of the detestable trap, with its fuse burning brightly. A few minutes of suspense, a mighty crash, a cloud of white smoke hanging over the green hill-top, and one of the most treacherous places that ever marred the face of nature's sweet earth was a harmless heap of dust and tumbled stones.

The House of Strange Stories

by

ANDREW LANG

*Andrew Lang (1844-1912) was born in Selkirk and edu-
cated at Edinburgh Academy, St Andrews University and
Balliol College, Oxford. He was one of the most famous
writers of his day, specializing in his interpretations of
mythology. He is probably chiefly remembered for his
series of children's books dealing with fairies, all named
with different colours (The Green Fairy Book, The Red
Fairy Book, etc.). He was a close friend of H. Rider Haggard and collaborated with him on The World's Desire.*

*Lang was also interested in the supernatural and real-life
mysteries. He researched a series of articles of his views
on famous mysteries, including the famous Kasper Hauser
and D. D. Hume, for The Cornhill Magazine, which were
later published under the title of Historical Mysteries
(1904). They reveal how much care Lang took to check
details and examine facts and theories when he produced
his books on the occult.*

*Lang's fiction has been almost forgotten, especially his
neglected volume of short stories, In The Wrong Paradise
(1886), from which 'The House of Strange Stories' is taken.
It is one of the stories featuring tales around the fireside
which were so much in vogue in the Victorian era. Incidentally, students of E. F. Benson should take especial
note of 'The Bachelor of Arts' Story' in this tale, for it seems
to form the germ of the idea used by Benson in his famous
'The Bus Conductor'.*

The House of Strange Stories, as I prefer to call it (though it is not known by that name in the county), seems the ideal place for a ghost. Yet, though so many people have dwelt upon its site and in its chambers, though the ancient Elizabethan oak, and all the queer tables and chairs that a dozen generations have bequeathed, might well be tenanted by ancestral spirits, and disturbed by rappings, it is a curious fact that there is *not* a ghost in the House of Strange Stories.

On my earliest visit to this mansion, I was disturbed, I own, by a not unpleasing expectancy. There *must*, one argued, be a shadowy lady in green in the bedroom, or, just as one was falling asleep, the spectre of a Jesuit would creep out of the priest's hole, where he was starved to death in the 'spacious times of great Elizabeth', and would search for a morsel of bread. The priest was usually starved out, sentinels being placed in all the rooms and passages, till at last hunger and want of air would drive the wretched man to give himself up, for the sake of change of wretchedness. Then perhaps he was hanged, or he 'died in our hands', as one of Elizabeth's officers euphemistically put it, when the Jesuit was tortured to death in the Tower.

'Does the priest of your "priest-hole" walk?' I asked the squire one winter evening in the House of Strange Stories.

Darkness had come to the rescue of the pheasants about four in the afternoon, and all of us, men and women, were sitting at afternoon tea in the firelit study, drowsily watching the flicker of the flame on the black panelling. The characters will introduce themselves, as they take part in the conversation.

'No,' said the squire, 'even the priest does not walk. Somehow very few of the Jesuits have left ghosts in country houses They are just the customers you would expect to "walk", but they don't.'

THE SQUIRE'S STORY

'There is, to be sure, one priestly ghost-story, which I will tell here just as I heard it from the Bishop of Dunchester himself. According to this most affable and distinguished prelate, he once arrived in a large country house shortly before dinner-time; he was led to his chamber, he dressed, and went down-stairs. Not knowing the plan of the house, he found his way into the library where the learned bishop remained for a few minutes, until the gong sounded for dinner, and a domestic, entering the apartment showed the prelate the way to the drawing-room, where the other guests were now assembled. The bishop, when the company appeared complete, and was beginning to manoeuvre towards the dining-room, addressed his host (whom we shall call Lord Birkenhead), and observed that the ecclesiastic had not yet appeared.

'What ecclesiastic?' asked his lordship.

'The priest,' replied the bishop, 'whom I met in the library.'

Upon this Lord Birkenhead's countenance changed some-what, and, with a casual remark, he put the question by. After dinner, when the ladies had left the men to their wine, Lord Birkenhead showed some curiosity as to 'the ecclesiastic', and learned that he had seemed somewhat shy and stiff, yet had the air of a man just about to enter into conversation.

'At that moment,' said the bishop, 'I was summoned to the drawing-room, and did not at first notice that my friend the priest had not followed me. He had an interesting and care-worn face,' added the bishop.

'You have certainly seen the family ghost,' said Lord Birkenhead; 'he only haunts the library, where, as you may imagine, his retirement is but seldom disturbed.'

'Then I must return, Lord Birkenhead, to your library,' said the bishop, 'and that without delay, for this appears to be a matter in which the services of one of the higher clergy, how-ever unworthy, may prove of incalculable benefit.'

'If I could only hope,' answered Lord Birkenhead (who was a Catholic) with a deep sigh, 'that his reverence would recog-nize Anglican orders!'

The bishop was now, as may be fancied, on his mettle, and without further parley, retired to the library. The rest of the men awaited his return.

In about half an hour the bishop reappeared, and a close observer might have detected a shade of paleness on his apos-tolic features, yet his face was radiant like that of a good man who has performed a good action. Being implored to relieve the anxiety of the company, the worthy prelate spoke as follows:

'On entering the library, which was illuminated by a single lamp, I found myself alone. I drew a chair to the fire, and, taking up a volume which chanced to be lying on the table, I composed myself to read. Thus, by an effort of will, I distracted myself from that state of "expectant attention" to which modern science attributes such phantoms and spectral appearances as can neither be explained away by a morbid condition of the liver, nor as caused by the common rat.

'I had not long been occupied when I became aware of the presence of another person in the room. I think my eyes had strayed from the volume, as I turned a page, to the table, on which I perceived the brown strong hand of a young man. Looking up, I beheld my friend the priest, who was indeed a man of some twenty-seven years of age, with a frank and open, though somewhat careworn, aspect. I at once asked if I could be of service to him in anything, and I trust I did not betray any wounding suspicion that he was other than a man of flesh and blood.

'"You can, indeed, my lord, relieve me of a great burden," said the young man, and it was apparent enough that he *did* acknowledge the validity of Anglican orders. "Will you kindly take from the shelf that volume of Cicero 'De Officiis,'" he said, —"remove the paper you will find there, and burn it in the fire on the hearth."

'"Certainly I will do as you say, but will you reward me by explaining the reason of your request?"

'"In me," said the appearance, "you behold Francis Wilton, priest. I was born in 1657, and, after adventures and an education with which I need not trouble you, found myself here as chaplain to the family of the Lord Birkenhead of the period. It chanced one day that I heard in confession, from the lips of Lady Birkenhead, a tale so strange, moving, and, but for the sacred circumstances of the revelation, so incredible, that my soul had no rest for thinking thereon. At last, neglecting my vow, and fearful that I might become forgetful of any portion of so marvellous a narrative, I took up my pen and committed the confession to the security of manuscript. Scarcely had I finished my unholy task when the sound of a distant horn told me that the hunt (to which pleasure I was passionately given) approached the demesne. I thrust the written confession into that volume of Cicero, hurried to the stable, saddled my horse with my own hands, and rode in the direction whence I heard the music of the hounds. On my way a locked gate barred my progress. I put Rupert at it, he took off badly, fell, and my spirit passed away in the fall. But not to the place of repose did my sinful spirit wing its flight. I found myself here in the library, where scarcely any one ever comes except the maids. When I would implore them to destroy the unholy document that binds me to earth, they merely scream; nor have I found any scion of the house, nor any guest, except your lordship, of more intrepid resolution or more charitable mood. And now, I trust, you will release me."

'I rose, stirred with pity; I took down the Cicero, and found a sheet of yellow paper covered with faded manuscript, which, of course, I did not read. I turned to the hearth, tossed on the fire the sere old paper, which blazed at once, and then, hearing the words *pax vobiscum*, I looked round. But I was alone. I returned to the dining-room; and that is all my story. Your maids need no longer dread the ghost of the library. He is released.'

'Well,' said one of the ladies, the young Miss Girton when the squire had finished the prelate's narrative, 'I don't call that much of a story. What was Lady Birkenhead's confession about? That's what one really wants to know.'

'The bishop could not possibly have read the paper,' said the Bachelor of Arts, one of the guests; 'not as a gentleman, nor a bishop.'

'I wish *I* had had the chance,' said the Girton girl.

'Perhaps the confession was in Latin,' said the Bachelor of Arts.

The Girton girl disdained to reply to this unworthy sneer.

'I have often observed,' she said in a reflective voice, 'that the most authentic and best attested bogies don't come to very much. They appear in a desultory manner, without any context, so to speak, and, like other difficulties, require a context to clear up their meaning.'

These efforts of the Girton girl to apply the methods of philology to spectres, were received in silence. The women did not understand them, though they had a strong personal opinion about their learned author.

MISS GIRTON'S STORY

'The only ghost *I* ever came across, or, rather, came within measurable distance of, never appeared at all so far as one knew.

'It was the Long Vacation before last,' said Miss Girton, 'and I went on a reading-party to Bantry Bay, with Wyndham and Toole of Somerville, and Clare of Lady Margaret's. Leighton coached us.

'Well, term-time was drawing near, and Bantry Bay was getting pretty cold, when I received an invitation from Lady Garryowen to stay with them at Dundellan on my way south. They were two very dear, old, hospitable Irish ladies, the last of their race, Lady Garryowen and her sister, Miss Patty. They were *so* hospitable that, though I did not know it, Dundellan was quite full when I reached it, overflowing with young people. The house has nothing very remarkable about it: a grey, plain building, with remains of the château about it, and a high park wall. In the garden wall there is a small round tower, just like those in the precinct wall at St Andrews. The ground floor is not used. On the first floor there is a furnished chamber with a deep round niche, almost a separate room. The first floor has long been fitted up as a bedroom and dressing-room, but it had not been occupied, and an old spinning-wheel in the corner must have been unused since '98, at least. I reached Dublin late—our train should have arrived at half-past six—it was ten before we toiled into the station. The Dundellan carriage was waiting for me, and, after an hour's drive, I reached the house. The dear old ladies had sat up for me, and I went to bed as soon as possible, in a very comfortable room. I fell asleep at once, and did not waken till broad day-

light, between seven and eight, when, as my eyes wandered
about, I saw, by the pictures on the wall, and the names on the
books beside my bed, that Miss Patty must have given up her
own room to me. I was quite sorry and, as I dressed, determined
to get her to let me change into any den rather than accept this
sacrifice. I went downstairs, and found breakfast ready, but
neither Lady Garryowen nor Miss Patty. Looking out of the
window into the garden, I heard, for the only time in my life,
the wild Irish keen over the dead, and saw the old nurse wailing and wringing her hands and hurrying to the house. As soon
as she entered she told me, with a burst of grief that Miss
Patty was dead.

'When I arrived the house was so full that there was literally
no room for me. But "Dundellan was never beaten yet," the
old ladies had said. There was still the room in the tower. But
this room had such an evil reputation for being "haunted" that
the servants could hardly be got to go near it, at least after
dark, and the dear old ladies never dreamed of sending any
of their guests to pass a bad night in a place with a bad name.
Miss Patty, who had the courage of a Bayard, did not think
twice. She went herself to sleep in the haunted tower, and left
her room to me. And when the old nurse went to call her in
the morning, she could not waken Miss Patty. She was dead.
Heart-disease, they called it. Of course,' added Miss Girton,
'I think, it was only a coincidence. But the Irish servants could
not be persuaded that Miss Patty had not seen whatever the
thing was that they believed to be in the garden tower. I don't
know what it was. You see the context was dreadfully vague,
a mere fragment.'

There was a little silence after the Girton girl's story.

'I never heard before in my life,' said the maiden aunt, at
last, 'of any host or hostess who took the haunted room themselves, when the house happened to be full. They always send
the stranger within their gates to it, and then pretend to be
vastly surprised when he does not have a good night. I had
several bad nights myself once. In Ireland too.'

'Tell us all about it, Judy,' said her brother, the squire.

'No,' murmured the maiden aunt. 'You would only laugh at

me. There was no ghost. I didn't hear anything. I didn't see anything. I didn't even *smell* anything, as they do in that horrid book by Wilkie Collins, "The Haunted Hotel." '

'Then why had you such bad nights?'

'Oh, I *felt*,' said the maiden aunt, with a little shudder.

'What did you *feel*, Aunt Judy?'

AUNT JUDY'S STORY

'I know you will laugh,' said the maiden aunt, abruptly entering on her nervous narrative. 'I felt all the time *as if somebody was looking through the window*. Now, you know, there couldn't be anybody. It was in an Irish country house where I had just arrived, and my room was on the second floor. The window was old-fashioned and narrow, with a deep recess. As soon as I went to bed I felt that some one was looking through the window, and meant to come in. I got up, and bolted the window, though I knew it was impossible for anybody to climb up there, and I drew the curtains, but I could not fall asleep. If ever I began to doze, I would waken with a start, and turn and look in the direction of the window. I did not sleep all night, and next night, though I was dreadfully tired, it was just the same thing. So I had to take my hostess into my confidence, though it was extremely disagreeable to seem so foolish. I only told her that I thought the air, or something, must disagree with me, for I could not sleep. Then, as some one was leaving the house that day, she implored me to try another room, where I slept beautifully, and afterwards had a very pleasant visit. But, the day I went away, my hostess asked me if I had been kept awake by anything in particular, for instance, by a feeling that some one was trying to come in at the window. Well, I admitted that I *had* a nervous feeling of that sort, and she said that she was very sorry, and that every one who slept in the room had exactly the same sensation. She supposed they must all have heard the history of the room, in childhood, and forgotten that they had heard it, and then been consciously reminded of it by reflex action. So I said I'd never heard the history of the room; but she said I *must* have, and so must all the people who felt as if some one was coming in by the window. And I said that it was rather a curious thing they should all forget they knew it, and all be reminded of it without being aware of it, and that, if she did not mind, I'd like to be reminded of it again. So she said that these objections had all been replied to and then she told me the history of the room. It only came to this, that, three generations before, the family butler (whom every one had always thought a most steady, respectable man), dressed himself up like a ghost, and got a ladder, and came in by the window to steal the diamonds of the lady of the house, and he frightened her to death, poor woman! That was all. But, ever since, people who sleep in the room don't sleep, so to speak, and keep thinking that some one is coming in by the casement. That's all; and I told you it was not an interesting story, but perhaps you will find more interest in the scientific explanation of all these things.'

The story of the maiden aunt, so far as it recounted her own experience, did not contain anything to which the judicial faculties of the mind refused assent. Probably the Bachelor of Arts felt that something a good deal more unusual was wanted, for he instantly started without being asked, on the following narrative.

THE BACHELOR OF ARTS' STORY

'I also was staying,' said the Bachelor of Arts, 'at the home of my friends in Scotland. The name of the house it is not necessary for me to give. The front of the castle looks forth on a somewhat narrow drive, bordered by black and funereal pines. On the night of my arrival at the castle, although I went late to bed, I did not feel at all sleepy. Something, perhaps, in the mountain air, or in the vicissitudes of baccarat, may have banished slumber. I had been lucky, and a pile of sovereigns and notes lay, in agreeable confusion, on my dressing-table. My feverish blood declined to be tranquillized, and at last I drew up the blind, threw open the latticed window, and looked out on the drive and the pine-wood. The faint and silvery blue of dawn was just wakening in the sky, and a setting moon hung, with a peculiarly ominous and wasted appearance, above the crests of the forest. But conceive my astonishment when I beheld, on the drive, and right under my window, a large and well-appointed hearse, with two white horses, with plumes complete, and attended by mutes, whose black staffs were tipped with silver that glittered pallid in the dawn.

'I exhausted my ingenuity in conjectures as to the presence of this remarkable vehicle with the white horses, so unusual, though, when one thinks of it, so appropriate to the chariot of Death. Could some belated visitor have arrived in a hearse? Could one of the domestics have expired, and was it the intention of my host to have the body thus honourably removed without casting a gloom over his guests?

'Wild as these hypotheses appeared, I could think of nothing better, and was just about to leave the window, and retire to bed, when the driver of the strange carriage, who had hither-to sat motionless, turned, and looked me full in the face. Never shall I forget the appearance of this man, whose sallow counte-nance, close-shaven dark chin, and small, black moustache, combined with a certain military air struck into me a certain indefinable alarm. No sooner had he caught my eye, than he gathered up his reins, raised his whip, and started the mortuary vehicle at a walk down the road. I followed it with my eyes till a bend in the avenue hid it from sight. So wrapt up was my spirit in the exercise of the single sense of vision that it was not till the hearse became lost to view that I noticed the entire absence of sound which accompanied its departure. Neither had the bridles and trappings of the white horses jingled as the animals shook their heads, nor had the wheels of the hearse crashed upon the gravel of the avenue. I was com-pelled by all these circumstances to believe that what I had looked upon was not of this world, and, with a beating heart, I sought refuge in sleep.

'Next morning, feeling far from refreshed, I arrived among the latest at breakfast. Almost all the men were out hunting or fishing.

'I tried to "lead up" to the hearse in conversation with the young ladies of the castle. I endeavoured to assume the languid and preoccupied air of the guest who, in ghost-stories, has had a bad night with the family spectre. I drew the conversation to the topic of apparitions, and even to warnings of death. I knew that every family worthy of the name has its omen: the Oxenhams a white bird, another house a brass band, whose airy music is poured forth by invisible performers, and so on. Of course I expected some one to cry, "Oh, we've got a hearse with white horses," for that is the kind of heirloom an ancient house regards with complacent pride. But nobody offered any remarks on the local omen, and even when I drew near the topic of hearses, one of the girls, my cousin, merely quoted, "Speak not like a death's-head, good Doll" (my name is Adolphus), and asked me to play at lawn-tennis.

'In the evening, in the smoking-room, it was no better, nobody had ever heard of an omen in this particular castle. Nay, when I told my story, for it came to that at last, they only laughed at me, and said I must have dreamed it. Of course I expected to be wakened in the night by some awful apparition, but nothing disturbed me. I never slept better, and hearses were the last things I thought of during the remainder of my visit. Months passed, and I had almost forgotten the vision, or dream, for I began to feel apprehensive that, after all, it *was* a dream. So costly and elaborate an apparition as a hearse with white horses and plumes complete, could never have been got up, regardless of expense, for one occasion only, and to frighten one undergraduate, yet it was certain that the hearse was not "the old family coach". My hosts had undeniably never heard of it in their lives before. Even tradition at the castle said nothing of a spectral hearse, though the house was credited with a white lady deprived of her hands, and a luminous boy.

'So it seemed just a dream or, at best, a story with no meaning or sequel. But sequel and meaning there were, and I saw both not too long afterwards.

'The next Easter Vacation after my visit to the castle, I went over to Paris with a friend, a fellow of my college. We drove to the hôtel and marched upstairs with our bags and baggage and jolly high stairs they were. When we had removed the soil of travel from our persons, my friend called out to me, "I say, Jones, why shouldn't we go down by the lift." "All right," said

I, and my friend walked to the door of the mechanical appa-
ratus, opened it, and got in. I followed him, when the porter
whose business it is to "personally conduct" the inmates of the
hotel, entered also, and was closing the door.

'His eyes met mine, and I knew him in a moment. I had seen
him once before. That sallow face, black, closely shaven chin,
furtive glance, and military bearing, were the face and the
glance and bearing of the driver of that awful hearse!

'In a moment—more swiftly than I can tell you—I pushed
past the man, threw open the door, and just managed, by a
violent effort, to drag my friend on to the landing. Then the
lift rose with a sudden impulse, fell again, and rushed, with
frightful velocity, to the basement of the hotel, whence we
heard an appalling crash, followed by groans. We rushed
downstairs, and the horrible spectacle of destruction that met
our eyes I shall never forget. The unhappy porter was expiring
in agony; but the warning had saved my life and my friend's.'

'I was that friend,' said I—the collector of these anecdotes;
'and so far I can testify to the truth of Jones's story.'

At this moment, however, the gong for dressing sounded,
and we went to our several apartments. Thus ended the night
of tales in the House of Strange Stories. Should you ever visit
it, you may well hear more.

The Invisible Eye

by

ERCKMANN-CHATRIAN

The Victorian era not only produced many fine writers of macabre tales in Britain, but all over Europe and America. Among the famous writers in this vein who flourished on the continent at this time can be listed Guy de Maupassant, Ernst Hoffmann, Wilhelm Meinhold, Honore de Balzac, Theophile Gautier, Gustave Flaubert, Villiers de L'Isle Adam and Joris Karl Huysmans.

Two other names, now almost forgotten, are those of Emile Erckmann (1822-1899) and Alexandre Chatrian (1826-1890) who collaborated on a long and extremely successful series of books before a quarrel and a lawsuit ended their partnership. Their main forte was historical fiction but they also produced some notable essays in terror and the supernatural. Their best collections in this vein were The Man-Wolf *(1876),* The Wild Huntsman *(1877) and* Strange Stories *(1880), though some of their books of stories not devoted solely to the macabre are still worth reading, such as* Popular Tales And Romances *(1872) and* Stories Of The Rhine *(1875).*

Many of this century's masters of terror have expressed approval of Erckmann-Chatrian's work, including M. R. James and H. P. Lovecraft. Indeed, Lovecraft said of this particular story that 'few short tales contain greater horror'. It is hard to think of a higher recommendation.

I

When I first started my career as an artist, I took a room in the roof-loft of an old house in the Rue des Minnesängers, at Nuremberg.

I had made my nest in an angle of the roof. The slates served me for walls, and the roof-tree for a ceiling: I had to walk over my straw mattress to reach the window; but this window commanded a magnificent view, for it overlooked both city and country beyond.

The old second-hand dealer, Toubec, knew the road up to my little den as well as I knew it myself, and was not afraid of climbing the ladder. Every week his goat's head, surmounted by a rusty wig, pushed up the trap-door, his fingers clutched the edge of the floor, and in a noisy tone he cried—

'Well, well, Master Christian, have we anything new?'

To which I answered—

'Come in: why the deuce don't you come in? I'm just finishing a little landscape, and want to have your opinion of it.'

Then his long thin spine lengthened itself out, until his head touched the roof; and the old fellow laughed silently.

I must do justice to Toubec: he never bargained with me. He bought all my pictures at fifteen florins apiece, one with the other, and sold them again at forty. He was an honest Jew.

This kind of existence was beginning to please me, and I was every day finding in it some new charm, when the city of Nuremberg was agitated by a strange and mysterious event.

Not far from my garret-window, a little to the left, rose the auberge of the Boeuf-gras, an old inn much frequented by the country-people. The gable of this auberge was conspicuous for the peculiarity of its form: it was very narrow, sharply pointed, and its edges were cut like the teeth of a saw; grotesque carvings ornamented the cornices and framework of its windows. But what was most remarkable was that the house which faced it reproduced exactly the same carvings and ornaments; every detail had been minutely copied, even to the support of the signboard, with its iron volutes and spirals.

It might have been said that these two ancient buildings reflected one another; only that behind the inn grew a tall oak, the dark foliage of which served to bring into bold relief the forms of the roof, while the opposite house stood bare against the sky. For the rest, the inn was as noisy and animated as the other house was silent. On the one side was to be seen, going in and coming out, an endless crowd of drinkers, singing, stumbling, cracking their whips; over the other, solitude reigned.

Once or twice a day the heavy door of the silent house opened to give egress to a little old woman, her back bent into a half-circle, her chin long and pointed, her dress clinging to her limbs, an enormous basket under her arm, and one hand tightly clutched upon her chest.

This old woman's appearance had struck me more than once; her little green eyes, her skinny, pinched-up nose, her shawl, dating back a hundred years at least; the smile that wrinkled her cheeks, and the lace of her cap hanging down upon her eyebrows—all this appeared strange, interested me, and made me strongly desire to learn who this old woman was, and what she did in her great lonely house.

I imagined her as passing there an existence devoted to good works and pious meditation. But one day, when I had stopped in the street to look at her, she turned sharply round and darted at me a look the horrible expression of which I know not how to describe, and made three or four hideous grimaces at me; then dropping again her doddering head, she drew her large shawl about her, the ends of which trailed after her on the ground, and slowly entered her heavy door.

'That's an old mad-woman,' I said to myself; 'a malicious, cunning old mad-woman! I ought not to have allowed myself to be so interested in her. But I'll try and recall her abominable grimace—Toubec will give me fifteen florins for it willingly.'

This way of treating the matter was far from satisfying my mind, however. The old woman's horrible glance pursued me everywhere; and more than once, while scaling the perpendicular ladder of my lodging-hole, feeling my clothes caught in a nail, I trembled from head to foot, believing that the old woman had seized me by the tails of my coat for the purpose of pulling me down backwards.

Toubec, to whom I related the story, far from laughing at it, received it with a serious air.

'Master Christian,' he said, 'if the old woman means you harm, take care; her teeth are small, sharp-pointed, and wonderfully white, which is not natural at her age. She has the Evil

Eye! Children run away at her approach, and the people of Nuremberg call her Fledermausse!'

I admired the Jew's clear-sightedness, and what he had told me made me reflect a good deal; but at the end of a few weeks, having often met Fledermausse without harmful consequences, my fears died away and I thought no more of her.

One night, when I was lying sound asleep, I was awoken by a strange harmony. It was a kind of vibration, so soft, so melodious, that the murmur of a light breeze through foliage can convey but a feeble idea of its gentle nature. For a long time I listened to it, my eyes wide open, and holding my breath the better to hear it.

At length, looking towards the window, I saw two wings beating against the glass. I thought, at first, that it was a bat imprisoned in my chamber; but the moon was shining clearly, and showed the wings of a magnificent night-moth, transparent as lace. At times their vibrations were so rapid as to hide them from my view; then for a while they would lie in repose, extended on the glass pane, their delicate articulations made visible anew.

This vaporous apparition in the midst of the universal silence opened my heart to the tenderest emotions; it seemed to me that a sylphid, pitying my solitude, had come to see me; and this idea brought the tears into my eyes.

'Have no fear, gentle captive—have no fear!' I said to it; 'your confidence shall not be betrayed. I will not retain you against your wishes; return to heaven—to liberty!'

And I opened the window.

The night was calm. Thousands of stars glittered in space. For a moment I contemplated this sublime spectacle, and the words of prayer rose naturally to my lips. But then, looking down, I saw a man hanging from the iron stanchion which supported the sign of the Boeuf-gras; the hair in disorder, the arms stiff, the legs straightened to a point, and throwing their gigantic shadow the whole length of the street.

The immobility of this figure, in the moonlight, had something frightful in it. I felt my tongue grow icy cold, and my teeth chattered. I was about to utter a cry; but by what mysterious attraction I know not, my eyes were drawn towards the opposite house, and there I dimly distinguished the old woman, in the midst of the heavy shadow, squatting at her window and contemplating the hanging body with diabolical satisfaction.

I became giddy with terror; my strength deserted me, and I fell down in a heap insensible.

I do not know how long I lay unconscious. On coming to myself I found it was broad day. Mingled and confused noises rose from the street below. I looked out from my window.

The burgomaster and his secretary were standing at the door of the Boeuf-gras; they remained there a long time. People came and went, stopped to look, then passed on their way. At length a stretcher, on which lay a body covered with a woollen cloth, was brought out and carried away by two men.

Then everyone else disappeared.

The window in front of the house remained open still; a fragment of rope dangled from the iron support of the sign-board. I had not dreamed—I had really seen the night-moth on my window-pane—then the suspended body—then the old woman!

In the course of that day Toubec paid me his weekly visit.

'Anything to sell, Master Christian?' he cried.

I did not hear him. I was seated on my only chair, my hands upon my knees, my eyes fixed on vacancy before me. Toubec, surprised at my immobility, repeated in a louder tone, 'Master Christian!—Master Christian!' then, stepping up to me, tapped me smartly on the shoulder.

'What's the matter?—what's the matter? Are you ill?' he asked.

'No—I was thinking.'

'What the deuce about?'

'The man who was hung—'

'Aha!' cried the old broker; 'you saw the poor fellow, then? What a strange affair! The third in the same place!'

'The third?'

'Yes, the third. I ought to have told you about it before; but there's still time—for there's sure to be a fourth, following the example of the others, the first step only making the difficulty.'

This said, Toubec seated himself on a box and lit his pipe with a thoughtful air.

'I'm not timid,' said he, 'but if anyone were to ask me to sleep in that room, I'd rather go and hang myself somewhere else! Nine or ten months back,' he continued, 'a wholesale furrier, from Tubingen, put up at the Boeuf-gras. He called for supper; ate well, drank well, and was shown up to bed in the room on the third floor which they call the "green chamber". The next day they found him hanging from the stanchion of the sign.

'So much for number one, about which there was nothing to be said. A proper report of the affair was drawn up, and the body of the stranger buried at the bottom of the garden. But about six weeks afterwards came a soldier from Neustadt; he had his discharge, and was congratulating himself on his return to his village. All the evening he did nothing but empty mugs of wine and talk of his cousin, who was waiting his return to marry him. At last they put him to bed in the green chamber, and the same night the watchman passing along the Rue des Minnesängers noticed something hanging from the signboard-stanchion. He raised his lantern; it was the soldier, with his discharge-papers in a tin box hanging on his left thigh, and his hands planted smoothly on the outer seams of his trousers, as if he had been on parade!

'It was certainly an extraordinary affair! The burgomaster declared it was the work of the devil. The chamber was examined; they replastered its walls. A notice of the death was sent to Neustadt, on the margin of which the clerk wrote—"Died suddenly of apoplexy."

'All Nuremberg was indignant against the landlord of the Boeuf-gras, and wished to compel him to take down the iron stanchion of his signboard, on the pretext that it put dangerous ideas in people's heads. But you may easily imagine that old Nikel Schmidt didn't listen with the ear on that side of his head.

'"That stanchion was put there by my grandfather," he said; "the sign of the Boeuf-gras has hung on it from father to son, for a hundred and fifty years; it does nobody any harm, it's more than thirty feet up; those who don't like it have only to look another way."

'People's excitement gradually cooled down, and for several months nothing happened. Unfortunately, a student from Heidelberg, on his way to the University, came to the Boeuf-gras and asked for a bed. He was the son of a pastor.

'Who could suppose that the son of a pastor would take into his head the idea of hanging himself to the stanchion of a public-house sign, because a furrier and a soldier had hung themselves there before him? It must be confessed, Master Christian, that the thing was not very probable—it would not have appeared more likely to you than it did to me. Well—'

'Enough! enough!' I cried; 'it is a horrible affair. I feel sure there is some frightful mystery at the bottom of it. It is neither the stanchion nor the chamber—'

'You don't mean that you suspect the landlord?—as honest a man as there is in the world, and belonging to one of the oldest families in Nuremberg?'

'No, no! Heaven keep me from forming unjust suspicions of anyone; but there are abysses into the depths of which one dares not look.'

'You are right,' said Toubec, astonished at my excited manner; 'and we had much better talk of something else. By-the-way, Master Christian, what about our landscape, the view of Sainte-Odile?'

The question brought me back to actualities. I showed the broker the picture I had just finished. The business was soon settled between us, and Toubec, thoroughly satisfied, went down the ladder, advising me to think no more of the student of Heidelberg.

I would very willingly have followed the old broker's advice, but when the devil mixes himself up with our affairs he is not easily shaken off.

II

In solitude, all these events came back to my mind with fright-ful distinctness.

The old woman, I said to myself, is the cause of all this;

she alone has planned these crimes, she alone has carried them into execution; but by what means? Has she had recourse to cunning only or really to the intervention of the invisible powers?

I paced my garret, a voice within me crying, 'It is not without purpose that Heaven has permitted you to see Fledermausse watching the agony of her victim; it was not without design that the poor young man's soul came to wake you in the form of a night-moth! No! all this has not been without purpose. Christian, Heaven imposes on you a terrible mission; if you fail to accomplish it, fear that you yourself may fall into the toils of the old woman! Perhaps at this moment she is laying her snares for you in the darkness!'

During several days these frightful images pursued me without cessation. I could not sleep; I found it impossible to work; the brush fell from my hand, and, shocking to confess, I detected myself at times complacently contemplating the dreadful stanchion. At last, one evening, unable any longer to bear this state of mind, I flew down the ladder four steps at a time, and went and hid myself beside Fledermausse's door, for the purpose of discovering her fatal secret.

From that time there was never a day that I was not on the watch, following the old woman like her shadow, never losing sight of her; but she was so cunning, she had so keen a scent that without even turning her head she discovered that I was behind her, and knew that I was on her track. But nevertheless, she pretended not to see me—went to the market, to the butcher's, like a simple housewife; only she quickened her pace and muttered to herself as she went.

At the end of a month I saw that it would be impossible for me to achieve my purpose by these means, and this conviction filled me with an inexpressible sadness.

'What can I do?' I asked myself. 'The old woman has discovered my intentions, and is thoroughly on her guard. I am helpless. The old wretch already thinks she sees me at the end of the cord!'

At length, from repeating to myself again and again the question, 'What can I do?' a luminous idea presented itself to my mind.

My chamber overlooked the house of Fledermausse, but it had no dormer window on that side. I carefully raised one of the slates of my roof, and the delight I felt on discovering that by this means I could command a view of the entire antique building can hardly be imagined.

'At last I've got you!' I cried to myself; 'you cannot escape me now! From here I shall see everything. You will not suspect this invisible eye—this eye that will surprise the crime at the moment of its inception! Oh, Justice! it moves slowly, but it comes!'

Nothing more sinister than this den could be imagined—a large yard, paved with moss-grown flagstones; a well in one corner, the stagnant water of which was frightful to behold; a wooden staircase leading up to a railed gallery, to the left, on the first floor, a drain-stone indicated the kitchen; to the right, the upper windows of the house looked into the street. All was dark, decaying, and dank-looking.

The sun penetrated only for an hour or two during the day the depths of this dismal sty; then the shadows again spread over it—the light fell in lozenge shapes upon the crumbling walls, on the mouldy balcony, on the dull windows.

Oh, the whole place was worthy of its mistress!

I had hardly made these reflections when the old woman entered the yard on her return from market. First, I heard her heavy door grate on its hinges, then Fledermausse, with her basket, appeared. She seemed fatigued—out of breath. The border of her cap hung down upon her nose, as, clutching the wooden rail with one hand, she mounted the stairs.

The heat was suffocating. It was exactly one of those days when insects of every kind—crickets, spiders, mosquitoes—fill old buildings with their grating noises and subterranean borings.

Fledermausse crossed the gallery slowly, like a ferret that feels itself at home. For more than a quarter of an hour she remained in the kitchen, then came out and swept the stones a little, on which a few straws had been scattered; at last she raised her head, with her green eyes carefully scrutinised every portion of the roof from which I was observing her.

By what strange intuition did she suspect anything? I know not; but I gently lowered the uplifted slate into its place, and gave over watching for the rest of that day.

The day following Fledermausse appeared to be reassured. A jagged ray of light fell into the gallery; passing this, she caught a fly, and delicately presented it to a spider established in an angle of the roof.

The spider was so large, that, in spite of the distance, I saw it descend then, gliding along one thread, like a drop of venom, seize its prey from the fingers of the dreadful old woman, and remount rapidly. Fledermausse watched it attentively; then her eyes half-closed, she sneezed, and cried to herself in a jocular tone—

'Bless you, beauty!—bless you!'

For six weeks I could discover nothing as to the power of Fledermausse: sometimes I saw her peeling potatoes, sometimes spreading her linen on the balustrade. Sometimes I saw her spin; but she never sang, as old women usually do, their quivering voices going so well with the humming of the spinning-wheel. Silence reigned about her. She had no cat— the favourite company of old maids; not a sparrow ever flew down to her yard, in passing over which the pigeons seemed to hurry their flight. It seemed as if everything were afraid of her look.

The spider alone took pleasure in her society.

I now look back with wonder at my patience during those long hours of observation; nothing escaped my attention, nothing was indifferent to me; at the least sound I lifted my slate. Mine was a boundless curiosity stimulated by an indefinable fear.

Toubec complained.

'What the devil are you doing with your time, Master Christian?' he would say to me. 'Formerly, you had something ready for me every week; now, hardly once in a month. Oh, you painters! As soon as they have a few kreutzer before them, they put their hands in their pockets and go to sleep!'

I myself was beginning to lose courage. With all my watching and spying, I had discovered nothing extraordinary. I was inclining to think that the old woman might not be so dangerous after all—that I had been wrong, perhaps, to suspect her. In short, I tried to find excuses for her. But one fine evening,

while, with my eye to the opening in the roof, I was giving
myself up to these charitable reflections, the scene abruptly
changed.

Fledermausse passed along her gallery with the swiftness of
a flash of light. She was no longer herself: she was erect, her
jaws knit, her look fixed, her neck extended; she moved with
long strides, her grey hair streaming behind her.

'Oh, oh!' I said to myself, 'something is going on!'

But the shadows of night descended on the big house, the
noises of the town died out, and all became silent. I was about
to seek my bed, when, happening to look out of my skylight,
I saw a light in the window of the green chamber of the Boeuf-
gras—a traveller was occupying that terrible room!

All my fears were instantly revived. The old woman's excitement explained itself—she scented another victim!

I could not sleep at all that night. The rustling of the straw of
my mattress, the nibbling of a mouse under the floor, sent a
chill through me. I rose and looked out of my window—I
listened. The light I had seen was no longer visible in the green
chamber.

During one of these moments of poignant anxiety—whether
the result of illusion or reality—I fancied I could discern
the figure of the old witch, likewise watching and listening.

The night passed, the dawn showed grey against my window-
panes, and, slowly increasing, the sounds and movements of
the re-awakened town arose. Harassed with fatigue and
emotion, I at last fell asleep; but my repose was of short
duration, and by eight o'clock I was again at my post of
observation.

It appeared that Fledermausse had passed a night no less
stormy than mine had been; for, when she opened the door
of the gallery, I saw that a livid pallor was upon her cheeks
and skinny neck. She had nothing on but her chemise and a
flannel petticoat; a few locks of rusty grey hair fell upon her
shoulders. She looked up musingly towards my garret; but she
saw nothing—she was thinking of something else.

Suddenly she descended into the yard, leaving her shoes at
the top of the stairs. Doubtless her object was to assure herself
that the outer door was securely fastened. She then hurried up

the stairs, three or four at a time. It was frightful to see! She rushed into one of the side rooms, and I heard the sound of a heavy box-lid fall. Then Fledermausse reappeared in the gallery, dragging with her a life-size dummy—and this figure was dressed like the unfortunate student of Heidelberg!

With surprising dexterity the old woman suspended this hideous object to a beam of the over-hanging roof, then went down into the yard to contemplate it from that point of view. A peal of grating laughter broke from her lips—she hurried up the stairs, and rushed down again, like a maniac; and every time she did this she burst into fresh fits of laughter.

A sound was heard outside the street door; the old woman sprang to the dummy, snatched it from its fastening, and carried it into the house; then she reappeared and leaned over the balcony, with outstretched neck, glittering eyes, and eagerly listening ears. The sound passed away—the muscles of her face relaxed, she drew a long breath. The passing of a vehicle had alarmed the old witch.

She then, once more, went back into her chamber, and I heard the lid of the box close heavily.

This strange scene utterly confounded all my ideas. What could that dummy mean?

I became more watchful and attentive than ever. Fledermausse went out with her basket, and I watched her to the top of the street; she had resumed her air of tottering age, walking with short steps, and from time to time half-turning her head, so as to enable herself to look behind out of the corners of her eyes. For five long hours she remained abroad, while I went and came from my spying-place incessantly, meditating all the while—the sun heating the slates above my head till my brain was almost scorched.

I saw at his window the traveller who occupied the green chamber at the Boeuf-gras; he was a peasant of Nassau, wearing a three-cornered hat, a scarlet waistcoat, and having a broad laughing countenance. He was tranquilly smoking his pipe, unsuspicious of anything wrong.

About two o'clock Fledermausse came back. The sound of her door opening echoed to the end of the passage. Presently she appeared alone, quite alone in the yard, and seated herself on the lowest step of the gallery-stairs. She placed her basket at her feet and drew from it, first several bunches of herbs, then some vegetables—then a three-cornered hat, a scarlet velvet waistcoat, a pair of plush breeches, and a pair of thick worsted stockings—the complete costume of a peasant of Nassau!

I reeled with giddiness—flames passed before my eyes.

I remembered those precipices that drew one towards them with irresistible power—wells that have had to be filled up because of persons throwing themselves into them—trees that have had to be cut down because of people hanging themselves upon them—the contagion of suicide and theft and murder, which at various times has taken possession of people's minds, by means well understood; that strange inducement, which makes people kill themselves because others kill themselves. My hair rose upon my head with horror!

But how could this Fledermausse—a creature so mean and wretched—have made discovery of so profound a law of nature? How had she found the means of turning it to the use of her sanguinary instincts? This I could neither understand nor imagine. Without more reflection, however, I resolved to turn the fatal law against her, and by its power to drag her into her own snare. So many innocent victims called for vengeance!

I hurried to all the old clothes-dealers in Nuremberg; and by the evening I arrived at the Boeuf-gras, with an enormous parcel under my arm.

Nikel Schmidt had long known me. I had painted the portrait of his wife, a fat and comely dame.

'Master Christian!' he cried, shaking me by the hand, 'to what happy circumstance do I owe the pleasure of this visit?'

'My dear Mr Schmidt, I feel a very strong desire to pass the night in that room of yours up yonder.'

We were on the doorstep of the inn, and I pointed up to the green chamber. The good fellow looked suspiciously at me.

'Oh! don't be afraid,' I said, 'I've no desire to hang myself.'

'I'm glad of it! I'm glad of it! for, frankly, I should be sorry—an artist of your talent. When do you want the room, Master Christian?'

'Tonight.'

'That's impossible—it's occupied.'

'The gentleman can have it at once, if he likes,' said a voice behind us; 'I shan't stay in it.'

We turned in surprise. It was the peasant of Nassau; his large three-cornered hat pressed down upon the back of his neck, and his bundle at the end of his travelling-stick. He had learned the story of the three travellers who had hung themselves.

'Such chambers!' he cried, stammering with terror; 'it's—it's murdering people to put them into such!—you—you deserve to be sent to the galleys!'

'Come, come, calm yourself,' said the landlord; 'you slept there comfortably enough last night.'

'Thank Heaven! I said my prayers before going to rest, or where should I be now?'

And he hurried away, raising his hands to heaven.

'Well,' said Master Schmidt, stupefied, 'the chamber is empty, but don't go into it to do me an ill turn.'

'I might be doing myself a much worse one,' I replied.

Giving my parcel to the servant-girl, I went and seated myself among the guests who were drinking and smoking.

For a long time I had not felt more calm, more happy to be in the world. After so much anxiety, I saw approaching my end—the horizon seemed to grow lighter. I know not by what formidable power I was being led on. I lit my pipe, and with my elbow on the table and a jug of wine before me, and sometimes rousing myself to look at the woman's house, I seriously asked myself whether all that had happened to me was more than a dream. But when the watchman came, to request us to vacate the room, graver thoughts took possession of my mind, and I followed, in meditative mood, the little servant-girl who preceded me with a candle in her hand.

III

We mounted the window flight of stairs to the third storey; arrived there, she placed the candle in my hand, and pointed to a door.

'That's it,' she said, and hurried back down the stairs as fast as she could go.

I opened the door. The green chamber was like all other inn bedchambers; the ceiling was low, the bed was high. After casting a glance round the room, I stepped across to the window.

Nothing was yet noticeable in Fledermausse's house, with the exception of a light, which shone at the back of a deep obscure bedchamber—a nightlight, doubtless.

'So much the better,' I said to myself, as I re-closed the window-curtains; 'I shall have plenty of time.'

I opened my parcel, and from its contents put on a woman's cap with a broad frilled border; then, with a piece of pointed charcoal, in front of the glass, I marked my forehead with a number of wrinkles. This took me a full hour to do; but after I had put on a gown and a large shawl, I was afraid of myself; Fledermausse herself was looking at me from the depths of the glass!

At that moment the watchman announced the hour of eleven. I rapidly dressed the dummy I had brought with me like the one prepared by the old witch. I then drew apart the window-curtains.

Certainly, after all I had seen of the old woman—her infernal cunning, her prudence, and her address—nothing ought to have surprised even me; yet I was positively terrified.

The light, which I had observed at the back of her room, now cast its yellow rays on her dummy, dressed like the peasant of Nassau, which sat huddled up on the side of the bed, its head dropped upon its chest, the large three-cornered hat drawn down over its features, its arms pendant by its sides, and its whole attitude that of a person plunged in despair.

Managed with diabolical art, the shadow permitted only a general view of the figure, the red waistcoat and its six rounded buttons alone caught the light; but the silence of night, the complete immobility of the figure, and its air of terrible dejection, all served to impress the beholder with irresistible force; even I myself, though not in the least taken by surprise, felt chilled to the marrow of my bones. How, then, would a poor countryman taken completely off his guard have felt? He would have been utterly overthrown; he would have lost all control of will, and the spirit of imitation would have done the rest.

Scarcely had I drawn aside the curtains than I discovered Fledermausse on the watch behind her window-panes.

She could not see me. I opened the window softly, the window over the way softly opened too; then the dummy appeared to rise slowly and advance towards me; I did the same, and seizing my candle with one hand, with the other threw the casement wide open.

The old woman and I were face to face; for, overwhelmed with astonishment, she had let the dummy fall from her hands. Our two looks crossed with an equal terror.

She stretched forth a finger, I did the same; her lips moved, I moved mine; she heaved a deep sigh and leant upon elbow, I rested in the same way.

How frightful the enacting of this scene was I cannot describe; it was made up of delirium, bewilderment, madness. It was a struggle between two wills, two intelligences, two souls, one of which sought to crush the other; and in this struggle I had the advantage. The dead were on my side.

After having for some seconds imitated all the movements of Fledermausse, I drew a cord from the folds of my petticoat and tied it to the iron stanchion of the signboard.

The old woman watched me with open mouth. I passed the cord round my neck. Her tawny eyeballs glittered; her features became convulsed—

'No, no!' she cried, in a hissing tone; 'no!'

I proceeded with the impassibility of a hangman.

Then Fledermausse was seized with rage.

'You're mad! you're mad!' she cried, springing up and clutching wildly at the sill of the window; 'you're mad!'

I gave her no time to continue. Suddenly blowing out my light, I stooped like a man preparing to make a vigorous spring, then seizing my dummy slipped the cord about its neck and hurled it into the air.

A terrible shriek resounded through the street; then all was silent again.

Perspiration bathed my forehead. I listened a long time.

At the end of an hour I heard far off—very far off—the cry of the watchman, announcing that midnight had struck.

'Justice is at last done,' I murmured to myself; 'the three victims are avenged. Heaven forgive me!'

I saw the old witch, drawn by the likeness of herself, a cord about her neck, hanging from the iron stanchion projecting from her house. I saw the thrill of death run through her limbs and the moon, calm and silent, rose above the edge of the roof, and shed its cold pale rays upon her dishevelled head.

As I had seen the poor young student of Heidelberg, I now saw Fledermausse.

The next day all Nuremberg knew that 'the Bat' had hung herself. It was the last event of the kind in the Rue des Minnesängers.

The Earth Draws

by

JONAS LIE

Another source of tales of terror during this era was the Scandinavian countries, which not only had their own special monster, the troll, but were also responsible for an enormous number of reports of sea serpents in the Norwegian fjords.

Among the more notable authors to appear from Scandinavia during this time were August Strindberg and Pelle Molin from Sweden, Jens Peter Jacobsen from Denmark, and from Norway, a formidable trio of Bjornsterne Bjornson, Henrik Ibsen and Jonas Lie.

Jonas Lie (1833-1908) attended the University of Christiana with both Bjornson and Ibsen, and studied law, which he practised for some time, then was forced to try his hand at literature after an unfortunate business deal. He sprang to sudden fame with his novel The Visionary (1870) and earned, again with Bjornson and Ibsen, a state stipend to continue his writing.

Nisbet Bain, who translated this story, says of Lie's writing that 'when he tells us some of the wild legends of his country, some of the grim tales on which he himself was brought up, he is at his most vivid and enthralling. We rarely hear of friendly elves or companionable gnomes from him. The supernatural beings that haunt those shores are malignant and malefic—they seem to hate man.'

One of Lie's rare books to be published in Britain was Weird Tales From Northern Seas (1893) and 'The Earth Draws' is one of those weird tales. This is about no friendly troll, but instead one of those spirits who, in words of Bain, 'are malignant and malefic—they seem to hate man.'

There was once a young salesman at the storekeeper's at Sörvaag.

He was fair, with curly hair, shrewd blue eyes, and so smart, and obliging, and handsome, that all the girls in the town got themselves sent on errands to the shop on purpose to see him. Moreover, he was so smart and skilful in everything he put his hand to, that the storekeeper would never part with him.

One day he went out to a fishing station for his principal.

The current was dead against him, so he rowed his boat close in shore. All at once he saw a little ring in the rocky wall just above high-water mark. He thought it was the sort of ring used for fastening boats, so he decided it would do no harm to rest a bit and have a snack of something, for he had been pulling at the oars since early morning.

But when he took hold of the ring to run his boatline through it, it fitted round his finger so tightly that he had to tug at it. He tugged, and with a rush out of the mountainside, came a large drawer. It was brimful of silk neckerchiefs and women's frippery. He was amazed, and stood pondering the matter.

Then he saw what looked like rusty flakes of iron in rows right over the whole mountainside, exactly resembling the slit of his own drawer.

He had now got the ring on his finger, and must needs try if it would open the other slits also. And thus he drew out drawer after drawer full of gold and silver bracelets, glass pearls, brooches and rings, laced caps, yarn, night-caps and woollen drawers, coffee, sugar, tobacco pipes, buttons, knives, axes, and scythes. He drew out many drawers; there was no end to the display they made.

But all round him he heard, as it were, the humming of a crowd and the tramp of seaboots. There was a hubbub, as if they were rolling hogsheads over a bridge and hoisting sails against the wind, and out to sea sounded the stroke of oars and the bumping of boats putting ashore.

Then he suddenly realized he had laid to his boat at a mooring-ring belonging to the underground folk, and had discovered their landing-place where they deposited their wares.

He stood there looking into a drawer of meerschaum pipes.

They were finer than he had thought possible to find in the whole world.

Then he felt the blow of a heavy hand which tried to thrust him aside; but, at the same time, some one laughed merrily close by. He saw a young woman in the fore-part of his boat. She was leaning, with broad shoulders and hairy arms, over a meal-sack. Her eyes laughed and shot forth sparks as from a smithy in the dark, but her face was oddly pale.

Then she vanished altogether.

He was glad when he got down into his boat again, pushed off and rowed away. But when he got out into the sound, and slackened speed a bit, he perceived that the ring was still on his finger.

His first thought was to tear it off and fling it into the sea; but then it seemed tighter than ever.

It was so curiously wrought and engraved that he examined it more curiously; and the longer he looked at it the stranger it gleamed and glistened. Turn it as he would to examine its spirals, he could never make out where they began and where they ended.

But as he sat there and looked at it, the black sparkling eyes of that pale face stood out more and more plainly before his eyes. He didn't exactly know whether he thought her ugly or handsome—the uncanny creature!

The ring he now meant to keep, come what might. And home he rowed, and said not a word to anybody of what had happened to him.

But from that day forth a strange restlessness came over him. When he was sweeping out the shop or measuring goods, he would suddenly stand there in a brown study, and fancy he was back at the landing-stage in the mountainside, and the black woman was laughing at him over the meal-sack.

He knew he must go back there once more, and put his ring to the test, though it might cost him his life.

And in the course of the summer his boat lay over at the mountainside in the same place as before.

When he had opened the drawer with his gold ring, he caught sight of the broad-shouldered woman. Her eyes sparkled, and had a wild look about them, and she peered curiously at him. And, every time he came, he seemed to be more expected, and she was more and more gladsome. They became quite old acquaintances, and she was always waiting for him there.

But at home he grew gloomy and silent. Yet, although he thought that it was sorcery, and her arms were hairy like a beast's, and although he really tried to keep away, nevertheless he could not help going thither, and whenever he had been away from her a whole week, she grew quite unmanageable, and laughed and shrieked when she saw him coming again.

And he always heard the noise and the bustle of many people all about him, but never could he see anything. It seemed to him, however, as if they all lay a little way off and pulled their boat aside for him to pass. His boat, too, was always nicely baled out, and the oars and sails righted and trimmed. The cable, too, was fastened for him whenever he came, and thrown to him whenever he went away.

Now and then she so managed it that he caught a glimpse into their warehouses and their bright halls in the mountain side, and at such times she seemed to be enticing him after her. And then, on his way home, he would shudder. 'What,' thought he, 'if the mountain wall were to shut to behind me?' and every time he was glad that he had been so far on his guard and had come off scot free.

And towards autumn, he grew more at his ease. He really made up his mind to try to give up these journeys. He set to work in real earnest, so that he had no time for thought, and plunged into his business with fiery impetuosity.

But when Christmas-time drew nigh with its snowflakes and darkness, such strange fancies came over him.

Whenever he went into dark nooks and corners, he saw the woman before him. She laughed and called to him, and shrieked and sent him messages in the wind. At last a strong desire came upon him, and one day he was unable to hold out any longer so off he went.

He fancied he caught a glimpse of her a long way off. She was casting huge boulders aside so as to see and follow the course of the boat, and she beckoned and greeted him through the drizzle and the mist. It was as though the current was bearing him thither all the time.

When he came up, the sea seethed and boiled for the crowds that were in it, though he saw them not. They waded out to him and drew his boat ashore, and steps and a bridge lay there ready for his feet. But right at the top she stood, and her breath came heavily, and she leaned towards him and drew him with those bold eyes of hers set in that face as pale as night. She went swiftly inland, looked behind her, and beckoned him after her; and then she threw open the door of an old iron safe in the midst of the wall.

On its shelves sparkled a bridal crown, and a shining girdle and breastplate and a kirtle, and all manner of bridal finery.

There she stood, and her breath came straining hot and heavy through her white teeth, and she smiled and ogled him archly. He felt her take hold of him, and it was as though a darkness fell around him.

Then all at once, as if in a gleam of twilight, he saw the whole trading-place, vast and wealthy and splendid, all round about him with its haven, warehouses, and trading-ships. She stretched out her hands and pointed to it, as if she would say that he should be the lord and master of the whole of it. A cold shiver ran through him; he perceived that it led right into the mountain. And out he rushed.

He cut the cable through with his knife, and wrenched the ring from his finger, and cast it into the sea, and off he rowed, so furiously that the sea foamed around him.

When he got home to his work again, and the bustle of the Christmas season began, he felt as if he had awakened from an evil nightmare. He felt so light of heart. He chatted gaily with customers over the counter, and his old life went on much the same as before. And everything he put his hand to went along as smooth as butter.

The tradesman's daughter now looked and smiled at him in shy admiration. Never had he remarked what taking ways were hers, or noticed how bonnie and bright the lassie was, and how graceful and supple she looked as she stood in the door-way. And ever since the tradesman's daughter had looked so strangely at him, he had no thought for any one but her.

He would lay awake at night, and reflect upon his grievous sin in lowering himself to the level of a supernatural monster, and glad was he that he had cast the ring away.

But on Christmas Eve, when the shop was shut and the house folks and servants were making ready for the festival in kitchen and parlour, the shopkeeper took him aside into his counting-house. If he liked his daughter, said he, there was no impediment that he could see. Let him take heart and woo her, for it had not escaped him how she was love-sick on his account. He himself, said the shopkeeper, was old, and would like to retire from business.

The good-looking shopman did not wait to be asked twice. He wooed straightway, and, before the Christmas cheer was on the table, he got yes for an answer.

Years passed and they thrived and prospered in house and home. They had pretty and clever children. He rejoiced in his wife; nothing was good enough for her, and honour and ease were her portion, both at home and abroad.

But in the seventh year, when it was drawing towards Yule-tide, a strange restlessness came over him. He wandered about by himself, and could find peace nowhere.

His wife fretted and sorrowed. She knew not what it could be, and it seemed to her that he oddly avoided her. He would wander for hours about the dark packhouse loft, among coffers and casks and barrels and sacks, and it was as though he disliked company when he was there.

Now it chanced on the day before Christmas Eve that one of the workpeople had to fetch something from the loft. There stood the master, deep in thought, by one of the meal-sacks, staring down on the ground before him.

'Don't you see the iron ring down in the floor there?' he asked.

But the man saw no ring.

'I see it there—the earth draws,' he sighed heavily.

On Christmas Eve he was nowhere to be found, though they searched for him high and low, and made inquiries about him everywhere amidst the Yule-tide bustle and merriment.

But late on Christmas Day while they were all running about in the utmost anxiety, not knowing whether they should lay the table or not, all at once in he came through the door.

He longed so much for both meat and drink, he said, and he was so happy and merry and jovial the whole evening through, that they all clean forgot the fright they had been in.

For a whole year afterwards he was chatty and sociable as before, and he made so much of his wife that it was quite absurd. He bore her in his hands, so to speak, and could not do enough for her.

But when it drew towards Yule-tide again, and the darkest time of the year, the same restlessness came over him. It was as though they only saw his shadow amongst them, and he went moping about the packhouse loft again.

On Christmas Eve the same thing happened as before—he disappeared. His wife and the people of the house went about in a terrible way, and were filled with astonishment and alarm.

And on Christmas Day he suddenly stepped into the room again, and was merry and jovial, as he generally was. But when the lights had burnt out, and they all had gone to bed, his wife could hold her tongue no longer : she burst into tears, and begged him to tell her where he had been.

Then he thrust her roughly from him, and his eyes shot sparks, as if he were crazy. He implored her, for their mutual happiness' sake, never to ask him such a question again.

Time went on, and the same thing happened every year. When the days grew dark, he moped about by himself, all gloomy and silent, and seemed bent upon hiding himself away from people; and on Christmas Eve he always disappeared, though nobody ever saw him go. And punctually on Christmas Day, at the very moment when they were about to lay the table, he all at once came in at the door, happy and contented with them all.

But just before every autumn, towards the dark days, always earlier than the year before, this restlessness came over him, and he moped about moodier and shyer of people than ever.

His wife never questioned him; but sorrow lay upon her, and it seemed to her to grow heavier and more crushing, since she seemed no longer able to take care of him, and he no longer seemed to belong to her.

Now one year, when it was again drawing nigh to Yule-tide,

he began roaming about as usual, heavy and cast down; and the day before Christmas Eve he took his wife along with him into the packhouse loft.

'Do you see anything there by the meal-sack?' he asked. But she saw nothing.

Then he gripped her by the hand, and begged and implored her to remain, and go with him there at night. As his life was dear to him, he said, he would fain try and stay at home that day.

In the course of the night he tightly grasped her hand time after time, and sighed and groaned. She felt that he was holding on to her, and striving hard, and with all his might, against *something*.

When morning came, it was all over. He was happier and lighter of mood than she had seen him for a long, long time, and he remained at home.

On that Christmas Eve there was such a hauling and a-carrying upstairs from both shop and cellar, and the candles shone till all the window-panes sparkled again. It was the first real festival he had ever spent in his own house, he said, and he meant to make a regular banquet of it.

But when, as the custom was, the people of the house came in one by one, and drank the health of their master and mistress, he grew paler and paler and whiter and whiter, as if his blood were being sucked out of him and drained away.

'The earth draws!' he shrieked, and there came a look of dreadful horror in his eyes.

Immediately afterwards he sat there—dead!

The Wondersmith

by

FITZ JAMES O'BRIEN

Poet and soldier Fitz James O'Brien (1828-1862) was born in Limerick and educated at Dublin University. It is not known exactly when he started writing but two of his earliest works were the poems Loch Ine *and* Irish Castles *which were later to be published in Edward Hayes' anthology* The Ballads Of Ireland (1856). *O'Brien went to London and is reported to have spent his inheritance, a sum of several thousand pounds, in less than two years. After this, he felt constrained to emigrate and went to America in 1852. Literary contacts soon ensured that he became a general favourite in New York's writing circles. His literary career in America was described by his friend and critic William Winter as being signalised 'by the production of some of the most original and beautiful poems and stories in the literature of his time'.*

He contributed to no less than fifty-two issues of Harper's Magazine, *and also wrote for the* New York Saturday Press, *the* Atlantic Monthly *and* Putnam's Magazine.

When the American Civil War broke out, he joined the 7th Regiment of the National Guard of New York, but left in search of action, which he duly found when he joined General Lander's staff. On 26th February, 1862, he was shot and badly wounded during a skirmish with Confederate cavalry. He died of his wound on 6th April, and was buried in Greenwood Cemetery, New York.

O'Brien is now chiefly remembered for his fantasies 'What Was it?' and 'The Diamond Lens'. Another of his fantasies, 'The Wondersmith', has suffered an eclipse over the last few decades, probably because of its length. It first appeared in the Atlantic Monthly, *October 1859, and was included in O'Brien's volume of tales* The Diamond Lens *(1887). I do not think it over fanciful to detect in this classic fantasy the original idea behind such popular macabre works as A. Merritt's* Burn Witch Burn *and Sarban's* The Doll Maker.

I

GOLOSH STREET AND ITS PEOPLE

Golosh Street is an interesting locality. All the oddities of trade seemed to have found their way thither and made an eccentric mercantile settlement. There is a bird-shop at one corner. Immediately opposite is an establishment where they sell nothing but ornaments made out of the tinted leaves of autumn, varnished and gummed into various forms. Further down is a second-hand book-stall. There is a small chink between two ordinary-sized houses, in which a little Frenchman makes and sells artificial eyes, specimens of which, ranged on a black velvet cushion, stare at you unwinkingly through the window as you pass, until you shudder and hurry on, thinking how awful the world would be if every one went about without eyelids. Madame Filomel, the fortune-teller, lives at No. 12 Golosh Street, second storey front, pull the bell on the left-hand side. Next door to Madame is the shop of Herr Hippe, commonly called the Wondersmith.

Herr Hippe's shop is the largest in Golosh Street, and to all appearance is furnished with the smallest stock. Beyond a few packing-cases, a turner's lathe, and a shelf laden with dissected maps of Europe, the interior of the shop is entirely unfurnished. The window, which is lofty and wide, but much begrimed with dirt, contains the only pleasant object in the place. This is a beautiful little miniature theatre,—that is to say, the orchestra and stage. It is fitted with charmingly painted scenery and all the appliances for scenic changes. There are tiny traps, and delicately constructed 'lifts', and real footlights fed with burning-fluid, and in the orchestra sits a diminutive conductor before his desk, surrounded by musical manikins, all provided with the smallest of violincellos, flutes, oboes, drums, and such like. There are characters also on the stage. A Templar in a white cloak is dragging a fainting female form to the parapet of a ruined bridge, while behind a great black rock on the left one can see a man concealed, who, kneeling, levels an arquebuse at the knight's heart. But the orchestra is silent; the conductor never beats the time, the musicians never play a note; the Templar never drags his victim an inch nearer to the bridge; the masked avenger takes an eternal aim with his weapon. This repose appears unnatural; for so admirably are the figures executed that they seem replete with life. One is almost led to believe, in looking on them, that they are resting beneath some spell which hinders their motion. One expects every moment to hear the loud explosion of the arquebuse,— to see the blue smoke curling, the Templar falling,—to hear the orchestra playing the requiem of the guilty.

Few people knew what Herr Hippe's business or trade really was. That he worked at something was evident; else why the shop? Some people inclined to the belief that he was an inventor, or mechanician. His workshop was in the rear of the store, and into that sanctuary no one but himself had admission. He arrived in Golosh Street eight or ten years ago, and one fine morning, the neighbours, taking down their shutters, observed that No. 13 had got a tenant. A tall, thin, sallow-faced man stood on a ladder outside the shop entrance, nailing up a large board, on which 'Herr Hippe, Wondersmith', was painted in black letters on a yellow ground. The little theatre stood in the window, where it stood ever after, and Herr Hippe was established.

But what was a Wondersmith? people asked each other. No one could reply. Madame Filomel was consulted; but she looked grave, and said that it was none of her business. Mr Pippel, the bird-fancier, who was a German, and ought to know best, thought it was the English for some singular Teutonic profession; but his replies were so vague that Golosh Street was as unsatisfied as ever. Solon, the little humpback, who kept the odd-volume book-stall at the lowest corner, could throw no light upon it. And at length people had to come to the conclusion that Herr Hippe was either a coiner or a magician, and opinions were divided.

———

II

A BOTTLEFUL OF SOULS

It was a dull December evening. There was little trade doing in Golosh Street, and the shutters were up at most of the shops. Hippe's store had been closed at least an hour.

Herr Hippe sat in his parlour, which was lit by a pleasant wood-fire. There were no candles in the room, and the flickering blaze played fantastic tricks on the pale grey walls. It seemed the festival of shadows. Processions of shapes, obscure and indistinct, passed across the leaden-hued panels and vanished in the dusk corners.

On a table close to where Herr Hippe sat was placed a large square box of some dark wood, while over it was spread a casing of steel, so elaborately wrought in an open arabesque pattern that it seemed like a shining blue lace which was lightly stretched over its surface.

Herr Hippe lay luxuriously in his arm-chair, looking meditatively into the fire. He was tall and thin, and his skin was of a dull saffron hue. Long, straight hair, sharply cut, regular features, a long, thin moustache, that curled like a dark asp around his mouth, the expression of which was so bitter and cruel that it seemed to distil the venom of the ideal serpent, and a bony, muscular form, were the prominent characteristics of the Wondersmith.

The profound silence that reigned in the chamber was broken by a peculiar scratching at the panel of the door. Herr Hippe started, raised his head, which vibrated on his long neck like the head of a cobra when about to strike, and uttered a strange guttural sound. The door opened and a squat, broad-shouldered woman, with large, wild, oriental eyes, entered softly.

'Ah! Filomel, you are come!' said the Wondersmith, sinking back in his chair. 'Where are the rest of them?'

'They will be here presently,' answered Madame Filomel, seating herself in an arm-chair.

'Have you brought the souls?' asked the Wondersmith.

'They are here,' said the fortune-teller, drawing a large pot-bellied black bottle from under her cloak. 'Ah! I have had such trouble with them!'

'Are they of the right brand,—wild, tearing, dark, devilish fellows? We want no essence of milk and honey, you know. None but souls bitter as hemlock or scorching as lightning will suit our purpose.'

'You will see, you will see. They are ethereal demons, every one of them. They are the pick of a thousand births. Do you think that I, old midwife that I am, don't know the squall of the demon child from that of the angel child, the very moment they are delivered? Ask a musician how he knows, even in the dark, a note struck by Thalberg from one struck by Liszt!'

'I long to test them,' cried the Wondersmith, rubbing his hands joyfully. 'I long to see how the little devils will behave when I give them their shapes. Ah! it will be a proud day for us when we let them loose upon the cursed Christian children! Through the length and breadth of the land they will go; wherever our wandering people set foot, and wherever they are, the children of the Christians shall die. Then we, the despised Bohemians, the gypsies, as they call us, will be once more lords of the earth, as we were in the days when the accursed things called cities did not exist, and men lived in the free woods and hunted the game of the forest. Toys indeed! Ay, we will give the little dears toys! toys that all day will sleep calmly in their boxes, seemingly stiff and wooden and without life,—but at night, when the souls enter them, will arise and surround the cots of the sleeping children, and pierce their hearts with their sharp little poisoned blades! Toys indeed! O, yes! I will sell them toys!'

And the Wondersmith laughed horribly, while the snaky moustache on his upper lip writhed as if it had truly a serpent's power and could sting.

'Have you got your first batch, Herr Hippe?' asked Madame Filomel. 'Are they all ready?'

'O, ay! they are ready,' answered the Wondersmith with gusto,—opening, as he spoke, the box covered with the blue steel lace-work; 'they are here.'

The box contained a quantity of exquisitely carved wooden manikins of both sexes, painted with great dexterity so as to present a miniature resemblance to nature. They were, in fact, nothing more than admirable specimens of those toys which children delight in placing in various positions on the table,—in regiments, or sitting at meals, or grouped under the stiff green trees which always accompany them in the boxes in which they are sold at the toy-shops.

The peculiarity, however, about the manikins of Herr Hippe was not alone the artistic truth with which the limbs and the features were gifted; but on the countenance of each little puppet the carver's art had wrought an expression of appalling wickedness. Every tiny face had its special stamp of ferocity. The lips were thin and brimful of malice; the small black bead-like eyes glittered with the fire of a universal hate. There was not one of the manikins, male or female, that did not hold in his or her hand some miniature weapon. The little men, scowling like demons, clasped in their wooden fingers swords delicate as a housewife's needle. The women, whose countenances expressed treachery and cruelty, clutched infinitesimal daggers, with which they seemed about to take some terrible vengeance.

'Good!' said Madame Filomel, taking one of the manikins out of the box and examining it attentively; 'you work well! These little ones are of the right stamp; they look as if they had mischief in them. Ah! here come our brothers.'

At this moment the same scratching that preceded the entrance of Madame Filomel was heard at the door, and Herr Hippe replied with a hoarse, guttural cry. The next moment two men entered. The first was a small man with very brilliant eyes. He was wrapt in a long shabby cloak, and wore a strange nondescript cap on his head. His companion was tall, long-limbed, and slender; and his dress, although of the ordinary cut, had a certain air of picturesqueness. Both the men possessed the same marked oriental type of countenance which distinguished the Wondersmith and Madame Filomel. True gypsies they seemed, who would not have been out of place telling fortunes, or stealing chickens in the green lanes of England, or wandering with their wild music and their sleight-of-hand tricks through Bohemian villages.

'Welcome, brothers!' said the Wondersmith; 'you are in
time. Sister Filomel has brought the souls, and we are about to
test them. Monsieur Kerplonne, take off your cloak. Brother
Oaksmith, take a chair. I promise you some amusement this
evening; so make yourselves comfortable. Here is something
to aid you.'

And while the Frenchman Kerplonne, and his tall companion,
Oaksmith, were obeying Hippe's invitation, he reached over
to a little closet let into the wall, and took thence a squat
bottle and some glasses, which he placed on the table.

'Drink, brothers!' he said; 'it is not Christian blood, but
good stout wine of Oporto. It goes right to the heart, and warms
one like the sunshine of the south.'

'It is good,' said Kerplonne, smacking his lips with
enthusiasm.

'Why don't you keep brandy? Hang wine!' cried Oaksmith,
after having swallowed two bumpers in rapid succession.

'Bah! Brandy has been the ruin of our race. It has made us
sots and thieves. It is a devil; may it be cursed!' cried Herr
Hippe passionately. 'It is a demon that stole from me my son,
the finest youth in all Courland. Yes! my son, the son of the
Waywode Balthazar, Grand Duke of Lower Egypt, died raving
in a gutter, with an empty brandy-bottle in his hands. Were
it not that the plant is a sacred one to our race, I would curse
the grape and the vine that bore it.'

This outburst was delivered with such energy that the three
gypsies kept silence. Oaksmith helped himself to another glass
of port, and the fortune-teller rocked to and fro in her chair,
too much overawed by the Wondersmith's vehemence of
manner to reply. Kerplonne took no part in the discussion, but
seemed lost in admiration of the manikins, which he took from
the box in which they lay, handling them with the greatest
care.

After the silence had lasted for about a minute, Herr Hippe
broke it with the sudden question, 'How does your eye get on,
Kerplonne?'

'Excellently, Duke. It is finished. I have it here.' And the
little Frenchman put his hand into his pocket and pulled out
a large artificial human eye. Its great size was the only thing

in this eye that would lead any one to suspect its artificiality. It was at least twice the size of life; but there was a fearful speculative light in its iris, which seemed to expand and contract like the eye of a living being, that rendered it a horrible staring paradox. It looked like the naked eye of the Cyclops, torn from his forehead, and still burning with wrath and the desire for vengeance.

The little Frenchman laughed pleasantly as he held the eye in his hand, and gazed down on that huge, dark pupil, that stared back at him, it seemed, with an air of defiance and mistrust.

'It is a devil of an eye,' said the little man, wiping the enamelled surface with an old silk pocket-handkerchief; 'it reads like a demon. My niece—the unhappy one—has a wretch of a lover, and I have a long time feared that she would run away with him. I could not read her correspondence, for she kept her writing-desk closely locked. But I asked her yesterday to keep this eye in some very safe place for me. She put it, as I knew she would, into her desk, and by its aid I read every one of her letters. She was to run away next Monday, the ingrate! but she will find herself disappointed.'

And the little man laughed heartily at the success of his stratagem, and polished and fondled the great eye.

'And you have been at work, too, I see, Herr Hippe. Your manikins are excellent. But where are the souls?'

'In that bottle,' answered the Wondersmith, pointing to the pot-bellied black bottle that Madame Filomel had brought with her. 'Yes, Monsieur Kerplonne,' he continued, 'my manikins are well made. I invoked the aid of Abigor, the demon of soldiery, and he inspired me. The little fellows will be famous assassins when they are animated. We will try them tonight.'

'Good!' cried Kerplonne, rubbing his hands joyously. 'It is close upon Christmas Day. We will fabricate millions of the little murderers by Christmas Eve, and sell them in large quantities; and when the households are all asleep, and the Christian children are waiting for Santa Claus to come, the small ones will troop from their boxes, and the Christian children will die. It is famous! Health to Abigor!'

'Let us try them at once,' said Oaksmith. 'Is your daughter,

Zonéla, in bed, Herr Hippe? Are we secure from intrusion?'

'No one is stirring about the house,' replied the Wonder-smith, gloomily.

Filomel leaned over to Oaksmith, and said in an undertone, 'Why do you mention his daughter? You know he does not like to have her spoken about.'

'I will take care that we are not disturbed,' said Kerplonne, rising. 'I will put my eye outside the door, to watch.'

He went to the door and placed his great eye upon the floor with tender care. As he did so, a dark form, unseen by him or his second vision, glided along the passage noiselessly, and was lost in the darkness.

'Now for it!' exclaimed Madame Filomel, taking up her fat black bottle. 'Herr Hippe, prepare your manikins!'

The Wondersmith took the little dolls out, one by one, and set them upon the table. While Madame Filomel uncorked the black bottle, Herr Hippe covered the dolls with a linen tent, which he took also from the box. This done, the fortune-teller held the mouth of the bottle to the door of the tent, gathering the loose cloth closely round the glass neck. Immediately tiny noises were heard inside the tent. Madame Filomel removed the bottle, and the Wondersmith lifted the covering in which he had enveloped his little people.

A wonderful transformation had taken place. Wooden and inflexible no longer, the crowd of manikins were now in full motion. The bead-like eyes turned, glittering, on all sides; the thin, wicked lips quivered with bad passions; the tiny hands sheathed and unsheathed the little swords and daggers. Episodes, common to life, were taking place in every direction. Here two martial manikins paid court to a pretty, sly-faced female, who smiled on each alternately, but gave her hand to be kissed to a third manikin, an ugly little scoundrel, who crouched behind her. There a pair of friendly dolls walked arm in arm, apparently on the best terms, while, all the time, one was watching his opportunity to stab the other in the back.

'I think they'll do,' said the Wondersmith, chuckling as he watched these various incidents. 'Treacherous, cruel, blood-thirsty. All goes marvellously well. But stay! I will put the grand test to them.'

So saying, he drew a gold dollar from his pocket, and let it fall on the table, in the very midst of the throng of manikins. It had hardly touched the table when there was a pause on all sides. Every head was turned towards the dollar. Then about twenty of the little creatures rushed towards the glittering coin. One, fleeter than the rest, leaped upon it and drew his sword. The entire crowd of little people had now gathered round this new centre of attraction. Men and women struggled and shoved to get nearer to the piece of gold. Hardly had the first Lilliputian mounted upon the treasure, when a hundred blades flashed back a defiant answer to his, and a dozen men, sword in hand, leaped upon the yellow platform and drove him off at sword point. Then commenced a general battle. The miniature faces were convulsed with rage and avarice. Each furious doll tried to plunge dagger or sword into his or her neighbour, and the women seemed possessed by a thousand devils.

'They will break themselves into atoms,' cried Filomel, as she watched with eagerness this savage *mêlée*. 'You had better gather them up, Herr Hippe. I will exhaust my bottle and suck all the souls back from them.'

'O, they are perfect devils! they are magnificent little demons!' cried the Frenchman, with enthusiasm. 'Hippe, you are a wonderful man!' The Wondersmith placed the linen tent over the struggling dolls, and Madame Filomel, who had been performing some mysterious manipulations with her black bottle, put the mouth once more to the door of the tent. In an instant the confused murmur within ceased. Madame Filomel corked the bottle quickly. The Wondersmith withdrew the tent, and, lo! the furious dolls were once more wooden-jointed and inflexible; and the old sinister look was again frozen on their faces.

'They must have blood, though,' said Herr Hippe, as he gathered them up and put them into their box. 'Mr Pippel, the bird-fancier, is asleep. I have a key that opens his door. We will let them loose among the birds; it will be rare fun.'

'Magnificent!' cried Kerplonne. 'Let us go on the instant. But first let me gather up my eye.'

The Frenchman pocketed his eye, after having given it a

polish with the silk handkerchief; Herr Hippe extinguished the lamp; Oaksmith took a last bumper of port; and the four gypsies departed for Mr Pippel's, carrying the box of manikins with them.

———

III

SOLON

The shadow that glided along the dark corridor, at the moment that Monsieur Kerplonne deposited his sentinel eye outside the door of the Wondersmith's apartment, sped swiftly through the passage and ascended the stairs to the attic. Here the shadow stopped at the entrance to one of the chambers and knocked at the door. There was no reply.

'Zonéla, are you asleep?' said the shadow, softly.

'O, Solon, is it you?' replied a sweet low voice from within. 'I thought it was Herr Hippe. Come in.'

The shadow opened the door and entered. There were neither candles nor lamp in the room; but through the projecting window, which was open, there came the faint gleams of the starlight, by which one could distinguish a female figure seated on a low stool in the middle of the floor.

'Has he left you without light again, Zonéla?' asked the shadow, closing the door of the apartment. 'I have brought my little lantern with me, though.'

'Thank you, Solon,' answered she called Zonéla; 'you are a good fellow. He never gives me any light of an evening, but bids me go to bed. I like to sit sometimes and look at the moon and the stars,—the stars more than all; for they seem all the time to look right back into my face, very sadly, as if they would say, "We see you, and pity you, and would help you, if we could." But it is so mournful to be always looking at such myriads of melancholy eyes! and I long so to read those nice books that you lend me Solon!'

By this time the shadow had lit the lantern and was a shadow no longer. A large head, covered with a profusion of long blonde hair, a beautiful pale face, lit with wide, blue, dreamy eyes; long arms and slender hands, attenuated legs, and—an enormous hump; such was Solon, the shadow. As soon as the humpback had lit the lamp, Zonéla arose from the low stool on which she had been seated, and took Solon's hand affectionately in hers.

Zonéla was surely not of gypsy blood. That rich auburn hair, that looked almost black in the lamp-light, that pale, transparent skin, tinged with an under-glow of warm rich blood, the hazel eyes, large and soft as those of a fawn, were never begotten of a Zingaro. Zonéla was about sixteen; her figure, although somewhat thin and angular, was full of the unconscious grace of youth. She was dressed in an old cotton print, which had been once of an exceedingly boisterous pattern, but was now a mere suggestion of former splendour; while round her head was twisted, in fantastic fashion, a silk handkerchief of green ground spotted with bright crimson. This strange head-dress gave her an elfish appearance.

'I have been out all day with the organ, and I am so tired, Solon!—not sleepy, but weary, I mean. Poor Furbelow was sleepy, though, and he's gone to bed.'

'I'm weary, too, Zonéla;—not weary as you are, though, for I sit in my little book-stall all day long, and do not drag round an organ and a monkey and play old tunes for pennies,— but weary of myself, of life, of the load that I carry on my shoulders'; and, as he said this, the poor humpback glanced sideways, as if to call attention to his deformed person.

'Well, but you ought not to be melancholy amidst your books, Solon. Gracious! If I could only sit in the sun and read as you do, how happy I should be! But it's very tiresome to trudge round all day with that nasty organ, and look up at the houses, and know that you are annoying the people inside; and then the boys play such bad tricks on poor Furbelow, throwing him hot pennies to pick up, and burning his poor little hands; and oh! sometimes, Solon, the men in the street make me so afraid,—they speak to me and look at me so oddly!—I'd a great deal rather sit in your book-stall and read.'

'I have nothing but odd volumes in my stall,' answered the

humpback. 'Perhaps that's right, though; for, after all, I'm nothing but an odd volume myself.'

'Come, don't be melancholy, Solon. Sit down and tell me a story. I'll bring Furbelow to listen.'

So saying, she went to a dusky corner of the cheerless attic room, and returned with a little Brazilian monkey in her arms, a poor, mild, drowsy thing. She sat down on her little stool, with Furbelow in her lap, and nodded her head to Solon, as much as to say, 'Go on; we are attentive.'

'You want a story, do you?' said the humpback, with a mournful smile. 'Well, I'll tell you one. Only what will your father say, if he catches me here?'

'Herr Hippe is not my father,' cried Zonéla, indignantly. 'He's a gypsy, and I know I'm stolen; and I'd run away from him, if I only knew where to run to. If I were his child, do you think that he would treat me as he does? make me trudge round the city, all day long, with a barrel-organ and a monkey, —though I love poor, dear little Furbelow,—and keep me up in a garret, and give me so little to eat? I know I'm not his child, for he hates me.'

'Listen to my story, Zonéla, and we'll talk of that afterwards. Let me sit at your feet';—and, having coiled himself up at the little maiden's feet, he commenced :—

'There once lived in a great city, just like this city of New York, a poor little hunchback. He kept a second-hand book-stall, where he made barely enough money to keep body and soul together. He was very sad at times, because he knew scarcely any one, and those that he did know did not love him. He had passed a sickly, secluded youth. The children of his neighbourhood would not play with him, for he was not made like them; and the people in the streets stared at him with pity, or scoffed at him when he went by. Ah! Zonéla, how his poor heart was wrung with bitterness when he beheld the procession of shapely men and fine women that every day passed him by in the thoroughfares of the great city! How he re-pined and cursed his fate as the torrent of fleet-footed firemen dashed past him to the toll of the bells, magnificently in their overflowing vitality and strength! But there was one consolation left him,—one drop of honey in the jar of gall, so sweet that it ameliorated all the bitterness of life. God had given him a deformed body, but his mind was straight and healthy. So the poor hunchback shut himself into the world of books, and was, if not happy, at least contented. He kept company with courteous paladins, and romantic heroes, and beautiful women; and this society was of such excellent breeding that it never so much as once noticed his poor crooked back or his lame walk. The love of books grew upon him with his years. He was remarked for his studious habits; and when, one day, the obscure people that he called father and mother—parents only in name—died, a compassionate book-vender gave him enough stock in trade to set up a little stall of his own. Here, in his book-stall, he sat in the sun all day, waiting for the customers that seldom came, and reading the fine deeds of the people of the ancient time, or the beautiful thoughts of the poets that had warmed millions of hearts before that hour, and still glowed for him with undiminished fire. One day, when he was reading some book, that, small as it was, was big enough to shut the whole world out from him, he heard some music in the street. Looking up from his book, he saw a little girl, with large eyes, playing an organ, while a monkey begged for alms from a crowd of idlers who had nothing in their pockets but their hands. The girl was playing, but she was also weeping. The merry notes of the polka were ground out to a silent accompaniment of tears. She looked very sad, this organ-girl, and her monkey seemed to have caught the infection, for his large brown eyes were moist, as if he also wept. The poor hunchback was struck with pity, and called the little girl over to give her a penny,—not, dear Zonéla, because he wished to bestow alms, but because he wanted to speak with her. She came, and they talked together. She came the next day,—for it turned out that they were neighbours,—and the next, and, in short, every day. They became friends. They were both lonely and afflicted, with this difference, that she was beautiful, and he—was a hunchback.'

'Why, Solon,' cried Zonéla, 'that's the very way you and I met!'

'It was then,' continued Solon, with a faint smile, 'that life seemed to have its music. A great harmony seemed to the poor cripple to fill the world. The carts that took the flour-barrels from the wharves to the store-houses seemed to emit joyous melodies from their wheels. The hum of the great business streets sounded like grand symphonies of triumph. As one who has been travelling through a barren country without much heed feels with singular force the sterility of the lands he has passed through when he reaches the fertile plains that lie at the end of his journey, so the humpback, after his vision had been freshened with this blooming flower, remembered for the first time the misery of the life that he had led. But he did not allow himself to dwell upon the past. The present was so delightful that it occupied all his thoughts. Zonéla, he was in love with the organ-girl.'

'O, that's so nice!' said Zonéla, innocently,—pinching poor Furbelow, as she spoke, in order to dispel a very evident snooze that was creeping over him. 'It's going to be a love-story.'

'Ah! but, Zonéla, he did not know whether she loved him in return. You forget that he was deformed.'

'But,' answered the girl gravely, 'he was good.'

A light like the flash of an aurora illuminated Solon's face for an instant. He put out his hand suddenly, as if to take Zonéla's and press it to his heart; but an unaccountable timidity seemed to arrest the impulse, and he only stroked Furbelow's head,—upon which that individual opened one large brown eye to the extent of the eighth of an inch, and, seeing that it was only Solon, instantly closed it again, and resumed his dream of a city where there were no organs and all the copper coin of the realm was iced.

'He hoped and feared,' continued Solon, in a low, mournful voice; 'but at times he was very miserable, because he did not think it possible that so much happiness was reserved for him as the love of this beautiful, innocent girl. At night, when he was in bed, and all the world was dreaming, he lay awake looking up at the old books against the walls, thinking how he could bring about the charming of her heart. One night, when he was thinking of this, he suddenly found himself in a beautiful country, where the light did not come from sun or moon or stars, but floated round and over and in everything like the atmosphere. On all sides he heard mysterious melodies sung by strangely musical voices. None of the features of the landscape was definite; yet when he looked on the vague harmonies of colour that melted one into another before his sight he was filled with a sense of inexplicable beauty. On every side of him fluttered radiant bodies, which darted to and fro through the illuminated space. They were not birds, yet they flew like birds; and as each one crossed the path of his vision he felt a strange delight flash through his brain, and straightway an interior voice seemed to sing beneath the vaulted dome of his temples a verse containing some beautiful thought. Little fairies were all this time dancing and fluttering around him, perching on his head, on his shoulders, or balancing themselves on his fingertips. "Where am I?" he asked. "Ah, Solon?" he heard them whisper, in tones that sounded like the distant tinkling of silver bells, "this land is nameless; but those who tread its soil, and breathe its air, and gaze on its floating sparks of light, are poets forevermore." Having said this, they vanished, and with them the beautiful indefinite land, and the flashing lights, and the illumined air; and the hunchback found himself again in bed, with the moonlight quivering on the floor, and the dusty books on their shelves, grim and mouldy as ever.'

'You have betrayed yourself. You called yourself Solon,' cried Zonéla. 'Was it a dream?'

'I do not know,' answered Solon; 'but since that night I have been a poet.'

'A poet?' screamed the little organ girl,—'a real poet, who makes verses which every one reads and every one talks of?'

'The people call me a poet,' answered Solon, with a sad smile. 'They do not know me by the name of Solon, for I write under an assumed title; but they praise me, and repeat my songs. But, Zonéla, I can't sing this load off of my back, can I?'

'O, bother the hump!' said Zonéla, jumping up suddenly. 'You're a poet, and that's enough, isn't it? I'm so glad you're a poet, Solon! You must repeat all your best things to me, won't you?'

Solon nodded assent.

'You don't ask me,' he said, 'who was the little girl that the hunchback loved.'

Zonéla's face flushed crimson. She turned suddenly away, and ran into a dark corner of the room. In a moment she returned with an old hand-organ in her arms.

'Play, Solon, play!' she cried. 'I am so glad that I want to dance. Furbelow, come and dance in honour of Solon the Poet.'

It was her confession. Solon's eyes flamed, as if his brain had suddenly ignited. He said nothing; but a triumphant smile broke over his countenance. Zonéla, the twilight of whose cheeks was still rosy with the setting blush, caught the lazy Furbelow by his little paws; Solon turned the crank of the organ, which wheezed out as merry a polka as its asthma would allow, and the girl and the monkey commenced their fantastic dance. They had taken but a few steps when the door suddenly opened, and the tall figure of the Wondersmith appeared on the threshold. His face was convulsed with rage, and the black snake that quivered on his upper lip seemed to rear itself as if about to spring upon the hunchback.

———

IV

THE MANIKINS AND THE MYNAHS

The four gypsies had left Herr Hippe's house cautiously, and directed their steps towards Mr Pippel's bird-shop. Golosh Street was asleep. Nothing was stirring in that tenebrous slum. As the gypsies moved stealthily along in the darkness they had a sinister and murderous air.

Mr Pippel's shop was but a short distance from the Wondersmith's house. A few moments, therefore, brought the gypsy party to the door, when, by the aid of a key which Herr Hippe produced, they silently slipped into the entry. Here the Wondersmith took a dark-lantern from under his cloak, re-

moved the cap that shrouded the light, and led the way into
the shop, which was separated from the entry only by a glass
door, that yielded, like the outer one, to a key which Hippe
took from his pocket. The four gypsies now entered the shop
and closed the door behind them.

It was a little world of birds. On every side, whether in large
or small cages, one beheld balls of various-coloured feathers
standing on one leg and breathing peacefully. Love-birds, nest-
ling shoulder to shoulder, English bullfinches, with ashen-
coloured backs; Java sparrows, fat and sleek and cleanly;
troupials, glossy and splendid in plumage; a cock of the rock,
gleaming, a ball of tawny fire; the campanero of Brazil, white
as snow,—these, with a humbler crowd of linnets, canaries,
robins, mocking-birds, and phoebes, slumbered calmly in their
little cages, that were hung so thickly on the wall as not to leave
an inch of it visible.

'Splendid little morsels, all of them!' exclaimed Monsieur
Kerplonne. 'Ah, we are going to have a rare beating!'

'So Pippel does not sleep in his shop,' said the English gypsy,
Oaksmith.

'No. The fellow lives somewhere up one of the avenues,'
answered Madame Filomel.

'Come,' said the Wondersmith, producing the box of manikins, 'get ready with souls, Madame Filomel. I am impatient to
see my little men letting out lives for the first time.' Just at the
moment that the Wondersmith uttered this sentence, the four
gypsies were startled by a hoarse voice issuing from a corner
of the room, and propounding in the most guttural tones the
intemperate query of 'What'll you take?' This sottish invitation had scarce been given, when a second extremely thick
voice replied from an opposite corner, in accents so rough
that they seemed to issue from a throat torn and furrowed
by the liquid of many bar-rooms, 'Brandy and water.'

'Hallo! who's here?' muttered Herr Hippe, flashing the light
of his lantern round the shop.

Oaksmith turned up his coat-cuffs, as if to be ready for a
fight; Madame Filomel glided, or rather rolled, towards the
door; while Kerplonne put his hand into his pocket, as if to

assure himself that his supernumerary optic was all right.

'What'll you take?' croaked the voice in the corner, once more.

'Brandy and water,' rapidly replied the second voice in the other corner. And then, as if by a concerted movement, a series of bibular invitations and acceptances were rolled backwards and forwards.

'What the devil can it be?' muttered the Wondersmith, flashing his lantern here and there. 'Ah! it is those mynahs.'

So saying, he stopped under one of the wicker cages that hung high up on the wall, and raised the lantern above his head, so as to throw the light upon that particular cage. The hospitable individual who had been extending all these hoarse invitations to partake of intoxicating beverages was an inhabitant of the cage. It was a large mynah-bird, who now stood perched on his crossbar, with his yellowish-orange bill sloped slightly over his shoulder, and his white eye cocked knowingly upon the Wondersmith. The respondent voice in the other corner came from another mynah, who sat in the dusk in a similar cage, also attentively watching the Wondersmith. These mynah-birds have a singular aptitude for acquiring phrases.

'What'll you take?' repeated the mynah, cocking his other eye upon Herr Hippe.

'*Mon Dieu!* what a bird!' exclaimed the little Frenchman. 'He is, in truth, polite.'

'I don't know what I'll take,' said Hippe, as if replying to the mynah; 'but I know what you'll get, old fellow! Filomel, open the cage-doors, and give me the bottle.'

Filomel opened, one after another, the doors of the numberless little cages, thereby arousing from slumber their feathered occupants, who opened their beaks, and stretched their claws, and stared with great surprise at the lantern and the midnight visitors.

By this time the Wondersmith had performed the mysterious manipulations with the bottle, and the manikins were once more in full motion, swarming out of their box, sword and dagger in hand, with their little black eyes glittering fiercely, and their white teeth shining. The little creatures seemed to scent their prey. The gypsies stood in the centre of the shop, watching the proceedings eagerly, while the Lilliputians made in a body towards the wall and commenced climbing from cage to cage. Then was heard a tremendous fluttering of wings, and faint, despairing squawks echoed on all sides. In almost every cage there was a fierce manikin thrusting his sword or dagger vigorously into the body of some unhappy bird.

The poor love-birds lay with their emerald feathers dabbled in their heart's blood, shoulder to shoulder in death as in life. Canaries gasped at the bottom of their cages, while the water in their little glass fountains ran red. The bullfinches wore an unnatural crimson on their breasts. The mocking-bird lay on his back, kicking spasmodically, in the last agonies, with a tiny sword-thrust cleaving his melodious throat in twain, so that from the instrument which used to gush with wondrous music only scarlet drops of blood now trickled. The manikins were ruthless. Their faces were ten times wickeder than ever, as they roamed from cage to cage, slaughtering with a fury that seemed entirely unappeasable.

Presently the feathery rustlings became fewer and fainter, and the little pipings of despair died away; and in every cage lay a poor murdered minstrel,—in every cage but two, and those two were high up on the wall; and in each glared a pair of wild, white eyes; and an orange beak, tough as steel, pointed threateningly down. With the needles which they grasped as swords all wet and warm with blood, and their beadlike eyes flashing in the light of the lantern, the Lilliputian assassins swarmed up the cages in two separate bodies, until they reached the wickets of the mynahs' cages. The first mynah to speak saw them coming,—had listened attentively to the many death-struggles of his comrades, and had, in fact, smelt a rat. Accordingly he was ready for the manikins. There he stood at the barbican of his castle, with his formidable beak couched like a lance. The manikins made a gallant charge. 'What'll you take?' was rattled out by the mynah, in a deep bass, as with one plunge of his sharp bill he scattered the ranks of the enemy, and sent three of them flying to the floor, where they lay with broken limbs. But the manikins were brave automata, and again they closed and charged the gallant mynah. Again the wicked white eyes of the bird gleamed, and again the orange bill dealt destruction. Everything seemed to be going on swimmingly for the mynah, when he found himself attacked in the rear by two treacherous manikins, who had stolen upon him from behind, through the lattice-work of the cage. Quick as lightning the mynah turned to repel this assault, but all too late; two slender, quivering threads of steel crossed in his poor body, and he staggered into a corner of the cage. His white eyes closed, then opened; a shiver passed over his body, beginning at his shoulder-tips and dying off in the extreme tips of the wings; he gasped as if for air, and then, with a convulsive shudder, which ruffled all his feathers, croaked out feebly his little speech, 'What'll you take?' Instantly from the opposite corner came the old response, still feebler than the question,—a mere gurgle, as it were, of 'Brandy and water.' Then all was silent. The mynah-birds were dead.

'They spill blood like Christians,' said the Wondersmith, gazing fondly on the manikins. 'They will be famous assassins.'

———

V

TIED UP

Herr Hippe stood in the doorway, scowling. His eyes seemed to scorch the poor hunchback, whose form, physically inferior, crouched before that baneful glare, while its head, mentally brave, reared itself as if to redeem the cowardice of the frame to which it belonged. Zonéla was frozen in the attitude of motion;—a dancing nymph in coloured marble; agility stunned; elasticity petrified.

Furbelow, astonished at this sudden change, and catching, with all the mysterious rapidity of instinct peculiar to the lower animals, the enigmatical character of the situation, turned his pleading melancholy eyes from one to another of the motionless three, as if begging that his humble intellect should be enlightened as speedily as possible. Not receiving the desired information, he, after the manner of trained animals, conceived that this unusual entrance, and consequent dramatic *tableau*, meant 'shop'. He therefore dropped Zonéla's hand, and pattered on his velvety little feet over towards the grim figure of the Wondersmith, holding out his poor little paw for the customary copper. He had but one idea drilled into him,—soulless creature that he was,—and that was alms. Furbelow frequently got more kicks than coppers, and the present supplication which he indulged in towards the Wondersmith was a terrible confirmation of the rule. The reply to the extended pleading paw was a kick. The long, nervous leg of the Wondersmith caught the little creature in the centre of the body and sent him whizzing across the room into a far corner, where he dropped senseless.

This vengeance which Herr Hippe executed upon Furbelow seemed to have operated as a sort of escape-valve, and he found voice. He hissed out the question, 'Who are you?' to the hunchback. 'Who are you? Deformed dog, who are you? What do you here?'

'My name is Solon,' answered the fearless head of the hunchback, while the frail, cowardly body shivered and trembled inch by inch into a corner.

'So you come to visit my daughter in the night-time, when I am away?' continued the Wondersmith, with a sneering tone that dropped from his snake-wreathed mouth like poison. 'You are a brave and gallant lover, are you not? Where did you win that Order of the Curse of God that decorates your shoulders? The women turn their heads and look after you in the street, when you pass, do they not? Lost in admiration of that symmetrical figure, those graceful limbs, that neck pliant as the stem that moors the lotus! Elegant, conquering, Christian cripple, what do you here in my daughter's room?'

Solon's feeble body seemed to sink into utter annihilation beneath the horrible taunts that his enemy hurled at him, while the large, brave brow and unconquered eyes still sent forth a magnetic resistance.

Suddenly the poor hunchback felt his arm grasped. A thrill seemed to run through his entire body. A warm atmosphere, invigorating and full of delicious odour, surrounded him. It appeared as if invisible bandages were twisted all about his limbs, giving him a strange strength. His sinking legs straightened. His powerless arms were braced. Astonished, he glanced round for an instant, and beheld Zonéla, with a world of love burning in her large lambent eyes, wreathing her round white arms about his humped shoulders. Then the poet knew the great sustaining power of love. Solon reared himself boldly.

'Sneer at my poor form,' he cried, in strong vibrating tones, flinging out one long arm and one thin finger at the Wondersmith. 'Humiliate me if you can. I care not. You are a wretch, and I am honest and pure. This girl is not your daughter. I do not fear you, Herr Hippe. There are stories abroad about you in the neighbourhood, and when you pass people say that they feel evil and blight hovering over their thresholds. You persecute this girl. You are her tyrant. You hate her. I am a cripple. Providence has cast this lump upon my shoulders. But that is nothing. I have come to see Zonéla because I love her,— because she loves me. You have no claim on her; so I will take her from you.'

Quick as lightning the Wondersmith had stridden a few paces, and grasped the poor cripple, who was yet quivering with the departing thunder of his passion. He seized him in his bony, muscular grasp, as he would have seized a puppet, and held him at arm's length, gasping and powerless; while Zonéla, pale, breathless, entreating, sank half-kneeling on the floor.

'Your skeleton will be interesting to science when you are dead, Mr Solon,' hissed the Wondersmith. 'But before I have the pleasure of reducing you to an anatomy, which I will assuredly do, I wish to compliment you on your power of penetration, or sources of information; for I know not if you have derived your knowledge from your own mental research or the efforts of others. You are perfectly correct in your statement that this charming young person is not my daughter. On the contrary, she is the daughter of a Hungarian nobleman who had the misfortune to incur my displeasure. I had a son, crooked spawn of a Christian!—a son, not like you, cankered, gnarled stump of life that you are,—but a youth tall and fair and noble in aspect, as became a child of one whose lineage makes Pharoah modern,—and being of good race, and dwelling in a country where his rank, gypsy as he was, was recognized, he mixed with the proudest of the land. One day he fell in with this accursed Hungarian, a fierce drinker of that devil's blood called brandy. My child until that hour had avoided this bane of our race. Generous wine he drank, because the soul of the sun, our ancestor, palpitated in its purple waves. But brandy, which is fallen and accursed wine, as devils are fallen and accursed angels, had never crossed his lips, until in an evil hour he was seduced by this Christian hog, and from that day forth his life was one fiery debauch, which set only in the black waves of death. I vowed vengeance on the destroyer of my child, and I kept my word. I have destroyed *his* child,— not compassed her death, but blighted her life, steeped her in misery and poverty, and now, thanks to the thousand devils, I have discovered a new torture for her heart. She thought to solace her life with a love-episode! She shall have her little crooked lover, sha'n't she? O, yes! she shall have him, cold and stark and livid, with that great, black, heavy hunch, which no back, however broad, can bear, Death, sitting between his shoulders!'

There was something so awful and demoniac in this entire speech and the manner in which it was delivered, that it petrified Zonéla into a mere inanimate figure, whose eyes seemed unalterably fixed on the fierce, cruel face of the Wondersmith. As for Solon, he was paralysed in the grasp of his foe. He heard, but could not reply. His large eyes, dilated with horror expressed unutterable agony.

The last sentence had hardly been hissed out by the gypsy when he took from his pocket a long, thin coil of whip-cord, which he entangled in a complicated mesh around the cripple's body. It was not the ordinary binding of a prisoner. The slender lash passed and repassed in a thousand intricate folds over the powerless limbs of the poor humpback. When the operation was completed, he looked as if he had been sewed from head to foot in some ingenious species of network.

'Now, my pretty lop-sided little lover,' laughed Herr Hippe, flinging Solon over his shoulder as a fisherman might fling a netful of fish, 'we will proceed to put you into your little cage

until your little coffin is quite ready. Meanwhile we will lock
up your darling beggar-girl to mourn over your untimely end.'

So saying, he stepped from the room with his captive, and
securely locked the door behind him.

When he had disappeared, the frozen Zonéla thawed, and
with a shriek of anguish flung herself on the inanimate body
of Furbelow.

VI

THE POISONING OF THE SWORDS

It was Christmas Eve, and eleven o'clock at night. All over the
land, curly heads were lying on white pillows, dreaming of the
coming of Santa Claus. Innumerable stockings hung by countless bedsides. Visions of beautiful toys, passing in splendid
pageantry through myriads of dimly lit dormitories, made
millions of little hearts palpitate in sleep.

It was on this night that the Wondersmith and his three
gypsy companions sat in close conclave in the little parlour
before mentioned.

There was a fire roaring in the grate. On a table, nearly in the
centre of the room, stood a huge decanter of port, that glowed
in the blaze which lit the chamber like a flask of crimson fire.
On every side, piled in heaps, inanimate, but scowling with
the same old wondrous scowl, lay myriads of the manikins, all
clutching in their wooden hands their tiny weapons. The
Wondersmith held in one hand a small silver bowl filled with
a green, glutinous substance, which he was delicately applying,
with the aid of a camel's-hair brush, to the tips of tiny swords
and daggers. A horrible smile wandered over his sallow face,—
a smile as unwholesome in appearance as the sickly light that
plays above reeking graveyards.

'Let us drink deep brothers,' he cried, leaving off his strange
anointment for a while, to lift a great glass, filled with
sparkling liquor, to his lips. 'Let us drink to our approaching

triumph. Let us drink to the great poison, Macousha. Subtle seed of Death,—swift hurricane that sweeps away Life,—vast hammer that crushes brain and heart and artery with its resistless weight,—I drink to it.'

'It is a noble concoction, Duke Balthazar,' said Madame Filomel, nodding in her chair as she swallowed her wine in great gulps. 'Where did you obtain it?'

'It is made,' said the Wondersmith, swallowing another great draught of wine ere he replied, 'in the wild woods of Guiana, in silence and in mystery. Only one tribe of Indians, the Macoushi Indians, know the secret. It is simmered over fires built of strange woods, and the maker of it dies in the making. The place, for a mile around the spot where it is fabricated, is shunned as accursed. Devils hover over the pot in which it stews; and the birds of the air, scenting the smallest breath of its vapour from far away, drop to earth with paralysed wings, cold and dead.'

'It kills, then, fast?' asked Kerplonne, the artificial-eye maker,—his own eyes gleaming, under the influence of the wine, with a sinister lustre, as if they had been fresh from the factory, and were yet untarnished by use.

'Kills?' echoed the Wondersmith, derisively; 'it is swifter than thunderbolts, stronger than lightning. But you shall see it proved before we let forth our army on the city accursed. You shall see a wretch die, as if smitten by a falling fragment of the sun.'

'What? Do you mean Solon?' asked Oaksmith and the fortune-teller together.

'Ah! you mean the young man who makes the commerce with books?' echoed Kerplonne. 'It is well. His agonies will instruct us.'

'Yes! Solon,' answered Hippe, with a savage accent. 'I hate him, and he shall die this horrid death. Ah! how the little fellows will leap upon him, when I bring him in, bound and helpless, and give their beautiful wicked souls to them! How they will pierce him in ten thousand spots with their poisoned weapons, until his skin turns blue and violet and crimson, and his form swells with the venom,—until his hump is lost in shapeless flesh! He hears what I say, every word of it. He

is in the closet next door, and is listening. How comfortable
he feels! How the sweat of terror rolls on his brow! How
he tries to loosen his bonds, and curses all earth and heaven
when he finds that he cannot! Ho! ho! Handsome lover of
Zonéla, will she kiss you when you are livid and swollen?
Here, Oaksmith, take these branches,—and you, Filomel,—and
finish the anointing of these swords. This wine is grand. This
poison is grand. It is fine to have good wine to drink, and good
poison to kill with; is it not?'—and, with flushed face and
rolling eyes, the Wondersmith continued to drink and use his
brush alternately.

The others hastened to follow his example. It was a horrible
scene: those four wicked faces; those myriads of tiny faces,
just as wicked; the certain unearthly air that pervaded the
apartment; the red, unwholesome glare cast by the fire; the wild
and reckless way in which the weird company drank the red-
illumined wine.

The anointing of the swords went on rapidly, and the wine
went as rapidly down the throats of the four poisoners. Their
faces grew more and more inflamed each instant; their eyes
shone like rolling fireballs; their hair was moist and dishevelled.
The old fortune-teller rocked to and fro in her chair. All four
began to mutter incoherent sentences, and babble unintelligible
wickednesses. Still the anointing of the swords went on.

'I see the faces of millions of young corpses,' babbled Herr
Hippe, gazing, with swimming eyes, into the silver bowl that
contained the Macousha poison,—'all young, all Christians,—
and the little fellows dancing, dancing, and stabbing, stabbing.
Filomel, Filomel, I say!'

'Well, Grand Duke,' snored the old woman, giving a violent
lurch.

'Where's the bottle of souls?'

'In my right-hand pocket, Herr Hippe';—and she felt, so
as to assure herself that it was there. She half drew out the black
bottle and let it slide again into her pocket,—let it slide again,
but it did not completely regain its former place. Caught by
some accident, it hung half out, swaying over the edge of the
pocket, as the fat midwife rolled backwards and forwards in
her drunken efforts at equilibrium.

'All right,' said Herr Hippe, 'perfectly right! Let's drink.'

He reached out his hand for his glass, and, with a dull sigh, dropped on the table, in the instantaneous slumber of intoxication. Oaksmith soon fell back in his chair, breathing heavily. Kerplonne followed. And the heavy, stertorous breathing of Filomel told that she slumbered also; but still her chair retained its rocking motion, and still the bottle of souls balanced itself on the edge of her pocket.

———

VII

LET LOOSE

Sure enough, Solon heard every word of the fiendish talk of the Wondersmith. For how many days he had been shut up, bound in the terrible net, in that dark closet, he did not know; but now he felt that his last hour was come. His little strength was completely worn out in efforts to disentangle himself. Once a day a door opened, and Herr Hippe placed a crust of bread and a cup of water within his reach. On this meagre fare he had subsisted. It was a hard life; but, bad as it was, it was better than the horrible death that menaced him. His brain reeled with terror at the prospect of it. Then, where was Zonéla? Why did she not come to his rescue? But she was, perhaps, dead. The darkness, too, appalled him. A faint light, when the moon was bright, came at night through a chink far up in the wall; and the only other hole in the chamber was an aperture through which, at some former time, a stove-pipe had been passed. Even if he were free, there would have been small hope of escape; but, laced as it were in a network of steel, what was to be done? He groaned and writhed upon the floor, and tore at the boards with his hands, which were free from the wrists down. All else was solidly laced up. Nothing but pride kept him from shrieking aloud, when, on the night of Christmas Eve, he heard the fiendish Hippe recite the programme of his murder.

While he was thus wailing and gnashing his teeth in darkness and torture, he heard a faint noise above his head. Then something seemed to leap from the ceiling and alight softly on the floor. He shuddered with terror. Was it some new torture of the Wondersmith's invention? The next moment, he felt some small animal crawling over his body, and a soft, silky paw was pushed timidly across his face. His heart leapt with joy.

'It is Furbelow!' he cried. 'Zonéla has sent him. He came through the stove-pipe hole.'

It was Furbelow, indeed, restored to life by Zonéla's care, and who had come down a narrow tube, that no human being could have threaded, to console the poor captive. The monkey nestled closely into the hunchback's bosom, and, as he did so, Solon felt something cold and hard hanging from his neck. He touched it. It was sharp. By the dim light that struggled through the aperture high up in the wall, he discovered a knife, suspended by a bit of cord. Ah! how the blood came rushing through the veins that crossed over and through his heart, when life and liberty came to him in this bit of rusty steel! With his manacled hands he loosened the heaven-sent weapon; a few cuts were rapidly made in the cunning network of cord that enveloped his limbs, and in a few seconds he was free!— cramped and faint with hunger, but free!—free to move, to use his limbs,—free to fight,—to die fighting, perhaps,—but still to die free. He ran to the door. The bolt was a weak one, for the Wondersmith had calculated more surely on his prison of cords than on any locks; and with a few efforts the door opened. He went cautiously out into the darkness, with Furbelow perched on his shoulder, pressing his cold muzzle against his cheek. He had made but a few steps when a trembling hand was put into his, and in another moment Zonéla's palpitating heart was pressed against his own. One long kiss, an embrace, a few whispered words, and the hunchback and the girl stole softly towards the door of the chamber in which the four gypsies slept. All seemed still; nothing but the hard breathing of the sleepers and the monotonous rocking of Madame Filomel's chair broke the silence. Solon stooped down and put his eye to the keyhole, through which a red bar of light streamed into the entry. As he did so, his foot crushed some brittle substance that lay just outside the door; at the same moment a howl of agony was heard to issue from the room within. Solon started; nor did he know that at that instant he had crushed into dust Monsieur Kerplonne's supernumerary eye, and the owner, though wrapt in a drunken sleep, felt the pang quiver through his brain.

While Solon peeped through the keyhole, all in the room was motionless. He had not gazed, however, for many seconds, when the chair of the fortune-teller gave a sudden lurch, and the black bottle, already hanging half out of her wide pocket, slipped entirely from its resting-place, and, falling heavily to the ground, shivered into fragments.

Then took place an astonishing spectacle. The myriads of armed dolls, that lay in piles about the room, became suddenly imbued with motion. They stood up straight, their tiny limbs moved, their black eyes flashed with wicked purpose, their thread-like swords gleamed as they waved them to and fro. The villainous souls imprisoned in the bottle began to work within them. Like the Lilliputians, when they found the giant Gulliver asleep, they scaled in swarms the burly sides of the four sleeping gypsies. At every step they took, they drove their thin swords and quivering daggers into the flesh of the drunken authors of their being. To stab and kill was their mission, and they stabbed and killed with incredible fury. They clustered on the Wondersmith's sallow cheeks and sinewy throat, piercing every portion with their diminutive poisoned blades. Filomel's fat carcass was alive with them. They blackened the spare body of Monsieur Kerplonne. They covered Oaksmith's huge form like a cluster of insects.

Overcome completely with the fumes of wine, these tiny wounds did not for a few moments awaken the sleeping victims. But the swift and deadly poison Macousha, with which the weapons had been so fiendishly anointed, began to work. Herr Hippe, stung into sudden life, leaped to his feet, with a dwarf army clinging to his clothes and his hands,—always stabbing, stabbing, stabbing. For an instant, a look of stupid bewilderment clouded his face; then the horrible truth burst upon him. He gave a shriek that curdled the air for miles and miles.

'Oaksmith! Kerplonne! Filomel! Awake! awake! We are

lost! The souls have got loose! We are dead! poisoned! O accursed ones! O demons, ye are slaying me! Ah! fiends of hell!'

Aroused by these frightful howls, the three gypsies sprang to their feet, to find themselves being stung to death by the manikins. They raved, they shrieked, they swore. They staggered round the chamber. Blinded in the eyes by the ever-stabbing weapons,—with the poison already burning in their veins like red-hot lead,—their forms swelling and discolouring visibly every moment,—their howls and attitudes and furious gestures made the scene look like a chamber in hell.

Maddened beyond endurance, the Wondersmith, half-blind, and choking with the venom that had congested all the blood-vessels of his body, seized dozens of the manikins and dashed them into the fire, trampling them down with his feet.

'Ye shall die too, if I die,' he cried, with a roar like that of a tiger. 'Ye shall burn, if I burn. I gave ye life,—I give ye death. Down!—down!—burn!—flame!'

The other gypsies, themselves maddened by approaching death, began hurling manikins, by handfuls, into the fire. The little creatures, being wooden of body, quickly caught the flames, and an awful struggle for life took place in the grate. Some of them escaped from between the bars and ran about the room, blazing, writhing in agony, and igniting the curtains and other draperies that hung around. Others fought and stabbed one another in the very core of the fire. Meantime, the motions of the gypsies grew slower and slower and their curses were uttered in choked guttural tones. The faces of all four were spotted with red and green and violet, their bodies were swollen to a frightful size, and at last they dropped on the floor.

The chamber was now a sheet of fire. The flames roared round and round, as if seeking for escape, licking every pro-jecting cornice and sill with greedy tongues. A hot, putrid breath came through the keyhole, and smote Solon and Zonéla like a wind of death. They clasped each other's hands with a moan of terror, and fled from the house.

The next morning, as Christmas Day was dawning and the happy children all over the great city were peeping from their beds into the myriads of stockings hanging near-by, the blue skies of heaven shone through a black network of stone and charred rafters. These were all that remained of the habitation of Herr Hippe, the Wondersmith.

The Basilisk

by

R. MURRAY GILCHRIST

Of all the stories and books I considered for this anthology of Victorian tales of terror, The Stone Dragon *(1894) by Robert Murray Gilchrist (1868-1917) was undoubtedly the most unique. And of the stories in that book,* The Basilisk *was probably the most outstanding.*

Gilchrist was a native and scholar of Derbyshire who wrote several books in the dialect of that region, which make interesting reading these days. He was also a regular contributor to newspapers and periodicals, including the National Observer *when it was edited by W. E. Henley. But of all his works,* The Stone Dragon *is the most singular, especially as he never repeated the style and genre that he employed in it. That he had a talent for the macabre is beyond question, but it is also worth noting as you read the story what a unique command of language Gilchrist had.*

About the story's content, I will say nothing; you must make up your own mind about it. But you are in for something special, I will say that. And as a clue, remember the definition of the basilisk: a fabulous creature with fiery, death-dealing eyes and breath.

Marina gave no sign that she heard my protestation. The embroidery of Venus's hands in her silk picture of The Judgment of Paris was seemingly of greater import to her than the love which almost tore my soul and body asunder. In absolute despair I sat until she had replenished her needle seven times. Then impassioned nature cried aloud : —

'You do not love me!'

She looked up somewhat wearily, as one debarred from rest. 'Listen,' she said. 'There is a creature called a Basilisk, which turns men and women into stone. In my girlhood I saw the Basilisk—I am stone!'

And, rising from her chair, she departed the room, leaving me in amazed doubt as to whether I had heard aright. I had always known of some curious secret in her life : a secret which permitted her to speak of and to understand things to which no other woman had dared to lift her thoughts. But alas! it was a secret whose influence ever thrust her back from the attaining of happiness. She would warm, then freeze instantly; discuss the purest wisdom, then cease with contemptuous lips and eyes. Doubtless this strangeness had been the first thing to awaken my passion. Her beauty was not of the kind that smites men with sudden craving : it was pale and reposeful, the loveliness of a marble image. Yet, as time went on, so wondrous became her fascination that even the murmur of her swaying garments sickened me with longing. Not more than a year had passed since our first meeting, when I had found her laden with flaming tendrils in the thinned woods of my heritage. A very Dryad, robed in grass colour, she was chanting to the sylvan deities. The invisible web took me, and I became her slave.

Her house lay two leagues from mine. It was a low-built mansion lying in a concave park. The thatch was gaudy with stonecrop and lichen. Amongst the central chimneys a foreign bird sat on a nest of twigs. The long windows blazed with heraldic devices; and paintings of kings and queens and nobles hung in the dim chambers. Here she dwelt with a retinue of aged servants, fantastic women and men half imbecile, who *salaamed* before her with eastern humility and yet addressed her in such terms as gossips use. Had she given them life they could not have obeyed with more reverence. Quaint things the women wrought for her—pomanders and cushions of thistledown; and the men were never happier than when they could tell her of the first thrush's egg in the thornbush or a sighting of the bitterns that haunted the marsh. She was their goddess and their daughter. Each day had its own routine. In the morning she rode and sang and played; at noon she read in the dusty library, drinking to the full of the dramatists and the platonists. Her own life was such a tragedy as an Elizabethan would have adored. None save her people knew her history, but there were wonderful stories of how she had bowed to tradition, and concentrated in herself the characteristics of a thousand wizard fathers. In the blossom of her youth she had sought strange knowledge, and had tasted thereof, and rued.

The morning after my declaration she rode across her park to the meditating walk I always paced till noon. She was alone, dressed in a habit of white with a loose girdle of blue. As her mare reached the yew hedge, she dismounted, and came to me with more lightness than I had ever beheld in her. At her waist hung a black glass mirror, and her half-bare arms were adorned with cabalistic jewels.

When I knelt to kiss her hand, she sighed heavily. 'Ask me nothing,' she said. 'Life itself is too joyless to be more embittered by explanations. Let all rest between us as now. I will love coldly, you warmly, with no nearer approaching.' Her voice rang full of a wistful expectancy : as if she knew that I should combat her half explained decision. She read me well, for almost ere she had done I cried out loudly against it :—'It can never be so—I cannot breathe—I shall die.'

She sank to the low moss-covered wall. 'Must the sacrifice be made?' she asked, half to herself. 'Must I tell him all?' Silence prevailed a while, then turning away her face she said : 'From the first I loved you, but last night in the darkness, when I could not sleep for thinking of your words, love sprang into desire.'

I was forbidden to speak.

'And desire seemed to burst the cords that bound me. In that moment's strength I felt that I could give all for the joy of being once utterly yours.'

I longed to clasp her to my heart. But her eyes were stern, and a frown crossed her brow.

'At morning light,' she said, 'desire died, but in my ecstasy I had sworn to give what must be given for that short bliss, and to lie in your arms and pant against you before another midnight. So I have come to bid you fare with me to the place where the spell may be loosed, and happiness bought.'

She called the mare : it came whinnying, and pawed the ground until she had stroked its neck. She mounted, setting in my hand a tiny, satin-shod foot that seemed rather child's than woman's. 'Let us go together to my house,' she said. 'I have orders to give and duties to fulfil. I will not keep you there long, for we must start soon on our errand.' I walked exultantly at her side, but, the grange in view, I entreated her to speak explicitly of our mysterious journey. She stooped and patted my head. ' 'Tis but a matter of buying and selling,' she answered.

When she had arranged her household affairs, she came to the library and bade me follow her. Then, with the mirror still swinging against her knees, she led me through the garden and the wilderness down to a misty wood. It being autumn, the trees were tinted gloriously in dusky bars of colouring. The rowan, with his amber leaves and scarlet berries, stood before the brown black-spotted sycamore; the silver beech flaunted his golden coins against my poverty; firs, green and fawn-hued, slumbered in hazy gossamer. No bird carolled, although the sun was hot. Marina noted the absence of sound, and without prelude of any kind began to sing from the ballad of the Witch Mother : about the nine enchanted knots, and the trouble-comb in the lady's knotted hair, and the master-kid that ran beneath her couch. Every drop of my blood froze in dread, for whilst she sang her face took on the majesty of one who traffics with infernal powers. As the shade of the trees fell over her, and we passed intermittently out of the light, I saw that her eyes glittered like rings of sapphires. Believing now that the ordeal she must undergo would be too frightful, I begged her to return. Supplicating on my knees—'Let me face the evil alone!' I said, 'I will entreat the loosening of the bonds. I will compel and accept any penalty.' She grew calm. 'Nay,' she said, very gently, 'if aught can conquer, it is my love alone. In the fervour of my last wish I can dare everything.'

By now, at the end of a sloping alley, we had reached the shores of a vast marsh. Some unknown quality in the sparkling water had stained its whole bed a bright yellow. Green leaves, of such a sour brightness as almost poisoned to behold, floated on the surface of the rush-girdled pools. Weeds like tempting

veils of mossy velvet grew beneath in vivid contrast with
the soil. Alders and willows hung over the margin. From where
we stood a half-submerged path of rough stones, threaded by
deep swift channels, crossed to the very centre. Marina put
her foot upon the first step. 'I must go first,' she said. 'Only once
before have I gone this way, yet I know its pitfalls better than
any living creature.'

Before I could hinder her she was leaping from stone to stone
like a hunted animal. I followed hastily, seeking, but vainly, to
lessen the space between us. She was gasping for breath,
and her heart-beats sounded like the ticking of a clock. When
we reached a great pool, itself almost a lake, that was covered
with lavender scum, the path turned abruptly to the right,
where stood an isolated grove of wasted elms. As Marina beheld
this, her pace slackened, and she paused in momentary
indecision; but, at my first word of pleading that she should
go no further, she went on, dragging her silken mud-bespattered
skirts. We climbed the slippery shores of the island (for island
it was, being raised much above the level of the marsh), and
Marina led the way over lush grass to an open glade. A great
marble tank lay there, supported on two thick pillars. Decayed
boughs rested on the crust of stagnancy within, and frogs,
bloated and almost blue, rolled off at our approach. To the
left stood the columns of a temple, a round, domed building,
with a closed door of bronze. Wild vines had grown athwart
the portal; rank, clinging herbs had sprung from the over-
teeming soil; astrological figures were chiselled on the broad
stairs.

Here Marina stopped. 'I shall blindfold you,' she said, taking
off her loose sash, 'and you must vow obedience to all I tell you.
The least error will betray us.' I promised, and submitted to the
bandage. With a pressure of the hand, and bidding me neither
move nor speak, she left me and went to the door of the
temple. Thrice her hand struck the dull metal. At the last
stroke a hissing shriek came from within, and the massive
hinges creaked loudly. A breath like an icy tongue leaped out
and touched me, and in the terror my hand sprang to the ker-
chief. Marina's voice, filled with agony, gave me instant pause.
'Oh, why am I thus torn between the man and the fiend? The

mesh that holds life in will be ripped from end to end! Is there no mercy?'

My hand fell impotent. Every muscle shrank. I felt myself turn to stone. After a while came a sweet scent of smouldering wood: such an Oriental fragrance as is offered to Indian gods. Then the door swung to, and I heard Marina's voice, dim and wordless, but raised in wild deprecation. Hour after hour passed so, and still I waited. Not until the sash grew crimson with the rays of the sinking sun did the door open.

'Come to me!' Marina whispered. 'Do not take off your blindfold. Quick—we must not stay here long. He is glutted with my sacrifice.'

Newborn joy rang in her tones. I stumbled across and was caught in her arms. Shafts of delight pierced my heart at the first contact with her warm breasts. She turned me round, and bidding me look straight in front, with one swift touch untied the knot. The first thing my dazed eyes fell upon was the mirror of black glass which had hung from her waist. She held it so that I might gaze into its depths. And there, with a cry of amazement and fear, *I saw the shadow of the Basilisk.*

The Thing was lying prone on the floor, the presentiment of a sleeping horror. Vivid scarlet and sable feathers covered its gold-crowned cock's-head, and its leathern dragon-wings were folded. Its sinuous tail, capped with a snake's eyes and mouth, was curved in luxurious and delighted satiety. A prodigious evil leaped in its atmosphere. But even as I looked a mist crowded over the surface of the mirror: the shadow faded, leaving only an indistinct and wavering shape. Marina breathed upon it, and, as I peered and pored, the gloom went off the plate and left, where the Thing had lain, the prostrate figure of a man. He was young and stalwart, a dark outline with a white face, and short black curls that fell in tangles over a shapely forehead, and eyelids languorous and red. His aspect was that of a wearied demon-god.

When Marina looked sideways and saw my wonderment, she laughed delightedly in one rippling running tune that should have quickened the dead entrails of the marsh. 'I have conquered!' she cried. 'I have purchased the fulness of joy!' And with one outstretched arm she closed the door before I could turn to look; with the other she encircled my neck, and, bringing down my head, pressed my mouth to hers. The mirror fell from her hand, and with her foot she crushed its shards into the dank mould.

The sun had sunk behind the trees now, and glittered through the intricate leafage like a charcoal-burner's fire. All the nymphs of the pools arose and danced, grey and cold, exulting at the absence of the divine light. So thickly · gathered the vapours that the path grew perilous. 'Stay, love,' I said. 'Let me take you in my arms and carry you. It is no longer safe for you to walk alone.' She made no reply, but, a flush arising to her pale cheeks, she stood and let me lift her to my bosom. She rested a hand on either shoulder, and gave no sign of fear as I bounded from stone to stone. The way lengthened deliciously, and by the time we reached the plantation the moon was rising over the further hills. Hope and fear fought in my heart : soon both were set at rest. When I set her on the dry ground she stood a-tiptoe, and murmured with exquisite shame : 'To-night, then, dearest. My home is yours now.'

So, in a rapture too subtle for words, we walked together, arm-enfolded, to her house. Preparations for a banquet were going on within : the windows were ablaze, and figures passed behind them bowed with heavy dishes. At the threshold of the hall we were met by a triumphant crash of melody. In the musicians' gallery bald-pated veterans played with flute and harp and viol-de-gamba. In two long rows the antic retainers stood, and bowed, and cried merrily : 'Joy and health to the bride and groom!' And they kissed Marina's hands and mine, and, with the players sending forth that half-forgotten tenderness which threads through ancient song-books, we passed to the feast, seating ourselves on the daïs, whilst the servants filled the tables below. But we made little feint of appetite. As the last dish of confections was removed a weird pageant swept across the further end of the banqueting-room : Oberon and Titania with Robin Goodfellow and the rest, attired in silks and satins gorgeous of hue, and bedizened with such late flowers as were still with us. I leaned forward to commend, and saw that each face was brown and wizened and thin-haired : so that their motions and their wedding paean felt goblin and discomforting; nor could I smile till they departed by the further door. Then the tables were cleared away, and Marina, taking my finger-tips in hers, opened a stately dance. The servants followed, and in the second maze, a shrill and joyful laughter proclaimed that the bride had sought her chamber....

Ere the dawn I wakened from a troubled sleep. My dream had been of despair : I had been persecuted by a host of devils, thieves of a priceless jewel. So I leaned over the pillow for Marina's consolation; my lips sought hers, my hand crept beneath her head. My heart gave one mad bound—then stopped.

A Dead Man's Teeth

by

S. BARING GOULD

The many and varied interests of S. Baring Gould (1834-1924) are best summarised by two of his written works— the hymn Onward Christian Soldiers *and* The Book Of Werewolves *(1865). Gould was at once Anglican priest, mythologist, poet, hymnographer, occult researcher, and, to round off this unique list, a squire-parson. This particular post was one of the last of its kind; Gould inherited the estate of Lew-Trenchard in 1881 and lived as owner and vicar until his death.*

He was the author of many books on many subjects— novels, travel, sermons, verse and his enduring folklore and supernatural studies. His short stories are few and far between, and ghost stories even scarcer. I was fortunate enough to be able to locate this rare item and present it here. It is one of the few stories of its kind (and in this collection) to include a small amount of humour. The actual 'ghost' involved is quite unique. I hope you enjoy it.

'Yes, sir, it is a grave, what you see there, and what is more I can tell you whose grave it is, or was. And there's a very curious story connected with that there grave, and if you don't mind sitting down on that piece of rock for five minutes, I'll tell you all about it.'

I was examining for geological purposes a quarry in Cornwall that had been opened in the side of a hill for the extraction of stone. I observed a sort of niche in the uppermost layer of rock, under the earth which rose some four feet above the surface of the rock.

The niche was about two feet deep and the same breadth, and the sides were cut perpendicularly. It was clearly artificial, and at once struck me as being a section of a grave. There was no churchyard interfered with, so that I supposed the grave was prehistoric, and at once inquired whether any bronze or flint weapons had been found when it was cut through.

'No, sir,' said the quarryman, 'nothing of the sort as far as I know; it was the top of the grave we cut through, and when we sent the pick into it, the gentleman's head came down into the quarry.'

'Gentleman's head? What gentleman's head?'

'Well, sir, I did not know at the time. It gave me a lot of trouble did that head, or rather the teeth from it. If you'll be so good as to sit down on that stone, I'll tell you all about it, and I reckon it will be worth your trouble. It's as curious a story as you have ever heard.'

'I will listen certainly. But excuse me one moment. I should like to crawl up the side of the quarry and examine the grave.'

'It's my lunch time, and I've nothing to do but to eat and talk for half-an-hour,' said the quarryman, 'so I'll tell you all the whole story, when you've been up and come down again. There'll be bones there. You'll find his neck; we cut off the head of the grave. But whatever you do, leave the bones alone. Don't carry any away with you in your pocket, or you'll be sorry.'

I made the exploration I required and found that a grave had been cut in the rock. Clearly, when the interment took place, those who made the grave did not consider that there was a sufficient depth of earth, and they had accordingly cut out a hole in the rock below the soil, to accommodate the dead man. Bones were still in situ. I could find no trace of coffin, but in all likelihood, if there had been one there, it had rotted away, and the gravelly soil from above had fallen in on all sides, and had taken the place of the wood as it decomposed. And if there had been a mound above the dead man, the sinking in after decomposition had caused it to disappear. There were bushes of heather above the grave, but nothing to indicate that a tomb had been in the place, as far as could be judged from above. Its presence would not have been guessed had it not been revealed by the operations of the quarrymen.

Having completed my observations, I returned to the bottom, and seated myself on the stone indicated by the workman. He occupied the top of another, and was engaged on a pie, from which he cut large pieces and thrust them between knife and thumb into his mouth. As he opened this receptacle I observed that the gums were ill-provided with teeth, so that mastication must be imperfect.

'You see, sir,' said the quarryman, 'when we cut that new slice we went slap through the head of the grave, and never knowed there was a grave there, till down came the head, like a snowball. It was my partner James Doune, as was up there wi' his pick. I was sitting here, and I'd just got out my dinner, when I heard James a-hollerin' to me to look out. I looked up, and saw that there skull come jumping down the side, and before I could get up down came the skull and flopped right among my victuals. There it sat in my lap, looking up in my face, as innocent as a babe, so it seemed to me.

'Well, sir, I dare say you know that there ain't a better preservative against toothache than to carry about a dead man's tooth in your pocket. Dead men's teeth don't lie about like empty snail shells, and I'd often wished to have one. I suffer terrible from my teeth. I've been kept raving with pain night after night, and one ain't up to work when one has been kept raving all night, either with teeth or babies. So you can imagine I was uncommon joyful when that head came bouncing into my lap. I found the teeth weren't particular tight in, and with my knife I easily got a tooth or two out; I thought I'd be square all round, so I got out a back tooth and an eye tooth and a front one. Then I thought I was pretty well set up and protected against toothache. I got my wife to sew 'em up in a bit o'silk and hung it round my neck. I may say this—from that day so long as I wore the dead man's teeth I never had a touch of the toothache.'

'And how long did you wear them?'

'Three days, sir.'

'Not more? Why did you not retain them?'

'I'll tell you why, if you'll listen to me.'

'Certainly. But what have you done with the skull?'

'Chucked it away. It weren't no good to nobody—least of

all to the owner. And for me—I'd got out of it all I wanted.'

'You have not got the teeth now?'

'No. I kept them for three days and then chucked them away.'

'Have you had toothache since?'

'Terrible; but I had what was worse when I had the teeth.'

'Well, go on and tell me what the "worse" was.'

'So I will, if you'll listen to me. Well, sir, I had them teeth done up in a bit of silk, and hung round my throat. The first night I went to bed, that was Saturday, I had the little bag round my neck. I hadn't hardly laid my head on the pillow when I found I wasn't no more what I ought to have been. In the first place, I hadn't gone to bed in my clothes, and no sooner was my head on my pillow than I was in a red coat and breeches and gaiters; and what is more, in the second place, I'd laid me down to rest, and I found myself on horseback, tearing over the country, jumping hedges, tally-hoing—me as never rode a horse in my life, and never tally-hoed, and wouldn't do it to save my soul. I knowed all the while I was doing wrong. I knowed I'd got to preach in our chapel next evening, the Sabbath Day—and here was I in a red coat, and galloping after the hounds, and tearing after a fox, and swearing awful! I couldn't help myself. I believe my face was as pink as my coat. I tried to compose my mouth to say Hallelujah, but I couldn't do it—I rapped out a—but, sir, I daren't even whisper what I then swore at the top o' my voice. It was terrible—terrible!'

I saw the quarryman's face bathed in perspiration. The thought of what he had gone through affected him, and his hand shook as he heaved a lump of pastry to his quivering lips.

'I tried to think I was in the pulpit; but it was no good; I was whacking into my cob, and kicking with spurs into her flanks, and away she went over a five-barred gate—it was terrible—terrible, to a shining light, sir,—such as I be.'

The man heaved a sigh and wiped his brow and cheeks, and rose with his pudding-bag.

'All the Sabbath Day after that,' continued the quarryman, 'I wasn't myself. It lay on my conscience that I'd done wrong; and when I preached in the evening, there was no unction in me, no more, sir, than you could have greased the fly-wheel of your watch with. I didn't feel happy, and it was with a heavy heart and a troubled head that I went to bed on the Sabbath night.' He heaved another sigh, and folded up his lunch-bag.

'Will you believe it, sir? No sooner had I closed my eyes than I was in a public-house. I—who've been in the Band of Hope ever since I was a baby. There I was, just out of the pulpit at Bethesda, and in the "Fox and Hounds" drinking. I tried to call out for ginger beer, but the words got altered in my throat to whisky toddy. And what was more, I was singing —roaring out at the top of my voice—

> "Come, my lads, let us be jolly,
> Drive away dull melancholy;
> For to grieve it is a folly
> When we meet together!" '

The quarryman covered his eyes with his hands—he was ashamed to look up.

'If that wasn't bad enough, the words that followed were worse—and I a teetotaller down to the ground,

> "Here's the bottle, as it passes,
> Do not fail to fill your glasses;
> Water drinkers are dull asses
> When they're met together."

'All the while I sang it I knew I was saying good-bye to my consistency, I was going against my dearest convictions. But I couldn't help myself, it was as though an evil spirit possessed me. I was myself and yet not myself. It was terrible—terrible —terrible!'

The quarryman swung his pasty bag, and smote his breast with it.

'That wasn't all,' he continued, and lowered his tone. 'There was an uncommon pretty barmaid with red rosy cheeks and curling black hair; and somehow I got my arm round her waist. I knowed my wife was looking on, and, sir, I knowed the consequences would be awful—awful—simply awful.'

The quarryman's head sank on his knees, he clasped his hands over the back of his head, and groaned for full five minutes. Presently he looked up, pulled himself together, and continued his narrative.

'The worst of all is behind. I was very busy on Monday, as I was on Mr Conybeare's committee. We were in for the election, and I'm tremendous strong as a Liberal, and I reckon I can influence a good many votes in my district of Cornwall. Well, sir, I'd been about canvassing for Mr Conybeare very hard, yet all the while I had a sort of deadly fear at my heart that what I'd been doing, both hunting and drinking, and swearing and singing, would come out in public, or would be thrown in my teeth by the Conservatives, and might damage the good cause. But no one said anything about it on Monday, and towards evening my mind was more at ease.

'I was very tired when I went to bed, for I had been working, as I said, very hard indeed, and persuading of obstinate politicians is worse than breaking stones for the road, and far worse than converting of obstinate sinners. No sooner had I laid my head on the pillow than—will you believe it, sir?—I was in the full swing of the election. I didn't know it was coming on so fast. I thought it about three weeks to go, but not a bit of it. They'd set up a polling place in the Board school, and there was I swaggering up to register my vote. There were placards—Unionist on one side, but I wouldn't look at them; on the other side were the Radical posters—from Mr Conybeare—and I knowed my own mind. If any man in England be true and loyal to the G.O.M. that's me. Well, sir, in I walked and gave my name, I knowed my number, and went as confident as possible into the little box and with my paper in one hand took the pencil in the other, wetted the pencil with my tongue to make sure it marked black enough, and then set down my cross. Will you believe it?—that spirit o' perversity and devilry had come over me once more, and I'd gone and voted Conservative.'

The quarryman staggered back, and I had just time to spring to his aid. He had fainted. I threw water over his face till he came round and by degrees he was himself again.

'Awful! awful! wasn't it?' said he. 'Well, sir, after that I would have nothing more to do with them teeth. They did it. I chucked 'em away; toothache would be better all night long than the trials I had to undergo when I had them dead man's teeth about me.'

'But have you not dreamed since?' I asked, looking at the pastry which, when he fainted, I had taken in my hand.

'Yes, sir, often, very often; but then my dreams since have always been Nonconformist, Temperance and Radical dreams—and them's wholesome.'

'You said something about knowing who it was whose grave you had disturbed?'

'Well, and so I believe I do. I did not know at the time, but afterwards, when I began to tell my story; then there was a talk about it and a raking and a grubbing among old folk's memories, and there was an old woman who said she could throw some light on the subject. Her tale was that about a hundred years ago, or more perhaps, she could not be sure, there lived at the Old Hall one Squire Trewenna. The Hall has been pulled down because of the mines, and the Trewennas are all gone. Squire Trewenna was a terrible man for hunting and drinking, and was, moreover, a regular Conservative. He was a fast chap, and no good to nobody but to dogs and horses, and before he died he begged that he might be buried on the brink of the moor where he'd ridden so often and enjoyed himself so much, and had killed a tremendous big fox in the last hunt he ever went out in before gout got to his stomach. And he said he wanted no headstone over him, that fox and hounds and horses might go over his grave. Well, folks forgot, as there was no headstone, where he lay, exact, and old Betty Tregellas says she believes what we cut into was Squire Trewenna's grave. I think so too, for how else was it that when I had those teeth about me I was so possessed by a spirit of unrighteousness and drinking and Conservatism? I reckon you've had a Board School education and been to the University, and are a learned man. Tell me, now, am I not right?'

The Doomed Man

by

DICK DONOVAN

Undoubtedly one of the most fertile regions for Victorian fiction was the sea, which held a fascination for many authors of the period. Few other fictional genres can have been so thoroughly researched (by sailors who later turned author) and yet still remain quite so unknown. Even today, it should be borne in mind, man has really only scratched the surface of the oceans. Consider how quickly new types of fish are investigated in search of new food sources by the simple expedient of fishing almost literally a few feet deeper. In the last century the sea was the vast unknown, full of monsters and mermaids, lost lands and phantom ships. Though successful ghost stories have been written around modern powered craft, the proper place for a nautical tale of terror is among the creaking timbers and flapping sails of an old sailing ship. Accordingly, I have selected two ghost stories set aboard sailing craft in the last century.

The success of BBC TV's The Onedin Line *probably owes much to the romantic image of the old sailing craft. This romantic image is aided by distance, though. Elizabeth Stuart Phelps Ward's story reminds us that the old ships were the scene of much brutality and misery, where the captain's word was law and power rested at a rope's end. The first tale is by Dick Donovan, who in real life was J. E. Preston Muddock, a prolific Victorian writer of thrillers. 'The Doomed Man' is from his 1899 volume* Tales Of Terror *and in it he uses all the traditional elements of life at sea on a sailing ship to heighten the atmosphere of*

*his tale, a ghost story which rises to a very effective
climax.*

It was in the year 1847, as our family business and trade were
spreading, that I opened a branch of our London house in Cuba,
and placed a trusted and experienced manager in charge. Unfortunately this gentleman died in 1850 of yellow fever, and
it became necessary that I should proceed at once to Cuba
to look into matters, and appoint a successor to the deceased
manager. A City friend recommended me to take passage in
a sailing vessel called the *Pride of the Ocean*, belonging to a
Liverpool firm, and then loading in the Liverpool docks, being
chartered to proceed direct to Cuba. I thereupon applied to
the owners, and engaged my passage in her. She was a full-
rigged ship of about a thousand tons, and was reputed to be
able to sail with a fair wind seventeen knots, being clipper
built.

I arrived in Liverpool on the very day that the ship was
advertised to sail. I was informed that she would leave the
dock at midnight, when it would be high-water, and that two
tugs would tow her beyond Holyhead. I did not reach Liverpool
until the evening, and drove at once from the railway station
to the vessel and got on board the ship as the dock gates were
being opened. Being very tired I went straight to bed, and the
next morning, as the sea was very rough, I could not get up, as
I am a poor sailor, and generally ill for three or four days at
the commencement of a voyage. On this occasion it was a full
week before I found my sea legs and sea stomach, and one
morning I took my place at the breakfast table for the first
time, and was welcomed and greeted by the captain, whom
I had not seen before. We were a very small party, as there
were only three passengers beside myself, one being a Spanish
lady who had been transacting some business in England on
behalf of her husband, who was a Cuban planter.

The captain's name was Jubal Tredegar, a native of Cornwall.
He was about fifty and had been at sea for over thirty years.
He had a swarthy sunburnt face, very dark hair, and black
eyes, with a full, rounded beard, but clean-shaven upper lip.

In every respect he was a typical sailor, save in one thing—
he was the most melancholy seaman I have ever come across.
It is proverbial of sailors that they are a rollicking, jovial set;
but this man was the exception to the rule, and he at once gave
me the impression that he had something on his mind. My
sympathies were in consequence of this aroused, and I mentally resolved that I would endeavour to win his confidence,
in the hope that I might be of use to him.

At first, however, I found that he was inclined to be taciturn,
and resent any attempt to draw him out; but I learnt from the
mate that Tredegar had commanded the ship for three voyages,
and was highly respected by the owners. He was a thoroughly
experienced navigator, and studied his owners' interests. There
was one thing I could not fail to note; he showed a disposition
to talk more to me than to any one else, and discovering that
he played a good game of cribbage—a game I was particularly
partial to—I got into closer touch with him, as one evening
he accepted my invitation to a game, and after that we played
whenever opportunity offered. But still he became neither
communicative nor talkative, and no subject I could start
appeared to have any interest for him.

We were playing one night in the cuddy after supper, when
I noticed that he seemed more than usually depressed, and
kept examining the barometer and casting an anxious eye up
through the skylight.

'What does the glass say, captain?' I asked at last.

'Well,' he answered, 'I think we are going to have a blow.
There is dirty weather about somewhere.'

When four bells (ten o'clock) struck we finished our game
and he went into his cabin, while I mounted the companion-
way to the poop, intending to smoke my usual cigar before
turning in. I had run short of cigars, and the captain had
promised to let me have a box of good Havanas, but not until
I reached the deck did I remember that I had not a single weed
in my case, so I went below again, and to the skipper's room,
intending to ask him for the cigars. Getting no response to my
knock I pushed the door open and was surprised to see him
seated at his table, so absorbed in gazing at the photograph of
a lady that he had not heard my knock. On perceiving me, he

hastily thrust the photograph into a drawer and jumped up.
I noticed him pass his hands over his eyes and turn away as if
ashamed, pretending to search for something on the top of a
chest of drawers. I thought it was an opportunity not to be
lost so I said to him :

'Pray excuse my intrusion; I knocked but you didn't hear me.
I would also take the liberty of saying I respect your emotion.
A man need not be ashamed of moist eyes when he gazes on
the face of some loved one who is far away. It's human. It
shows a kindly heart, an impressionable mind!'

He turned suddenly and, putting out his hand to me, said :
'Thank you, thank you, Mr Gibling! You are a good sort. A
little sympathy sometimes is not a bad thing, and, hardened
old shellback as I am, I suppose I've got a soft spot somewhere.
But, excuse me, I must go on deck.'

I made known my errand, and having procured the box of
cigars for me from his locker, I carried them to my cabin, and
he went on deck, and when I had opened the box and taken
two or three cigars out I followed him. The night was very
dark. Nearly all the sails were set. There was an unpleasant,
lumpy sea, and the wind was blowing in fitful gusts.

The captain ordered the watch to shorten sail, but before the
order was entirely carried out a squall struck us, and the
vessel heeled over tremendously and commenced to fly
through the water, churning the sea around her into white,
flashing, phosphorescent froth. Anyone who has ever made
a voyage in a sailing ship knows the apparent, and often real,
confusion that ensues when a sudden squall strikes the vessel.
At such times the wind will frequently blow for a few minutes
with hurricane force, and it is no unusual thing for sails to be
split to ribbons—even for spars to be carried away. Given a
dark night, a heavy squall, a rough sea, rent sails, and the land
lubber who is unmoved must be made of very stern stuff. The
rifle-like report and cracking of the long shreds of the torn sail
are alarming enough to the inexperienced; but when you add
to this the rattling of the ropes, the banging of blocks, the
groaning of the ship's timbers, the harsh creaking of the spars,
the roar, swish and hiss of the waves, the great masses of boiling
white foam that spread around, and the hoarse voices of men

on deck to unseen men up above on the yard-arms in the mysterious darkness, there is at once a scene which tests the nerves of the landsman to a very considerable extent.

The squall that struck the *Pride of the Ocean* was very heavy, and the main topsail went to ribbons. The skipper, who was a perfect seaman, issued his orders rapidly, but with judgment and a display of self-possession, while his officers ably seconded him. Three or four times he came close to me as he shifted his position on the poop, the better to make his voice heard above the howling of the wind. I did not attempt to address him, knowing full well that at such a moment he required to concentrate all his attention on his duties. Once, when he came near me, I heard him mutter—'My God, my God, have pity on me!' It may be imagined to what an extent I was affected by this utterance. Had he said, 'Have pity on *us*,' I should at once have jumped to the conclusion that we were all in danger, but the cry for pity was for himself alone. It set me pondering, and connecting it with his usual melancholy, and the sad and distressful expression of his face, I was not only puzzled but anxious. A few minutes later, as the ship did not pay off as rapidly as she should have done, Captain Tredegar ran to the wheel to help the helmsman to jam the rudder harder over, and as he glanced at the binnacle and his features were illumined by the light from the lamp, I was perfectly startled by his ghastly pallor. To such an extent was I moved that I rushed to him and asked if he was ill. With a powerful sweep of his right arm he moved me from before him, and in tones of terror exclaimed—'There it is again! There, out there on the crest of that wave!' I peered into the darkness, but could see nothing save the phosphorescent gleam of the tumbling sea.

By this time I was quite unnerved, for a dreadful thought took possession of me. I thought that the skipper was suffering from incipient madness.

In a few minutes, having got the wheel well over, he called one of the watch aft to assist the steersman, and he himself went forward to the break of the poop, and continued to give his orders. By this time the men had got the flying ropes and flapping sails under control, and, the dark scud in the heavens driving to leeward before the hurricane blast, the moon peeped through the ragged film and threw a weird, ghostly gleam of shimmering light over the swirling waters, while the track of the squall could be followed as it drove down the heavens.

As is often the case, at the tail of the great blast was a deluge. It was as if some huge door in the sky had been opened and the waters fell out in a cataract. I hurried below, as I had no desire to be soaked to the skin, and when I reached the cuddy I found the Spanish lady passenger seated at the table, looking very scared and unhappy.

'Oh, Mr Gibling,' she exclaimed, 'is there any danger? What an awful storm!'

I assured her that all was well, and that the rain would probably bring a dead calm.

'Did you see the captain?' she asked, still displaying great agitation.

There was something in her manner and the tone of her voice that struck me as peculiar, and I replied:

'Yes. I saw him on deck.'

'Ah, but I mean here. He has just come down and gone to his room. I spoke to him, but he would not answer me. He looked awful. I am sure there is something queer about him. His eyes seemed bulging from his head, and if he had seen a ghost he couldn't have been whiter. He is either ill or going mad. Do go to him.'

The lady's words did not tend to allay my own fears and suspicions, but, anxious not to add to her alarm, I said with an air of assumed indifference:

'The fact is, I suppose, he is over-anxious. Not that there is anything to fear, I am sure. We are in the squall zone, you know, but there is every prospect of making a good passage. However, I will go and talk to the captain.'

So saying, I left her, and made my way to the skipper's state room. I knocked as usual, but again there was no response; so I pushed the door open, and found Captain Tredegar seated in his chair, his body bent over the table, and his face hidden by his arms. His cap had fallen off and was lying on the table, and I noted that his hands were opening and shutting in a spasmodic, nervous way. It was no time for ceremony. I

should have been dull indeed not to recognize that the man
was suffering. I therefore went to his side, and laying my hand
on his shoulder said sympathetically :

'Excuse me, Captain Tredegar, but you are not well. Can
I do anything for you ? Do make a confidant of me. Believe
me I am not actuated by mere vulgar curiosity. Pray command my services if I can be of any use.'

He lifted his head up. I had never seen before in any human
face such a pronounced look of nervous horror. His eyes
wandered about the room; the corners of his mouth twitched,
and he sobbed like a child that had cried itself into a state
of physical exhaustion. I was positively alarmed, and my first
impulse was to run for assistance. As if divining my thoughts
he seized my wrist in his powerful hand, and said in a broken
voice :

'Pardon me, sir, you are very good. I am suffering from an
attack to which I am at rare intervals subject; but I shall be
all right directly. Please don't make a scene. There is some
rum there in that bottle, give me a little drop. It will set me up.'

Although I was doubtful whether rum was the proper
remedy in such a case, I could not resist his appealing manner,
and taking the bottle from the rack I poured into a glass about
a table-spoonful.

'Oh, more than that, more than that,' he cried. 'Fill the glass
nearly.'

Perhaps at any other time I should have argued against his
request, but I let the rum run from the bottle until the tumbler
was quite half-full. He clutched it with trembling hand, and
poured the contents at one gulp down his throat.

'Thanks, thanks,' he said, as he recovered his breath and
placed the glass on the table. 'That will put new life into me.
I feel better already.'

He rose, shuddered as he did so, and took his sou'wester
and oilskin from a peg. He put a hand on each of my shoulders,
and looking me in the face, said with an impressive earnest-
ness :

'Mr Gibling, I am more than obliged to you. Add to my
obligation, will you, by promising not to mention to anyone
that you have seen me in one of my strange moods.'

'Certainly I will,' I replied. 'You may trust me. And, as I have said, if I can be of service command me.'

'Very well; some day I may put you to the test,' he answered; 'good-night, and God bless you.'

He left me, and I heard him clatter up the gangway in his great boots. As I crossed towards my own cabin the Spanish lady was still sitting at the cuddy table.

'Have you been with the captain?' she asked.

'I have,' I replied.

'How is he?'

'He is all right,' I answered lightly.

She glanced about the cuddy as if to make sure no one was listening, and then, bending towards me as if inviting confidence, she said in a half whisper:

'Do you know, Mr Gibling, when the captain came down from the deck a little while ago there was such a peculiar look in his face that I could almost have fancied he—'

She stopped suddenly in her speech, visibly shuddered, and put her pretty white fingers before her eyes. After an awkward pause I broke the silence by saying:

'Almost fancied he—what?'

'He had seen some gruesome and unnatural sight.'

I laughed, though I had an inkling of her meaning, for strangely enough a vague, phantom-like thought had been troubling me; but I could not define it, could not give it shape; now at her words it was clear enough, and an uncontrollable impulse impelled me to give it utterance:

'Ghosts, you mean,' and I laughed at my own words, for the idea seemed to me utterly ridiculous. But not so to the lady. Her face assumed a graver aspect, and her eyes betrayed that whatever my views might be her mind was made up.

'What I mean is, he has seen a vision,' she remarked, with awe in her voice.

'Oh, nonsense,' I exclaimed. 'Hobgoblins and bogeys belong to the period of our childhood. When we come to years of discretion we should cease to be childish.'

My remark annoyed her. She rose and curled her lip disdainfully. 'I am not childish and I don't talk nonsense,' she said, as she swept past me without so much as giving me a chance to apologize. I felt annoyed with myself for having been so tactless, but otherwise laughed mentally at what I considered the absurdity of the position.

A few minutes later I went on deck to finish my final smoke before turning in. The rain had ceased and the air was delightfully cool. The wind had gone, the sky was a mass of picturesque clouds with fantastic outlines. Here and there groups of stars were visible, and with chastened light, as if shining through gauze, the moon made a silver pathway over the face of the deep until it blended with the horizon in impenetrable blackness, which rounded off the weird scene. The captain had discarded his oilskins, which were lying on the top of a hencoop, and he was leaning on his elbows over the taffrail, complacently smoking a cigar, and absorbed apparently in the contemplation of the phosphoric display that flashed and glistened under the ship's counter as she fell and rose to the swell. I approached him. He straightened up, turned his back to the rail, folded his arms across his breast, and puffing at his cigar as he cast a scrutinizing eye aloft at the flapping sails, he said in a cheerful tone:

'Quite a contrast to a little while ago, isn't it, Mr Gibling? But it's the sort of weather we must expect in these latitudes.'

I was struck by his changed manner. He seemed so cheerful and light-hearted. He wasn't the same man I had seen down in the cabin half an hour ago.

'Yes, I suppose so,' I remarked, for the sake of saying something.

'It's not your first voyage to sea, is it?' he asked.

'No.'

'Have you been to Cuba before?'

'Oh yes.'

'Ah! then you will know pretty well what kind of voyage it is.'

I told him that I knew fairly well what one might expect on such a voyage at that time of the year, and we continued to chat pleasantly for a little while until six bells struck (eleven o'clock). 'All's well!' came in solemn tones from the look-out man on the fo'c'stle.

'Well, I think I shall turn in,' said the captain, as he threw

the stump of his cigar overboard, glanced up aloft, then at the
binnacle, and calling the second officer who was on watch, and
telling him to keep the ship on the same course until the morning, he moved towards the companion-way, and I followed.
When we reached the saloon he put out his hand. As I took
it he said 'Good-night,' and immediately added in lower tones,
'Don't forget your promise.'

I turned in and tried to sleep, but for a long time tossed
about, thinking of what had passed, and trying to account for
the captain's strange behaviour; but the more I thought the
more I got puzzled, and I came to the conclusion there was
some strange mystery about him. I saw through my port the
sun beginning to redden the eastern horizon before sleep came
to me. I did not waken until long after the usual breakfast
hour, so I breakfasted alone.

When I went on deck I noticed the Spanish lady reclining
in a deck-chair. She was reading a book, and perhaps that
accounted for her taking no notice of me as I bowed and said
'Good-morning.'

The sun was shining brilliantly. The sky was cloudless save
on the horizon, where there were woolly banks. A steady little
breeze just kept the sails full, and the short, choppy waves
danced and flashed in the sunlight. The captain was not on
deck, and I was informed by the second mate that he had not
turned out yet. Wishing to propitiate the Spanish lady passenger, I carried a camp stool to where she was sitting, and
in the most fascinating manner I was capable of commanding
I asked if I could sit beside her. She smiled sweetly, and
accorded her gracious permission. We said some commonplace things about the weather; she descanted on the tropical
beauties of Cuba, and criticized rather severely the English
climate; while as for London, she spoke of it with scorn and
much shrugging of shoulders.

When she paused, I embraced the opportunity to turn the
trend of conversation by saying :

'I am afraid that I was a little rude to you last night,' but
I hardly expected such a blunt reply as she made.

'Yes, you were exceedingly rude, and I hate rude men.'

'I hope you don't hate me,' I cried, laughingly.

'Oh no, not quite. You're a Londoner, you see.'

This was very severe. I confess I was hardly prepared for it, and I was tempted to say something cutting in reply, but checked myself, bowed, and merely remarked:

'Which is not my fault. Therefore pity me rather than blame me.'

'Certainly I do that,' she replied, with an amusing seriousness. 'But look here; answer me this. Why should you have been rude last night when I said what I did about the captain?'

'Madame,' I said, as I laid my hand on my heart and bowed, 'believe me I had no intention of being rude; but the fact is, I am a somewhat commonplace, matter-of-fact man, and I have no belief in anything that is said to be due to supernatural causes.'

'Supernatural or not supernatural,' she retorted, 'there are things going on around us which certainly cannot be explained by any known laws.'

'Possibly, and yet I doubt it,' I replied, with a sceptical smile.

'Well, your obtuseness is your own affair,' she said, with a shrug of her shoulders; 'but now, look here, Mr Gibling, permit me to make a little prophecy. Captain Tredegar has something awful on his mind. He sees visions, and will ultimately go mad.'

Her words startled me. For the first time I was inclined to regard her seriously, in one respect at least; that was the ultimate madness of the skipper. That thought had haunted me, but I had tried to put it away. Even to my somewhat dulled perception it had been made evident that a man who could act as Tredegar had acted on the previous night was a victim to some obscure form of mental disease which might ultimately destroy him. Now the lady spoke with such an absence of vagueness that I asked her if she had known the captain long, and if she was acquainted with his past history.

'Indeed, no,' she exclaimed. 'I never saw the man in my life until I joined the ship in Liverpool.'

'Then why do you speak with such an air of self-conviction?'

'I speak as I think. I think as I know.'

'But how do you know?'

'Well, you are stupid,' she exclaimed, with a show of exasperation. 'I know, because I have a sense you don't possess. I was born where the sun shines. I have beliefs you have not. I believe that men who do evil in this world can be haunted into madness by the disembodied spirits of those they injure. Now you may laugh and sneer as much as you like, sir, but I tell you this : when Captain Tredegar came down to the cabin last night his face clearly indicated that he had been terrified by something not human, and I saw madness written large in his eyes.'

I should be wanting in common honesty if I failed to say that this woman's remarks put certain rambling thoughts of my own into shape, impressed me in a way that a short time previously I should have been ashamed to own to. They set me pondering, and I tried to recall every act, word, look and gesture of the captain's, with the result that I had to admit there was something strange about him. At that moment Captain Tredegar himself came on deck. His breezy, jovial manner, and smiling bronzed face, seemed to make the conversation about him ridiculous, and tended to confound the prophet who had talked of madness.

He bowed politely to the lady, and chatted to her pleasantly. He greeted me with a cheery 'Good-morning,' and expressed a hope that neither of us had been much alarmed by the squall of the previous evening. He said the passage was going to be a splendid one; one of the best he had ever made; and if, as he anticipated we should do, we picked up a good slant of wind when we had made a little more westing, we should reach Cuba several days before the time we were expected.

The mate now came on deck and he and the captain walked to the break of the poop. When he was out of earshot I turned to the lady and said :

'He doesn't look much like a man who is given to seeing visions and is doomed to madness, does he ?'

'You cannot see beneath the mask,' she replied, with another contemptuous curl of her lip; and she added somewhat mysteriously, 'Wait, wait, wait,' repeating the word three times, with a rising inflection on each repetition. Then she turned

to her book again, as if she wished me to understand that she
would say no more. I took the hint, and making a show of
stretching my limbs, I rose and began to pace up and down.
The subject of the conversation between me and the lady
continued to occupy my thoughts against my will, and the
more I thought the more like a riddle did the captain appear
to me. I was really astonished to find myself taking so much
interest in him. If Captain Tredegar had been a relative of
mine, my own brother, in fact, I could hardly have felt more
anxious or more desirous to solve the mystery that seemed to
surround him. His appearance that morning, and his appearance
and behaviour of the night before, were in such violent contrast
that to put it down to the merely varying moods to which
we are all liable was not satisfactory enough. What puzzled
me more than anything else was his behaviour during the storm.
To suppose that he was a coward and lost his nerve in a passing squall was absurd on the face of it. In the very height of
the storm he delivered his orders with coolness and judgment,
as I could testify, but what did he mean by exclaiming: 'There
it is again! There, out there on the crest of that wave'? Then
again, why the appeal to God to pity him? Having perplexed
and fretted myself until I felt quite confused, I found myself
unable to alter the original opinion I had formed, which was
that Captain Tredegar was liable to attacks of mental aberra-
tion, and that being so he was not a fit person to have charge
of a valuable vessel and her living freight.

Viewing the matter from this point, I came to the conclusion,
rightly or wrongly, that it was my bounden duty as an honest
man to make representations to his owners as to the skipper's
state of mind; for surely no one would say that a man liable
to attacks of temporary mania was the proper person to be in
charge of a ship. As I came to this decision I heard the captain
call out from the break of the poop:

'Make eight bells.'

The boatswain struck the hour on the bell, and 'eight bells'
was roared out by the men about the decks. I was recalled
to a sense of my surroundings and as the skipper passed me,
he said cheerily:

'Well, Mr Gibling. It's time to splice the main brace, isn't it?'

I may explain for the benefit of those who have not made a voyage to sea that it is customary in most passenger vessels for the passengers to partake of a glass of liquor of some kind at noon, eight bells. This, in nautical phraseology, is termed 'splicing the main brace'. It is the most interesting period of the twenty-four hours to lands-people, because the captain and his officers having taken their sights, as it is called, they proceed to work them out, in order to discover the position of the ship; that is, her latitude and longitude, and that being done, it is marked on the chart.

As I accompanied the skipper to the cuddy, I began to think that perhaps after all I was doing him a wrong, and it would be unfair to say anything to his owners until I had received stronger proof that my suspicions were well founded. Certainly, as he sat at the table making his calculations and working out the position, he not only seemed the perfection of physical fitness, but fully endowed with keen and sound intelligence. As I noted this I came to the conclusion that it was no less my duty to suspend my judgment—than to watch closely and wait patiently.

I wish it to be distinctly understood that at this period of the voyage I was halting between two opinions. On the one hand, I considered Captain Tredegar peculiar in many respects —a man of mystery, in short—and on the other, I was painfully anxious not to do him an injustice. It will also be noted that the conclusions arrived at by the Spanish lady, who was an emotional and superstitious woman, were not in accordance with my own. For according to her views, the captain's strange behaviour was the result of seeing visions; according to mine, he suffered from intermittent mania, which was probably traceable to a too free indulgence in rum or other potent liquors. Not that I had ever seen him the worse for drink, but he took a good deal more than was good for him, in my opinion, though it did not affect him as it would have done others who were not so case-hardened.

For the next few days our progress was not very satisfactory, owing to the light, variable winds. For a steamer it would have been almost ideal weather, but dependent as we were on the winds, it was very tantalizing. During this time the skipper continued in his bright, cheery mood, and every evening at a fixed hour we sat down in the cabin for a game of cribbage. I took to studying him very closely, and from many little signs I saw I felt pretty certain that a great deal of his light-hearted manner was assumed. Occasionally I noted a strange wild look came into his eyes, and his cheeks paled as though some deadly fear had seized him. A mere casual observer would have failed to notice these signs, but my perception had been quickened. I was ever on the alert, on the watch, and there was not much that escaped me.

A change came at last. One evening when I expected the skipper to take part in the usual game of cribbage he brusquely and rudely refused, and I saw the half-sullen, half-terrified expression in his face again. I thought it very peculiar that his mood should synchronize with a change in the weather. The barometer had been falling all day, and it was only too evident that we were going to have a dirty night. As the sun got low in the heavens, heavy banks of clouds came up, and the wind rapidly strengthened, until we had to shorten sail to such an extent that very little canvas remained set. The captain seemed extremely anxious. He walked up and down the poop in a restless, nervous way. Occasionally he stopped to gaze windward, and sometimes he muttered to himself. I resolved at last to speak to him, anxious and preoccupied as he was. So I went boldly up to him and said:

'We are evidently in for a change, don't you think so?'

He turned upon me with a dark, lowering face, his brow knit, and his whole manner that of one straining under suppressed passion.

'Yes, I do,' he answered excitedly, 'damn you. Anyway, I'm a doomed man.'

He walked rapidly away without another word, and I stood for some little time dumbfounded. Anyone who could speak in such a manner was surely mad, and I seriously considered it was my business to take counsel with my fellow passengers, if not with the officers of the ship, for a mad captain ought to be relieved of his responsible duties in the interest of every soul on board. But before I could stir away the man himself came back to me, and said in a most pathetic and appealing way that went to my heart :

'Pray pardon my rudeness, Mr Gibling. You don't know how I'm troubled. I am suffering dreadfully, and if you knew all you would pity rather than blame me.'

'Why not place me in possession of the information, then?' I asked. He put his hand to his eyes for a moment or two and shuddered.

'It is so dreadful, so horrible,' he muttered mysteriously, speaking rather to himself than me.

'All the more reason, then, why you should take me into your confidence,' I said.

'Yes—perhaps you are right. I will. Come to my cabin in half an hour and I will tell you the awful story.'

Further conversation was interrupted by the bursting of a squall accompanied by heavy rain, while a long swell that came up was a sure precursor of the coming gales, of which squalls were only the heralds.

I at once descended to the cabin to get out of the rain, but quite half an hour passed before the captain came down. He passed me without speaking, but called the steward and ordered some tea to be taken to his cabin. And when another half-hour had elapsed the steward brought me a message to the effect that Captain Tredegar wished to see me in his room. The weather had now become very bad and the ship was labouring heavily. I found the captain seated at his table with a small Bible open before him, but which he closed and tossed into his bunk as I entered. He looked pale, ill, and careworn. He asked me to sit down, and remarked :

'You have shown much interest in me, sir, and instinctively I feel I can place confidence in you. The time has now come for me to speak, or be dumb for evermore. I am a doomed man. My fate is sealed, and it is that fearful certainty that weighs upon me like a ton of lead.'

His words and manner seemed to me unmistakably to indicate insanity, and I could not repress a feeling of alarm. He must have guessed my thoughts, for he said quickly :

'Don't alarm yourself, and bear with me patiently; my brain is perfectly clear, and I know what I am doing, although a stranger might be disposed to think I was labouring under a distempered imagination. But it is not so. An awful fear takes possession of me and unmans me. It paralyses my faculties and renders life a curse instead of a blessing.'

'A fear of what?' I asked.

'Of the dead,' he answered solemnly.

I looked hard at him again. That surely was not the answer of a sane man.

'What nonsense,' I said a little sharply. 'What harm can the dead do to the living? I gave you credit for being stronger minded than that. It is clear to me now that you are allowing yourself to sink into a morbid, nervous condition, that must end disastrously. Why on earth should you embitter your existence by imaginary evils? Shake yourself free of morbid, gloomy forebodings; be a man, and if you are a just one you need fear nothing, not even the living, let alone the dead.'

He did not attempt to interrupt this little outburst on my part, which perhaps was hardly justified. But I could not restrain myself. I was compelled to give vent to my thoughts.

'You mean well, Mr Gibling,' he remarked, with perfect self-possession, when I had finished speaking, 'and I understand your feelings; but before condemning me, before allowing your wrath to run away with your judgment, be patient and listen to me as you promised to do. This may be the only opportunity that will ever occur for me to tell you my story.'

'Pray proceed,' I remarked; 'perhaps I have been somewhat hasty; you will find, however, that I am a good listener, and under any circumstances you may count on my sympathy.'

He remained silent for some minutes, his elbows on the table, his hands clasping his face, his eyes seemingly fixed on vacancy. He started and came to himself again.

'Mr Gibling,' he began, 'I have a very strange story to tell you if you care to listen to it. Whatever your feelings are now, however sceptical you may be, I fancy your views will undergo a change by the time I have done. I repeat that I am a doomed man. My sands have nearly run out, and I must say what I have to say now or never.'

'Please go on,' I said as he paused, evidently waiting for me to speak.

'Very well,' he continued, 'I'll begin at the beginning. As you know, I am a Cornishman; I come from a race of seamen; the salt of the sea flows in my veins. What education I received was got at a school in Devonshire, where I passed nearly nine years of my life. At that school I had a chum. We were inseparable. We were more like brothers. His name was Peter Gibson. He was three or four years my senior, and was a rough, wild, boorish sort of fellow; not good at picking up the routine knowledge of a school training, but as sharp as a needle, with an insatiable thirst for stories of fighting and adventure. In this line he would read everything he got hold of, and one day he said to me: "Jubal, I intend to go to sea, and I'm going to be a devil; will you stick to me?" he asked.

' "Yes," I answered in a moment of boyish enthusiasm. He had great influence over me. I looked up to him as my superior, and regarded him as a leader.

' "You swear it?" he demanded.

' "Yes," I said again.

'Whereupon he made me go down on my knees, hold both my hands up to heaven, and take a solemn oath that I would stick to him, go with him wherever he went, and do whatever he did.

'Now you must remember I was a youngster at this time, and what I did was only what a boy might be expected to do. Gibson certainly had a good deal of influence over me. He was a masterful sort of fellow, with a great, bulky, powerful frame, while his pluck won my admiration. He funked at nothing, and could lick every boy in the neighbourhood.

'We left school about the same time, and though his father, who was pretty well off, wanted to put him in business, Peter declared he would go to sea. I had been intended for a seafaring life from my cradle. The males of my family always went to sea. The result of his determination was that he and I found ourselves fellow apprentices on board a full-rigged vessel going out to the East Indies. She was a trader, and during a voyage of nearly four years we visited a great many places in the East; saw a great deal of the world, and experienced fair and foul weather from the very best to the very worst. As might have been expected, Peter picked up seamanship very rapidly, and became one of the smartest sailors on board. My regard for him and his liking for me had never altered, and when we returned to Liverpool we were as much chums as ever.

'We were only at home two months when we were transferred to another ship belonging to the same owners, and rated as A.B.'s. This voyage we sailed to Vancouver round the Horn, and from there we came down in ballast to Monte Video, and loaded up with a general cargo for home. At this time there was a civil war going on in the Argentine Republic, and of course at Monte Video we heard a great deal of talk about it. Gibson used to get very excited over the war news, and over and over again he tried to persuade me to clear out from the ship and go with him to do some fighting. He'd no sympathies with either one side or the other, and I don't think he even knew what the row was about, but he wanted some fighting; fight was in his blood, and he was pining for what he called fun. I preferred, however, to keep a straight course, as my people before me had done. I wanted to gradually mount the ladder until I reached the top, and I knew that the quixotic expedition he proposed would have defeated my object. I therefore declined to fall in with his views. It riled him for a time, but at last he admitted that he had no right to try and persuade me against my will; but as far as he was concerned he was going. And go he did, much to my regret, I must confess. Although it went somewhat against my grain, I helped him to secretly get on shore, and some money that I had I handed over to him.

'We spent our last night together at a *café* in Monte Video; and when the time came for us to part he wrung my hand, and I was cut up in a way I had never been before. After that I saw no more of him, nor did I hear anything of him for ten years, when we met again under very extraordinary circumstances.

'I was then mate of a splendid barque called the *Curlew*, hailing from Bristol. We had taken out a cargo of iron to Bilbao; there the ship was chartered by the Spanish Government to convey five hundred soldiers and a quantity of specie to Havana. The *Curlew* was an exceptionally fine vessel, with unusually good 'tween deck space, and therefore very suitable as a transport. We made a good passage to Havana, landed the troops, but were told we should have to retain the specie for a few days until some grandee or other came to receive it. He happened then to be up the country, but was expected back in the course of a week. As we had made a quicker passage than was expected, it had thrown him out in his calculations. Well, of course, it didn't matter to us much, as our charter provided for our return to Bilbao; and, equally of course, so long as we were employed by the Spanish authorities we sailed under the Spanish flag.

'The second night after our arrival I went on shore, and in strolling through the town my attention was arrested by a sign over the door of a drinking-place. It read, "Old England, kept by Will Bradshaw." This and the sound of English voices induced me to enter, and I found the place pretty well crowded with sailor men and Spanish women of a disreputable class. I saw at once the sort of house it was, and as I did not consider it advisable for me as chief mate of a Government vessel to be seen there, I was for clearing out again when I noticed a big, brawny, powerfully-built fellow mixing drinks behind the bar. He was unmistakably an Englishman. His face was burnt brown. He had a dark, bushy beard, and looked like a man who had a large spice of the devil in him. Despite the beard the face seemed familiar to me, and when I heard him call out an order to one of his waiters, the voice left me no longer in doubt. It was the voice of Peter Gibson. So I pushed my way through the crowd to the counter, for it was not likely I could leave without renewing acquaintance with my old chum, and I asked, "Isn't your name Peter Gibson?"

' "No, it isn't," he yelled. "I'm Will Bradshaw, the boss of this place." I was taken aback for a minute, for I was sure I couldn't be mistaken. Then it flashed on me that Peter had a reason for being known as Will Bradshaw; so I pulled out a pocket-book, wrote my name on a leaf, tore it out, and handed it to him. I saw a look of surprise come into his eyes and his face change colour. Then he grasped my hand and wrung it, told an assistant to look after the place, and asking me to follow him, he led the way by a side entrance to a large garden at the back of the house, where seats were placed under the palm trees, and a few coloured lamps were hung up. Nearly every seat was occupied by men and women, and negro waiters were attending to their wants.

'Peter took me to a remote corner of the garden, where there was a sort of summer-house on a knoll.

'"We can have a quiet yarn here," he said. Then he called one of the negroes and told him to bring a bottle of wine, and that done, he began in his old masterful way to ask me questions about my career during the past ten years. I told him straight; but when I questioned him he shirked my questions, simply saying, "Well, I've had a lot of roughing, old chap, and have been in some queer corners. I drifted down here about two years since, just as the former proprietor of this shanty went off the hooks with Yellow Jack. I made a bid for the place and got it, but had to give bills for the greater part of the purchase money, and I've still got a lot of millstones round my neck. I'm rather sick, and think of chucking it and going on the rampage again.'

'We yarned away for two hours, when I had to go, and naturally I asked him to come and see me on board the vessel. He turned up the next day, and the day after that; and I told him as an item of news that my skipper was going into the country on the morrow for a few days to shoot with a party of friends, and that I should be in charge; and I invited him to come on board and have dinner with me in the evening, an invitation he readily accepted.

'When he turned up he had a friend with him, a Spaniard who spoke good English, and whom he introduced to me as Alonzo Gomez. He said he wanted me to know this man, as he was a good sort, and might be of use to me. He was described as a planter, but I couldn't help thinking there was a good deal more of the loafer than the planter about him. However, he was very polite, as most Spaniards are, and as he seemed to be rather an amusing cuss, I thought I had judged him too harshly. Of course, I gave my guests a good feed, and made the steward open some champagne. During the dinner Peter asked me a lot of questions about the ship, and how much Spanish money we had on board, and where it was kept. If it had been anyone else, and at any other time, I should have resented these questions, but I felt there was no harm in answering my old schoolfellow and shipmate.

'When the dinner was over Peter said that for old acquaintance sake we must have a jorum of rum punch, and that he would make it. So I told the steward to get the necessary ingredients, and Peter set to work to concoct the liquor. I don't remember much more after that. I didn't come to my senses until the next morning. I found on turning out that the steward was ill, and on my going to him he told me that my friends had given him some of the punch. It had made him sick at first, and afterwards he fell into a heavy sleep from which he had not long awakened, and that he was then suffering from a frightful headache and a heavy, drowsy feeling. That was precisely my condition; but I attributed it to not having drunk wisely, but too well. The second mate, who had been on shore the previous night, undertook to do certain work I had to attend to; and having given the steward some medicine from the medicine chest, I went and turned in once more, and slept pretty well the whole day. Anyway, I did not turn to again until the following morning.

'In the course of that day, the high official who was to receive the specie came on board with an escort, and commanded the strong room in the afterpart of the cabin to be opened, and the specie brought out. I at once procured the keys from a safe in the captain's cabin, and on going to the strong room, I was surprised and alarmed to find that the various seals put upon the door at Bilbao were broken, and they had been broken quite recently, as two or three days before I had examined them and found them all right. My alarm and confusion increased when, having got the door open, we discovered that two of the boxes, one containing Bank of Spain notes and the other gold dollars, had been burst open, and partly rifled of their contents. Altogether a sum in notes and gold equivalent to twenty thousand pounds had been stolen.

'The big-wig was in a great state, and at once sent on shore for a magistrate and a lot of military officers, and began an inquiry there and then; and I, having been in charge of the ship for some days, was practically put on trial.

'Perhaps I needn't tell you that I felt I could at once name the thief. His name was Peter Gibson, alias Will Bradshaw. He and his Spanish chum had drugged me and the steward; of that I had no doubt then, and as all the crew had gone on shore except the boatswain and the cook, and two of the hands who were on duty at the gangway, it was easy for the rascals to carry out their nefarious scheme of getting at the specie.

'Now, I'm not talking mere words to you when I tell you that it went against my grain to denounce my old schoolfellow and shipmate, and at first I resolved that I wouldn't. But, after all, a chap's own interests have to be counted first, and as Gibson had been mean hound enough to drug me and carry off money under my care, I didn't see why I should screen him. So I denounced him, and in a very short time he was under arrest. But even then he might have escaped conviction had it not been for his stupidity in keeping the bank-notes. His friend, who was also arrested, turned out to be a notorious character with a most evil reputation, and was looked upon as an expert in picking locks. The task they had set themselves of stealing the money was comparatively easy, as all the conditions were in their favour, and I fell a too easy victim to their cunning.

'Well, of course, I had to attend the trial and give evidence. The crime was considered very serious indeed, as Government property had been stolen and Government seals unlawfully broken. The offence was called a first-class one, and the penalty was death. No such sensation had been provided for Havana for many a long day. It was considered better than a bull-fight.

'To make a long story short, the result of it all was that the two rascals were convicted and sentenced to be shot. The verdict cut me to the heart, and as only a short shrift was allowed the culprits, as the sentence was to be carried out in twenty-four hours, I obtained permission to visit Gibson. I found him in rather a dejected state, seated in a courtyard of the gaol which was guarded by soldiers. As soon as he saw me he seemed to go mad, reviled me in language that was of would haunt me and drive me to madness by appearing to me a pretty fiery character, then cursed me and swore that he on dark nights at sea. "You are a doomed man," he said, "and will come to a sudden and terrible end. I leave my curse to you."

'I tried to reason with him, but I might as well have tried to reason with an enraged wild cat in the jungle. He did nothing but utter curses on me, and recognizing how hopeless it was to try and appease him, I withdrew, and the next morning he and his pal were shot at daybreak.

'Although I was much cut up by the way he had treated me, I did not attach any importance to either his curses or his threats. I wasn't altogether free from superstition, what sailor is, but I quite believed that when a person was dead he was done with. I soon began to find out, however, that I was wrong, for some weeks later, when we were on our passage back to Bilbao, I had the middle watch one night, just as we got into the Bay of Biscay. It was a wild night, and we were close hauled under double reefed topsails. Suddenly out of the waves came a glowing figure. It was Gibson's spectre. He shrieked at me, and I heard his curses again, and again he told me I was doomed.

'Since then I've seen him often. He has kept his word. He has haunted me, and is driving me mad and hounding me to death. Yes, I am doomed. I feel it and know it. Nothing can avert the doom.

'You know my story now. Don't ridicule it; don't laugh at me; for to me it's a terribly serious business, and I feel that I shall never see the dear woman I love again.'

He ceased speaking, and I noticed the wild, scared look in his eyes which I had seen before. The perspiration was streaming down his face, he appeared to be suffering great mental agony. I tried to soothe him, but it was no use, and he kept on repeating that he was doomed.

Now let me say here at once that I did not believe the captain had seen any real supernatural appearance. I regarded him as a highly imaginative and sensitive man. On such a man Gibson's curses and threats would be sure to make a very deep impression. It could hardly be otherwise, seeing that the two men had practically grown up together. They had been school-mates and shipmates, and Gibson's violent end must have affected his once friend in no ordinary degree. Long dwelling upon the dramatic scene in the prison at Havana, the day previous to the execution, had taken such a hold on the skipper's imagination that he had worried himself into a belief in a mere chimera of the brain. To him, no doubt, the visions were real enough, although they were nothing more than disturbed brain fancies.

Such was the theory I consoled myself with, and I determined there and then to use every possible endeavour to get the captain out of his morbid condition, and prove to him by gentle reasoning that he was simply a victim to his own gloomy fears. I was so far successful at that moment that I induced him to turn in, having first of all called the mate down and given him certain instructions; then I compounded him a simple soothing draught from ingredients in the medicine chest, and at his own request I sat by him and read certain passages in the Bible, until he fell into a sound sleep.

I was considerably exercised in my own mind as to the proper course I ought to adopt, and I was tempted at first to take the Spanish lady into my confidence, and discuss the matter with her. But this idea was put out of my head at once, for she was sitting in the cuddy, as she usually did in the evening, where she passed her time either reading or in doing needlework. She saw that I came from the captain's cabin, and tackled me.

'How is the skipper?' she asked.

'He is a little indisposed tonight, but will be all right tomorrow, no doubt,' I answered.

'Not he,' she exclaimed. 'I tell you that man's a haunted man, and will either go mad or commit suicide.'

Remembering how dogmatically she had expressed herself on a previous occasion on the subject of supernatural visitations, I deemed it desirable not to enter into any discussion, and I also made up my mind that it would be a fatal mistake to let her know the captain's story, so I merely said, in answer to her statement, 'I hope not,' and passed to my cabin.

Now I want to repeat here, and for very obvious reasons,

what were the views I held at this stage. I considered that the captain was suffering from a distressing nervous illness, the result of long pondering over an incident which could not fail to make a tremendous impression on him. But not for a moment did I entertain any belief in the supernatural. Necessarily I was exceedingly anxious, for there was no doctor on board, I had no medical knowledge myself, and we could not hope to reach our destination for another three weeks. There was every prospect then of the prognostications about a fine and rapid passage being falsified. The barometer had been steadily falling for some time, and all the indications were for bad weather. I knew that in that latitude, at that time of year, heavy storms were not uncommon, and it seemed likely that we should experience them. The anxious state of my mind kept me awake for some time, revolving all sorts of schemes, but nothing that seemed to me satisfactory. Eight bells midnight sounded, and I heard the mate come out of his room and go on deck to take the watch. I slipped out of bed, put on my dressing-gown and slippers, and stole over to the captain's cabin. To my intense relief I found he was sleeping soundly.

As the motion of the vessel made it evident there was a heavy sea on, I went up the companion-way to see what the weather was like. It was a wild, weird night. A south-west gale was blowing and a tremendous sea running. There was no moon, but the stars shone with a superb lustre wherever the ragged, storm-driven scud allowed them to be seen. I passed a few words with the mate, and asked him what he thought of the weather.

'It's a bad wind for us,' he answered, 'and the heavy squalls that come up every now and then prevent our setting much sail. But if I were skipper, I would crack on and let things rip. I'd drive the ship even at the risk of losing canvas.'

'Why don't you do so, as it is?' I asked. 'You've got charge of the deck for the next four hours, and have practically a free hand.'

'No I haven't,' he answered. 'I've got to obey orders, though I think sometimes, between you and me, sir, that the old man's got a bee in his bonnet.'

'What makes you think that?' I queried, my interest in the

skipper making me anxious to hear what the mate had to say.

'Well, I think it's because he's given to seeing the devil, or something as bad.'

I laughed, although I was serious enough; and being anxious to draw the officer out, I remarked:

'Well, I shouldn't say it's quite as bad as that; but he is ill, there is no doubt about it, and wants looking after.'

'I should think he does,' was the reply, given with peculiar decisiveness. Then, bending his head towards me, the better to make himself heard without raising his voice too much, for the howling of the wind made it difficult to hear sometimes, he added, 'Look here, Mr Gibling, will you give me your promise that, if I express an opinion, it won't go any farther?'

'Yes, I think you may trust me,' I answered.

'Well, look here, sir, if you have any influence with the old man, you should persuade him to keep his room for the rest of the passage. And if he won't, I say that in his own interest and the interest of everyone on board this craft, that he should be made to stay there.'

Never before had the mate been so outspoken to me, and it was further evidence, if I needed any, that the skipper's condition had not escaped the observation of others; and I seriously determined to act on the suggestion, and use every effort to induce the captain to keep his room.

As a slight shift in the wind here necessitated the mate ordering the watch to trim the yards, I went below, and, feeling thoroughly exhausted, I drank a glass of whisky, and turning in, fell asleep. I must have slept between three and four hours, when I awoke with a start, for overhead was a tremendous hubbub. The tramping of heavily-booted feet, the rattling of cordage, the shaking of sails; while the ship, which was heeled over at an unusual angle, was quivering. I hastily donned my dressing-gown, and rushed on deck. A very heavy squall had struck us, and had torn the main-sail out of the bolt ropes. 'All hands' had been called on deck, and what with the shrieking wind and roaring sea, and the hoarse voices of the sailors, the situation seemed alarming enough to a landsman like myself. A lurch of the ship drove me down to the lee rail against the mizzen shrouds, which I clung to for dear life. Suddenly I felt myself gripped round the waist, and a body seemed to fall at my feet. I realized in an instant that it was the captain. He had only his shirt and trousers on. His feet were bare, his head was bare. So much I was able to make out in the darkness that wasn't altogether darkness, for a few stars still shone.

'For the love of God, for the sake of the Christ that was crucified, save me!' shrieked the unhappy man, as he crouched on his knees and linked his hands round my body.

'Don't give way like this,' I said, feeling almost distracted myself. 'Come, let me lead you down to your cabin. The mate will look after the ship. She is in good hands.'

It seemed as if the unhappy man did not understand what I had said to him, for pointing to the sea, he cried in a voice of acute terror:

'There, there, don't you see it? there on that wave? Oh, my God, it's awful!'

Mechanically I turned my eyes to where he pointed, and to my astonishment I saw what appeared to me to be a pale, lambent flame, shapeless and blue and nebulous. But I was conscious of thinking to myself that this was some natural phenomenon, like the well-known St Elmo's fire. Slowly, however, even as I watched (for my eyes were riveted on that light by some strange fascination), I saw the shapeless mass grow brighter. Then for the first time it seemed to dawn upon me that I was gazing upon something unearthly. My heart leaped to my mouth at the conviction, and a cold shivering thrilled through my body. I tried to shut out the vision, but my eyes would not close; I was under some spell, against which I had no power of resistance.

As I gazed, the flame assumed shape; the shape of a human being. I distinguished a face, wan and ghastly. The eyes were lustreless and fixed, like those of a dead man. In the naked body were many wounds, and from these wounds blood spurted out in streams, and as it seemed to me made the sea around crimson. I shuddered with horror at this dreadful sight; my knees bent under me, and I was on the point of sinking down, when I made a supreme effort and rallied. For the skipper was still clinging to me. I felt his weight, I heard his groans, but I saw nothing save that spectral figure with the gory streams pouring from its body.

Panting and breathless, a cold perspiration bursting through every pore, and with a feeling as if the scalp of my head was shrinking to nothing, I continued to gaze. The figure remained motionless, but its dull, glazed, dead eyes riveted themselves upon me and I could not endure their gaze. I felt my brain maddening with terror; driven to frenzy I made a supreme effort to lift the captain in my arms and carry him bodily down to his room. But he broke from me. He made a flying leap from the poop to the waist of the ship; then another flying leap over the rail into the dark seething waters. I heard the heavy splash his falling body made. One long, piercing shriek filled the air as he floated astern.

I remember little more. There was a cry of 'Man overboard!' a wild rush of feet; a hasty cutting away of lifebuoys; hoarse voices mingling with flapping sails. How I got below I don't know, but I found myself lying in my berth with the Spanish lady standing over me, putting eau de cologne on my temples.

'Do you feel better now?' she asked in a not unkindly way.

'Yes, thank you,' I answered, feeling confused; 'but tell me, what does it mean? What has happened?'

'Why, don't you know?' she exclaimed; 'the captain has jumped overboard. I told you what would happen. He was haunted and went mad, I suppose. Anyway the poor fellow's gone.'

'And how did I get here?' I asked, with a dreadful sinking sensation at the heart and a dazed numb feeling in the brain.

'Well, you tumbled down the companion-way and were insensible when the stewards picked you up. You fainted, I suppose, with fright, eh?'

'I don't know, I don't know,' I murmured. 'It's all a dream.'

'Now tell me and speak the truth,' she said, in a commanding tone. 'Did you see anything?'

'Yes.'

'What?'

'The vision of a bleeding man.'

'Ah!' she exclaimed triumphantly, 'how about your scepticism now, eh?'

I had to confess that, according to my belief, I had seen the spectre of a man bleeding from several wounds; but still I thought it was nothing more than a delusion.

'But the captain was with you?'

'Yes.'

'And he saw it?'

'I have reason to think so.'

'Then were you both deluded? Anyway, poor fellow, he was deluded to his death. For he has perished.'

I could not enter into any argument. I felt too ill and distressed. I thanked her for her attention, and begged that she would leave me, as I thought I could sleep. She complied with this request, but I tossed and dreamed nightmare dreams, and dreamed and tossed for hours. It took me several days to recover from that awful shock to the nerves; indeed, I don't think I have ever quite recovered, or that I ever shall. I need scarcely say that from the moment the poor demented captain took that flying leap into the sea nothing more was ever seen of him, and an entry of his suicide was made in the log-book, and I signed it. On our arrival at Havana an inquiry was held by the British Consul, and I was called upon to state what I knew. I confined myself to saying that the captain believed that he saw a vision occasionally. He was very greatly affected, and I presume his brain gave way. I did not attempt to speak of my own awful experience. It was not necessary. Even if I had done so how could I have hoped to be believed? And yet I had seen with my own eyes. I, a scoffer in such matters, had been convinced, and what I have written here I solemnly declare to be true. Perhaps somebody cleverer than I, and more learned than I, may be able to explain away the mystery, but for me it will remain an awful, appalling mystery until I cease to breathe. Then, perhaps—who knows?—I may be able to solve it.

Kentucky's Ghost

by

ELIZABETH STUART PHELPS WARD

*For our second tale from the Victorian maritime era, we
turn to the American, Elizabeth Stuart Phelps Ward
(1844-1911). Born in Boston, she was the daughter of
Elizabeth Stuart Phelps, a popular writer of religious
novels of the time. She married the writer Herbert Ward,
and they collaborated on several books. One of her best
collections was* Men, Women And Ghosts *(1869) in which
she produced some absorbing studies of the moral ghost
story so very much in vogue in the middle of the nine-
teenth century. 'Kentucky's Ghost' comes from this collection and is a convincing story of life on board during those
violent days. The wealth of detail about life at sea makes
it hard to remember that it was in fact written by a
woman, while the supernatural climax is a good reminder
of just how skilled women were at writing ghost stories in
those days.*

True? Every syllable.

That was a very fair yarn of yours, Tom Brown, very fair for
a landsman, but I'll bet you a doughnut I can beat it.

It was somewhere about twenty years ago that we were
laying in for that particular trip to Madagascar.

We cleared from Long Wharf in the ship *Madonna*,—which
they tell me means, My Lady, and a pretty name it was; it was
apt to give me that gentle kind of feeling when I spoke it, which
is surprising when you consider what a dull old hull she was,
never logging over ten knots, and uncertain at that. It may
have been because of Moll's coming down once in a while in the

days that we lay at dock, bringing the boy with her, and sitting up on deck in a little white apron, knitting. She was a very good-looking woman, was my wife, in those days, and I felt proud of her,—natural, with the lads looking on.

I used to speak my thought about the name sometimes, when the lads weren't particularly noisy, but they laughed at me mostly. I was rough enough and bad enough in those days; as rough as the rest, and as bad as the rest, I suppose, but yet I seemed to have my notions a little different from the others. 'Jake's poetry', they called 'em.

We were loading for the East Shore trade. There isn't much of the genuine, old-fashioned trade left in these days, except the whisky branch. We had a little whisky in the hold, I remember, that trip, with a good stock of knives, red flannel, hand-saws, nails, and cotton. We were hoping to be at home again within the year. We were well-provisioned, and Dodd the cook made about as fair coffee as you're likely to find in the galley of a trader. As for our officers, when I say the less said of them the better, it ain't so much that I mean to be disrespectful as that I mean to put it tenderly. Officers in the merchant service, especially if it happens to be the African service, are quite often brutal men, and about as fit for their positions as if they'd been imported for the purpose a little indirect from Davy Jones's locker.

Well; we weighed, along the last of the month, in pretty good spirits. The *Madonna* was as seaworthy as any eight-hundred-tonner in the harbour, even if she was clumsy; we turned in, some sixteen of us or thereabouts, into the fo'castle,—a jolly set, mostly old messmates, and well content with one another; and the breeze was stiff from the west, with a fair sky.

The night before we were off, Molly and I took a walk upon the wharves after supper. I carried the baby. A boy, sitting on some boxes, pulled my sleeve as we went by, and asked me, pointing to the *Madonna*, if I would tell him the name of the ship.

'Find out for yourself,' said I, not overpleased to be interrupted.

'Don't be cross with him,' says Molly. The baby threw a kiss at the boy, and Molly smiled at him through the dark. I don't suppose I should ever have remembered the lubber from that day to this, except that I liked the looks of Molly smiling at him through the dark.

My wife and I said good-bye the next morning in a little sheltered place among the lumber on the wharf; she was one of your women who never like to do their crying before folks.

She climbed on the pile of lumber and sat down, a little flushed and quivery, to watch us off. I remember seeing her there with the baby till we were well down the channel. I remember noticing the bay as it grew cleaner, and thinking that I would break off swearing; and I remember cursing Bob Smart like a pirate within an hour.

The breeze held steadier than we'd looked for, and we'd made a good offing and discharged the pilot by nightfall. Mr Whitmarsh, the mate, was aft with the captain. The boys were singing a little; the smell of the coffee was coming up, hot and homelike, from the galley. I was up in the maintop when all at once there came a cry and a shout; and, when I touched deck, I saw a crowd around the fore-hatch.

'What's all this noise for?' says Mr Whitmarsh, coming up and scowling.

'A stow-away, sir! A boy stowed away!' said Bob, catching the officer's tone quick enough. He jerked the poor fellow out of the hold, and pushed him along to the mate's feet.

I say 'poor fellow', and you'd never wonder why if you'd seen as much of stowing away as I have.

I'd as lief see a son of mine in a Carolina slave-gang as to see him lead the life of a stow-away. What with the officers feeling that they've been taken in, and the men, who catch their cue from their superiors, and the spite of the lawful boy who was hired in the proper way, he don't have what you may call a tender time.

This chap was a little fellow, slight for his years, which might have been fifteen. He was palish, with a jerk of thin hair on his forehead. He was hungry, and homesick, and frightened. He looked about on all our faces, and then he cowered a little, and lay still just as Bob had thrown him.

'We—ell,' says Whitmarsh, very slow, 'if you don't repent your bargain before you go ashore, my fine fellow, —— me, if

I'm mate of the *Madonna*! and take that for your pains!'

Upon that he kicks the poor little lubber from quarter-deck to bowsprit and goes down to his supper. The men laugh a little, then they whistle a little, then they finish their song quite gay and well acquainted, with the coffee steaming away in the galley. Nobody has a word for the boy,—bless you, no!

I'll venture he wouldn't have had a mouthful that night if it had not been for me; and I can't say as I should have bothered myself about him, if it had not come across me sudden, while he sat there rubbing his eyes quite violent, that I had seen the lad before; then I remembered walking on the wharves, and him on the box, and Molly saying softly that I was cross to him.

Seeing that my wife had smiled at him, and my baby thrown a kiss at him, it went against me not to look after the little rascal a bit that night.

'But you've got no business here, you know,' said I; 'nobody wants you.'

'I wish I was ashore!' said he,—'I wish I was ashore!'

With that he begins to rub his eyes so very violent that I stopped. There was good stuff in him too; for he choked and winked at me, and made out that the sun was on the water and he had a cold in the head.

I don't know whether it was on account of being taken a little notice of that night, but the lad always hung about me afterwards; chased me round with his eyes in a way he had, and did odd jobs for me without the asking.

One night before the first week was out, he hauled alongside of me on the windlass. I was trying a new pipe so I didn't give him much notice for a while.

'You did this job up shrewd, Kent,' said I, by and by; 'how did you steer in?'—for it did not often happen that the *Madonna* got out of port with a stow-away in her hold.

'Watch was drunk; I crawled down ahind the whisky. It was hot and dark. I lay and thought how hungry I was,' says he.

'Friends at home?' says I.

Upon that he gives me a nod, very short, and gets up and walks off whistling.

The first Sunday out that chap didn't know any more what to do with himself than a lobster just put on to boil. Sunday's cleaning day at sea, you know. The lads washed up, and sat round, little knots of them, mending their trousers. Bob got out his cards. Me and a few mates took it comfortable under the to'gallant fo'castle (I being on watch below), reeling off the stiffest yarns we had in tow. Kent looked on a while, then listened to us a while, then walked off.

By and by says Bob, 'Look over there!' and there was Kent, sitting curled away in a heap under the stern of the long-boat. He had a book. Bob crawls behind and snatches it up, unbeknown, out of his hands; then he falls to laughing as if he would strangle, and gives the book a toss to me. It was a bit of Testament, black and old. There was writing on the yellow leaf which ran :—

'Kentucky Hodge,
'from his Affecshunate mother
'who prays, For you evry day, Amen.'

The boy turned red, then white, and straightened up quite sudden, but he never said a word, only sat down again, and let us laugh it out. I've lost my reckoning if he ever heard the last of it. He told me one day how he came by the name, but I forget exactly. Something about an old uncle died in Kentucky, and the name was moniment-like, you see. He used to seem cut up a bit about it at first, for the lads took to it famously; but he got used to it in a week or two, and seeing as they meant him no unkindness, took it quite cheery.

One other thing I noticed was that he never had the book about after that. He fell into our ways next Sunday more easy.

They don't take the Bible as a general thing, sailors don't; though I will say that I never saw the man at sea who didn't give it the credit of being an uncommon good yarn.

But I tell you, Tom Brown, I felt sorry for that boy. It's punishment enough for a little scamp like him leaving the honest shore, and folks at home that were a bit tender of him maybe, to rough it on a trader, learning how to slush down a back-stay, or tie knots with frozen fingers in a snow-squall.

But that's not the worst of it, by no means. If ever there was a cold-blooded, cruel man, with a wicked eye and a fist like a mallet, it was Job Whitmarsh. And I believe, of all the trips I've taken, him being mate of the *Madonna*, Kentucky found him at his worst. Bradley the second mate was none too gentle in his ways, but he never held a candle to Mr Whitmarsh. He took a spite to the boy from the first, and he kept it up to the last.

I've seen him beat that boy till the blood run down in little pools on deck; then send him up, all wet and red, to clear the to'sail halliards; and when, what with the pain and faintness, he dizzied a little, and clung to the ratlines, half blind, he would have him down and flog him till the cap'n interfered,—which would happen occasionally on a fair day when he had taken just enough to be good-natured. He used to rack his brains for the words he slung at the boy working quiet enough beside him. If curses had been a marketable article, Whitmarsh would have made his fortune. Then he used to kick the lad down the fo'castle ladder; he used to work him, sick or well, as he wouldn't have worked a dray-horse; he used to chase him all about the deck at the rope's end; he used to mast-head him for hours on the stretch; he used to starve him out in the hold. It didn't come in my line to be over-tender, but I turned sick at heart, Tom, more than once, looking on helpless, and me a great stout fellow.

I remember a thing McCallum said one night; McCallum was a Scot,—an old fellow with grey hair; told the best yarns on the fo'castle.

'Mark my words, shipmates,' says he. 'When Job Whitmarsh's time comes to go as straight to hell as Judas, that boy will bring his summons. Dead or alive, that boy will bring his summons.'

One day I recollect that the lad was sick with fever, and took to his hammock. Whitmarsh drove him on deck, and ordered him aloft. I was standing near by, trimming the spanker. Kentucky staggered for'ard a little and sat down. There was a rope's-end there, knotted three times. The mate struck him.

'I'm very weak, sir,' says he.

He struck him again. He struck him twice more. The boy fell over a little, and lay where he fell.

I don't know what ailed me, but all of a sudden I seemed

to be lying off Long Wharf, with Molly in a white apron with her shining needles, and the baby a-play in his red stockings about the deck.

'Think if it was him!' says she, or she seems to say,—'think if it was *him*!'

And the next I knew I'd let slip my tongue in a jiffy, and given it to the mate in a way I'll bet Whitmarsh never got before. And the next I knew after that they had the irons on me.

'Sorry about that, eh?' said he, the day before they took 'em off.

'*No*, sir,' says I. And I never was. Kentucky never forgot that. I had helped him occasional in the beginning,—learned him how to veer and haul a brace, let go or belay a sheet,—but let him alone generally speaking, and went about my own business. That week in irons I really believe the lad never forgot.

One Saturday night, when the mate had been uncommon furious that week—Kentucky turned on him, very pale and slow (I was up in the mizzen-top, and heard him quite distinct).

'Mr Whitmarsh,' says he,—'Mr Whitmarsh,'—he draws his breath in,—'Mr Whitmarsh,'—three times,—'you've got the power and you know it, and so do the gentlemen who put you here; and I'm only a stow-away boy, and things are all in a tangle, but *you'll be sorry yet for every time you've laid your hands on me!*'

He hadn't a pleasant look about the eyes either, when he said it.

Fact was, that first month on the *Madonna* had done the lad no good. He had a surly, sullen way with him, some'at like what I've seen about a chained dog. At the first, his talk had been clean as my baby's, and he would blush like any girl at Bob Smart's stories; but he got used to Bob, and pretty good, in time, at small swearing.

I don't think I should have noticed it so much if it had not been for seeming to see Molly and the knitting-needles, and the child upon the deck, and hearing her say, 'Think if it was *him*!'

Well, things went along just about so with us till we neared

the Cape. It's not a pretty place, the Cape, on a winter's voyage.
I can't say as I ever was what you may call scared after the first
time rounding it, but it's not a pretty place.

I don't seem to remember much about Kent till there come
a Friday at the first of December. It was a still day, with a
little haze, like white sand sifted across a sunbeam on a kitchen
table. The lad was quiet-like all day, chasing me about with
his eyes.

'Sick?' says I.

'No,' says he.

'Whitmarsh drunk?' says I.

'No,' says he.

A little after dark I was lying on a coil of ropes, napping it.
The boys were having the Bay of Biscay quite lively, and I
waked up on the jump in the choruses. Kent came up. He was
not singing. He sat down beside me, and first I thought I
wouldn't trouble myself about him, and then I thought I
would.

So I opens one eye at him encouraging. He crawls up a little
closer to me. It was rather dark where we sat, with a great
greenish shadow dropping from the mainsail. The wind was up
a little, and the light at helm looked flickery and red.

'Jake,' says he all at once, 'where's your mother?'

'In—heaven!' says I, all taken aback.

'Oh!' says he. 'Got any women-folks at home that miss you?'
asks he, by and by.

Said I, 'Shouldn't wonder.'

After that he sits still a little with his elbows on his knees;
then he peers at me sidewise a while; then said he, 'I s'pose
I've got a mother to home. I ran away from her.'

That was the first time he had ever spoke about his folks
since he came aboard.

'She was asleep down in the south chamber,' says he. 'I got
out the window. There was one white shirt she'd made for
meetin' and such. I've never worn it out here. I hadn't the
heart. It has a collar and some cuffs, you know. She had a headache making of it. She's been follering me round all day, sewing
that shirt. When I come in she would look up bright-like and
smiling. Father's dead. There ain't anybody but me. All day

long she's been follering of me round.'

So then he gets up, and joins the lads, and tries to sing a little; but he comes back very still and sits down. We could see the flickery light upon the boys' faces, and on the rigging, and on the cap'n, who was damning the bosun a little aft.

'Jake,' says he, quite low, 'look here. I've been thinking. Do you reckon there's a chap here—just one, perhaps—who's said his prayers since he came aboard?'

'*No!*' said I, quite short: for I'd have bet my head on it.

I can remember, as if it was this morning, just how the question sounded, and the answer. I can't seem to put it into words how it came all over me. The wind was turning brisk, and we'd just eased her with a few reefs; Bob Smart, out furling the flying jib, got soaked; me and the boy sitting silent, were spattered. I remember watching the curve of the great swells, mahogany colour, with the tip of white, and thinking how like it was to a big creature hissing and foaming at the mouth, and thinking all at once something about Him holding of the sea in a balance, and not a word bespoke to beg His favour respectful since we weighed our anchor, and the cap'n yonder calling on Him just that minute to send the *Madonna* to the bottom, if the bosun hadn't disobeyed his orders about the squaring of the after-yards.

'From his Affecshunate mother who prays, For you evry day, Amen,' whispers Kentucky, presently, very soft, 'The book's tore up. Mr Whitmarsh wadded his old gun with it. But I remember.'

Then said he; 'It's almost bedtime at home. She's setting in a little rocking-chair,—green one. There's a fire, and the dog. She sets all by herself.'

Then he begins again: 'She has to bring in her own wood now. There's a grey ribbon on her cap. When she goes to meetin' she wears a grey bonnet. She's drawed the curtains and the door is locked. But she thinks I'll be coming home sorry some day,—I'm sure she thinks I'll be coming home sorry.'

Just then there comes the order, 'Port watch ahoy! Tumble up there lively!' so I turns out, and the lad turns in, and the night settles down a little black, and my hands and head are full. Next day it blows a clean, all but a bank of grey, very thin and still which lay just abeam of us.

The sea looked like a great purple pincushion, with a mast or two stuck in on the horizon for the pins. 'Jake's poetry', the boys said that was.

By noon that little grey bank had grown up thick, like a wall. By sundown the cap'n let his liquor alone, and kept the deck. By night we were in chop-seas, with a very ugly wind.

'Steer small, there!' cries Whitmarsh, growing hot about the face,—for we made a terribly crooked wake, with a broad sheer, and the old hull strained heavily,—'steer small there, I tell you! Mind your eye now, McCallum, with your fore-sail! Furl the royals! Send down the royals! Cheerily, men! Where's that lubber Kent? Up with you, lively now!'

Kentucky sprang for'ard at the order, then stopped short. Anybody as knows a royal from an anchor wouldn't have blamed the lad. It's no play for an old tar, stout and full in size, sending down the royals in a gale like that; let alone a boy of fifteen years on his first voyage.

But the mate takes to swearing and Kent shoots away up,— the great mast swinging like a pendulum to and fro, and the reef-points snapping, and the blocks creaking, and the sails flapping to that extent as you wouldn't consider possible unless you'd been before the mast yourself. It reminded me of evil birds I've read of, that stun a man with their wings.

Kent stuck bravely as far as the cross-trees. There he slipped and struggled and clung in the dark and noise a while, then comes sliding down the back-stay.

'I'm not afraid, sir,' says he; 'but I cannot do it.'

For answer Whitmarsh takes to the rope's-end. So Kentucky is up again, and slips and struggles and clings again, and then lays down again.

At this the men begin to grumble a little.

'Will you kill the lad?' said I. I get a blow for my pains, that sends me off my feet none too easy; and when I rub the stars out of my eyes the boy is up again, and the mate behind him with the rope. Whitmarsh stopped when he'd gone far enough. The lad climbed on. Once he looked back. He never opened his lips; he just looked back. If I've seen him once since, in my thinking, I've seen him twenty times,—up in the shadow of the great grey wings, looking back.

After that there was only a cry, and a splash, and the *Madonna* racing along with the gale at twelve knots. If it had been the whole crew overboard, she could never have stopped for them that night.

'Well,' said the cap'n, 'you've done it now.'

Whitmarsh turned his back.

By and by, when the wind fell, and the hurry was over, and I had the time to think a steady thought, being in the morning watch, I seemed to see the old lady in the grey bonnet setting by the fire. And the dog. And the green rocking-chair. And the front door, with the boy walking in on a sunny afternoon to take her by surprise.

Then I remember leaning over to look down, and wondering if the lad were thinking of it too, and what had happened to him now, these two hours back, and just about where he was, and how he liked his new quarters, and many other strange and curious things.

And while I sat there thinking, the Sunday-morning stars cut through the clouds, and the solemn Sunday-morning light began to break upon the sea.

We had a quiet run of it, after that, into port, where we lay about a couple of months or so, trading off for a fair stock of palm-oil, ivory, and hides. The days were hot and purple and still. We hadn't what you might call a blow till we rounded the Cape again, heading for home.

It was just about the spot that we lost the boy that we fell upon the worst gale of the trip. It struck us quite sudden. Whitmarsh was a little high. He wasn't apt to be drunk in a gale, if it gave him warning sufficient.

Well, somebody had to furl the main-royal again, and he pitched on to McCallum. McCallum hadn't his beat for fighting out the royal in a blow.

So he piled away lively, up to the to'-sail yard. There, all of a sudden, he stopped. Next we knew he was down like lightning.

His face had gone very white.

'What's up with *you*?' roared Whitmarsh.

Said McCallum, *'There's somebody up there, sir.'*

Screamed Whitmarsh, 'You're an idiot!'

Said McCallum, very quiet and distinct: 'There's somebody up there, sir. I saw him quite plain. He saw me. I called up. He called down. Says he, *"Don't you come up!"* and hang me if I'll stir a step for you or any other man tonight!'

I never saw the face of any man alive go the turn that mate's face went. If he wouldn't have relished knocking the Scotchman dead before his eyes, I've lost my guess. Can't say what he would have done to the old fellow, if there'd been any time to lose.

He'd the sense left to see there wasn't overmuch, so he orders out Bob Smart direct.

Bob goes up steady, with a quid in his cheek and a cool eye. Half-way amid to'-sail and to'gallant he stops, and down he comes, spinning.

'Be drowned if there ain't!' said he. 'He's sitting square upon the yard. I never see the boy Kentucky, if he isn't sitting on that yard. *"Don't you come up!"* he cries out,—*"don't you come up!"*'

'Bob's drunk, and McCallum's a fool!' said Jim Welch, standing by. So Welch volunteers up, and takes Jaloffe with him. They were a couple of the coolest hands aboard—Welch and Jaloffe. So up they goes, and down they comes like the rest, by the run.

'He beckoned of me back!' says Welch. 'He hollered not to come up! not to come up!'

After that there wasn't a man of us would stir aloft, not for love nor money.

Well, Whitmarsh he stamped, and he swore, and he knocked us about furious; but we sat and looked at one another's eyes, and never stirred. Something cold, like a frost-bite, seemed to crawl along from man to man, looking into one another's eyes.

'I'll shame ye all, then, for a set of cowardly lubbers!' cries the mate; and what with the anger and the drink he was as good as his word, and up the ratlines in a twinkle.

In a flash we were after him,—he was our officer, you see,

and we felt ashamed,—me at the head, and the lads following after.

I got to the futtock shrouds, and there I stopped, for I saw him myself,—a palish boy, with a jerk of thin hair on his forehead; I'd have known him anywhere in this world or t'other. I saw him just as distinct as I see you, Tom Brown, sitting on that yard quite steady with the royal flapping like to flap him off.

I reckon I've had as much experience fore and aft, in the course of fifteen years at sea, as any man that ever tied a reef-point in a nor'easter; but I never saw a sight like that, not before nor since.

I won't say that I didn't wish myself on deck; but I stuck to the shrouds, and looked on steady.

Whitmarsh, swearing that that royal should be furled, went on and went up.

It was after that I hear the voice. It came from the figure of the boy upon the upper yard.

But this time it says, 'Come up! Come up!' And then, a little louder, 'Come up! Come up! Come up!' So he goes up, and next I knew there was a cry,—and next a splash,—and then I saw the royal flapping from the empty yard, and the mate was gone, and the boy.

Job Whitmarsh was never seen again.

The Weird Woman

ANONYMOUS

I have reserved this story till last, for it really sums up all that was good about the Victorian world of the macabre. The many elements that make it up—the family curse, the haunted house, the Christmas festivities amid swirling snow, the desperate chase on horseback—are characteristic of so many tales of terror of the period. Indeed, it could only have meant something in this period. To see what I mean, try bringing it up to date; try changing horse for car, or grange for semi-detached. The world of shadows and superstition that was Victorian England, so well depicted in this 1871 tale, was unique. While the foundations of so much of our present knowledge of subjects like medicine, public health, electricity, chemistry and agriculture, were being, if not laid, at least mapped out, people could still believe in the existence of devils and demons. And why not? A good ghost story is pure entertainment. It was not until well into the twentieth century that ghost stories began to have a deeper significance and to become allegorical; in fact, to lose their charm. No mental effort is required to read 'The Weird Woman', no seeking for hidden meanings; there are no complexities of plot, no allegory on the state of the world. And so it should be. At what other point in literary history could a man, standing over the body of his fiancée, say such a line as this:

'Speak, hound! Or, by heaven, this night shall witness two murders instead of one!'

Those were the days.

My brother Oswald and I had long been orphans. Our parents —of good position, but small means—having succeeded in placing us tolerably well in life—I, as an officer in the Indian army, my brother as a barrister—died, leaving us little more than their blessing.

We had no nearer relation to us than ourselves—neither sister, sweetheart, nor wife—and our mutual affection was great. In fact, we were all in all to each other, having no more family ties than Cicely Mostyn, a cousin, who dwelt in Scotland, and an eccentric, rich, old bachelor uncle, the head of the Tregethans, and the possessor of Holme Grange, North Wales, an estate which had belonged to our race for centuries.

Having stated that Uncle Jaffery was rich, old, and a bachelor, it follows that we nephews paid him much deference, and regarded with veneration, as with curiosity, the iron safe, which, on our visits to the Holme, our worthy relative, with a gloating chuckle informed us held his last will and testament.

'It *must* come to one of you—to one,' he ever concluded. 'Wouldn't you like to know which? There'll be rare fighting and scratching. You are true Tregethans. I only regret dying, because I shan't see it!'

In vain we strove to discover which of us he most favoured. Had we not felt his pride of family would prevent it, we might have feared his bequeathing his wealth to a hospital, and cutting us off without a shilling.

As it was, we never got a penny from him while living, but struggled on as we could, I, with my pay, Oswald with his briefs, till the joyous—yes, I own that was how we regarded it—intelligence reached us that Uncle Jaffery had died suddenly in his bed.

No sooner, however, was the breath out of the old man's body, than his eccentricity and dislike to his kin began to display themselves. Only Oswald and I were to attend his funeral; not a woman was to be present, while his coffin was to be kept above ground till midnight of Christmas Day, when it was to be deposited in the family vault. In conclusion, he peremptorily ordered that his will should not be opened nor read till an exact twelvemonth, to the very hour, after that date, when a ball was to be given, and all the neighbouring gentry invited. During the intervening period, Holme Grange was to be shut up, the old housekeeper, who had been in the Tregethans' service from childhood, being left in sole charge. A month, however, before the prescribed year expired, Oswald, myself, and our cousin Cicely were to make the Grange our home.

To uninformed ears the latter command appeared simple enough, but to those who knew the ancient traditions of our race it bore a deep significance; for those ancient traditions affirmed that no two Tregethans, after they had reached man or woman's estate, could dwell many weeks together under the roof of Holme Grange without dire quarrels ensuing, which, in past ages, had ended in a life's enmity, or death. The oldest inhabitant knew it as 'The Tregethans' Curse'.

Oswald and I, conscious of the strong affection binding us, had frequently laughed at these old women's tales, and as the eventful Christmas drew near, jestingly wrote that, if we quarrelled with any one, it must be with Cicely Mostyn, whom we remembered as a bright-eyed, fair-complexioned, golden-haired lassie of six, who had termed us 'rough laddies', and who had needed high bribery and corruption, in the form of fruit and sugar-plums, before she would consent to be kissed.

One bleak, wintry, November night, just returned from India, I was being carried express through the English counties to Wales. The allotted time had expired, and I was hastening to the dead man's appointed rendezvous for the living.

The snow had fallen heavily during the day—so heavily as often to impede our progress, and once or twice even threatened to extinguish the engine fires. Trees and hedgerows were laden with it; but November had covered it from view by a veil of fog, till the arrival of December and the keen north wind.

At the station I found the carriage waiting to drive me to the Grange, four miles distant. The horses, like the coachman, were fat from long idleness, and dragged slowly through the heavy country lanes, till—the fog everywhere, the snow only glinting occasionally through it, and the wind whistling over the bleak hills—I thought the Grange would never come in view. I knew the turn of the road at which it generally could be seen; but now we had proceeded more than half-way up the oak avenue before it loomed forth from the dull grey night.

It was a vast building of red brick, somewhat of the Elizabethan style, with modern additions added quaintly here and there. The roof was gabled, the chimneys eccentric, while, above all, rose a bell tower.

The bell yet remained, though the rope had long rotted away; and when the rushing hurricanes from the hills swung it creakingly to and fro, occasionally the ponderous clapper striking the rusty sides, sent forth a low, hollow groaning sound, especially ghostly in the night season.

The reception-rooms were in the front—the more homely at the back; thus, as the carriage drew up, not a light broke the vast frontage to bid me welcome, while the footman's knock reverberated mournfully in the large hall within.

In a moment, however, many lights gleamed, and the door opening, the old housekeeper stood curtseying to receive me. 'And so you are the first at the old place, Master Frank? You are the first, and you are welcome!' she remarked, as—I having warmly shaken her mittened hands—taking a lamp from the servant, she led the way to the back of the house. 'Mr Oswald comes by the last train, and Miss Cicely does not arrive until tomorrow.'

We traversed a long, high corridor; and the light, casting our shadows in ghostly proportions on the walls, dark with age, gave an awesome, chilling aspect to one returning after years of absence to the home of his forefathers. The place, too, owing to its being so long shut up, possessed a damp, musty smell, which crept through the blood as did the fog without.

'It's been a dull time here, Master Frank, and I'm glad it's over, and that Tregethan voices are again to sound in the old rooms. I've made everything as comfortable as I could.'

In speaking, she threw wide a door, disclosing beyond the family dining apartment—the ceiling low, the walls oak-panelled, that reflected the glorious fire of logs which crackled on the spacious hearth, while a lamp burned brightly on the centre table.

The aspect, so different to the other portion, cheered me, as wine cheers a fainting man; and, advancing, I exclaimed,

'Ah, this looks like home indeed! Now, my dear old friend, come and tell me all the news; it's long since we two had a chat together.'

'Always the same—always the same, Master Frank,' replied the housekeeper, highly gratified—'ever ready to flatter an old woman by listening to her chattering. But there, I'll do your bidding. True the place was your ancestors', and must interest you. So there is the mulled claret, and now, Master Frank, you sit down and get warm, while I sit here.'

We each took our seat, and garrulously the old lady talked, while I listened.

Meanwhile the wind, which had risen in fury rattled the window-panes, and the fog began to lift—not without a struggle, though growing brighter one moment, to be denser the next.

'I should think Oswald will scarcely risk the road tonight,' I abruptly remarked. 'The wind is a tempest; while once or twice I fancy I have seen snowflakes.'

'Maybe, he'll stop the night at Llandudyn; and perhaps it's better, though we at Holme count nothing of these storms. We are used to them, and the Grange, is strong enough to stand their fury,' rejoined the housekeeper. Then, with a cough, as if to dismiss the subject, she continued some domestic piece of intelligence which I, thinking of my brother, had interrupted.

Another hour passed. The Grange clock had beaten out ten; and, owing partly to the heat of the fire, partly to the rather prosy talk of my companion, I was dozing in my chair, when I was aroused by a sharp, startling cry.

I glanced quickly up, and my surprise changed to alarm, as my eyes rested on the housekeeper.

She sat erect in her chair, rigid as in death, her head half-turned over her shoulder to the window, her face corpse-like in hue, her lips parted, her grey eyes dilated, and one hand raised as to arrest attention. Her attitude was that of attentive listening; her expression denoted unspeakable horror.

Had she gone mad?

Pulling myself up on my seat, I gazed at her in perplexity. Was it a case of catalepsy? Should I address her? Should I summon aid?

Before I could decide, she had sprung to her feet, her horror increasing; and darting to my side, as I also arose, clinging to me in mortal terror, her face still bent on the large recessed lattice window, she cried, 'Oh Master Frank, did you not hear it? Heaven aid us! Listen, listen! There—it's there! Ah, woe to the house of Tregethan! Blood—blood is again to stain its threshold!'

I stood utterly bewildered. What did the old woman mean? Had she, indeed, lost her reason? She was trembling like a leaf.

'My good Mrs Lloyd,' I ejaculated, 'what, in heaven's name, is the matter?'

'Matter? What, are you a Tregethan, and cannot hear it?' she asked, lifting her white face to mine. 'There—there, it is coming again! Listen!'

Leaning forward, I instinctively obeyed.

There certainly was a singular sound in the storm—a strange, floating, weird shriek—blending with the tempest, yet not of it.

'I hear what you mean,' said I; 'but it is only the wind among the hills. The storm is terrific.'

She shook her head with a smile.

'Wind?' she repeated. 'No, no; I've lived long enough among the hills, and heard tempests enough to know the difference between them and that cry. I tell you, when it is heard, evil and bloodshed is coming to the Tregethans. I am seventy now, but only once have I heard it before: then its warning was verified. It was before you, Master Frank, were born.'

'Do you mean,' I asked impressed, despite myself, and catching so much of her awe as to speak in whispers, 'when my uncle Jaffery and my father quarrelled?'

'Yes; it ended in a foolish, boyish duel in the plantation. Still, blood was shed; but, praise to heaven, that time life was spared. Ah, hark! It comes; three—three times—and nearer, nearer!' cried the old woman, frantically wringing her hands. 'The Lord be with us! Perhaps *she* will come; then bitter is the woe indeed!'

'She—whom?' I asked.

'The Weird Woman.'

Despite the effect the singular scene was beginning to have

over me, I could not prevent a smile; but it speedily vanished. The housekeeper, approaching the table, had extinguished the lamp; then, returning, knelt crouching on the hearthrug at my feet, as if for protection, as, extending her aged, wrinkled hand towards the casement, she said, in a low, thrilling whisper, 'Look, Master Frank, at the window. Never move your gaze from it, if you would see her, for the Woman with the Dead Eyes goes by like a flash. Wait.'

Carried away by her strange manner, as though my will was subservient to hers, I complied.

A death-like silence reigned in the apartment, illumined only by the fire-light, which threw grotesque forms on the dark panelling, gave movement to the pictures of my ancestors suspended upon it, and darted bright, shifting lights on the broad lattice, beyond which was darkness, and the beating, howling wind.

I kept my eyes riveted upon the window. I no longer seemed to have a will of my own. A spell was on me. Minutes were as hours, marked by the quick breathing of the old housekeeper at my feet.

As I looked, the pall of darkness was abruptly broken; and —yes—I swear it—amid the gloom, there swelled out the floating form of a woman, her trailing garments of a dull red brown, saturated by rain, clung about her limbs; her long, red hair, streamed over her partly exposed shoulders. Her face was turned towards the room—towards us.

What a face!—cold, colourless, deathly white, as the hueless lips—with two large, dark, awful eyes gleaming forth, dilated as by some unearthly horror—blended with malignant triumph. But what was more awful yet, the eyes were dead fixed, staring, as if plucked from the face of a corpse—a face to freeze the blood of the strongest—to overturn the brain of the weakest.

The housekeeper shrieked aloud, and buried her face in her hands, while with an ejaculation of fear, I sank into my chair.

The whole had passed in a few seconds. The Weird Woman, with the Dead Eyes had indeed flashed by; but, ere she vanished, the long, bony, narrow hand had been directed at *me*; and, shivering as with an ague, I cowered under the icy stare.

The logs falling together aroused me; and angry, both with

myself and the housekeeper, I leaped up, exclaiming, 'Why, Mrs Lloyd, what an absurd donkey you have been making me by these old tales; listening to such stories the mind's eye could conjure up anything. Pray, let us have the lamp again.'

She looked fixedly at me, as quietly she arose.

'You *saw* it, Master Frank,' she said. 'There is evil coming. Pray heaven it is not to you!'

'Nonsense!' I retorted, irritably. 'I could swear you had been reared among the hills. I gazed long enough to people the air with phantoms, and make my eyes ache to bursting. There, take off the glasses. Where is a light?'

'Stay, Master Frank'—and she laid her hand impressively on my arm, as I bent to the logs—'promise not to tell a soul of this. It will be better not.'

'Tell! not very likely, my good old lady, that I shall seek to make myself a laughing-stock,' I rejoined. 'Your claret was rather too abundant, I imagine, for its fumes to create such visions.'

Mrs Lloyd shook her head.

'You are trying to deceive yourself, Master Frank. You wish *not* to believe it; but mark my words, before the year is out, you'll have cause to recall this night. Hark! here comes your brother.'

Carriage wheels were sounding in the avenue. Seizing the lamp in my hand, I hastened to the door.

It had been already opened as I reached it.

Oswald was coming up the broad steps, the snow falling about him.

'My dear Oswald!' I exclaimed, hurrying forward. 'So, here you are, old fellow!'

'Yes,' he laughed, 'like a certain personage, when he quits the lower regions—in a perfect whirlwind.'

He extended his hand. As I took it in mine, the bell in the tower gave one prolonged boom, which, echoing dolefully, fled away to the hills, where it was broken and lost.

I could not suppress the start it caused me. There appeared something ominous in the occurrence. As I turned to conduct Oswald to the dining-room, my eyes rested on the housekeeper's features. They were perfectly white. She, too, had noticed the chill boom of the bell in the tower.

I found Oswald much changed; study, and the hard fight for gentlemanly subsistence, seemed to have bitten into his nature. Two wrinkles had sprung up from the eyebrows to the forehead, adding to the intellectuality of the countenance. The small mouth was graver, while the dark eyes were less mirthful, with an inner look, as of one brooding on silent thought. This, however, seemed to wear off as we conversed together on past, present, and future, enjoying the sumptuous supper prepared by the housekeeper, who did not appear again that night.

The hour was late before we separated; and soon after, wearied by my day's journey, I was sleeping heavily.

Towards morning, when slumber grew lighter, I was troubled by a strange dream. It seemed to come in rapid snatches—nothing was continuous. All I felt certain upon was, that Oswald and the Weird Woman played parts in it.

Once I was battling my way over a barren waste, the wind and rain dashing full in my teeth. Yet I never swerved. It appeared compulsory that I should hurry on, though my feet felt bound with lead. Abruptly, a river was before me; there was no way to cross it, save by swimming. I plunged in. The water pressed so warm and heavy about my limbs that, with difficulty, I could move. Then the moon broke forth, and with a scream of horror, I saw that the river was one of blood, whilst Oswald, his face white, his dark eyes hateful, was regarding me with fiendish malice from the bank.

I scrambled out, sick and dizzy. My brother had vanished, but I hastened on. Then came a fearful rushing of waters in my ears; again Oswald and the Woman with the Dead Eyes were there; but a mist enveloped what took place. When I awoke, I could remember nothing. I was merely conscious that, despite the water being frozen in the caraffes and ewers, I was bathed in perspiration, and hanging half out of bed, my head within a few inches of the floor.

As my eyes opened, I was trembling violently, like one seized by panic. Speedily recovering myself, and assuming a more comfortable position, I drew the clothes about me, for I soon began to shiver, and exclaimed, 'Confound that old house-

keeper, for giving me the nightmare! Whatever was I dreaming about?'

But all my efforts to recall it were in vain. During the ensuing morning—nay, for *days* after—the dream haunted me, bringing with it a vague dread; but at the very instant I believed the subject of it was becoming lucid, a cloud enveloped it, giving it the shape of a reflection in a blurred mirror.

By the next morning the fog had disappeared before the hurricane wind, which, proud of its victory, had subsided into a low, purring breeze, and the sun shone out with a warmth that recalled the sweet-smelling, fallen leaves of autumn. It was just the right day for the advent of youth and beauty, and Cicely Mostyn was to arrive that morning, under the chaperonage of Mrs Bruce, an elderly connection on the father's side.

Oswald and I had gone on the terrace to await her, but by some mistake the ladies missed the carriage sent to the station, and, taking a fly, had dismounted at the lodge-gates to walk up the avenue. Thus the first sight we had of Cicely Mostyn, was when—while we were chatting carelessly, cigar in mouth, listening for the carriage-wheels—she suddenly emerged from under the shadow of the oaks, into the full sunlight, within a few paces of the terrace—Mrs Bruce leaning on her arm.

Was this the prim, staid little 'lassie, wi' the lint-white locks', about whom Oswald and I had been recalling many a childish incident? This young, beautiful girl, her soft cheek dimpled like a summer brook, who, stopping abruptly, half-shyly, half-curiously, regarded us?

Ah, Cissy, Cissy! that was the moment to me, which a man never forgets, whatever be his alloted span. It was the joy of heaven comprised in one delicious, earthly second.

Cicely Mostyn was about middle height, and only eighteen. Her form was slim and graceful; every move, every pose displaying new charms. Her complexion was transparently clear, flushed with a delicate rose tint. Her eyes were dark, arch, mirthful, yet tender; her mouth a Cupid's treasury of smiles and man-traps; her hair like threads of brightest shimmering gold. But why describe her? Suffice it, that from that moment

Cicely Mostyn was all the world to me.

I could not remove my gaze from her, not even to note the effect her loveliness had had on Oswald; but, side by side, we advanced to give our cousin greeting.

Cicely was muffled up in furs; her face peeping from beneath a coquettish hat, trimmed with blue ribbons, and when she spoke, it was with the most delightful hint of the Scottish accent imaginable. Winningly, yet bashfully, she returned our salutation, then introduced her companion.

Mrs Bruce was stout, with a matronly dignity; had soft, grey hair, bright happy eyes, and a face to smile at youth's innocent follies, as if the fleeting years had not wholly made her forget that period in her own existence. She was a kindly adviser and friend.

With two such pleasant additions to the Holme Grange household, it need scarcely be said that the days passed rapidly. We talked, we played, we sang, we walked, rode, drove, and skated, when the weather permitted it. All the while, Christmas came creeping towards us—the Christmas that was to proclaim to whom the Holme should belong, and as each moment of the present became past, my love grew stronger.

I made no effort to hide my passion. It was as open as the natural timidity that a man truly in love experiences in the presence of her he adores, will permit; especially when indifferent persons are by. What my faltering tongue refused to utter, however, I left with full confidence to my eyes and fingers. The one was eloquent in ardent glances, the other in trembling touches.

There was, though, a circumstance which gave me considerable uneasiness. I had a presentiment—nay, more than a presentiment—that Oswald and I were rivals—that he, too, loved Cicely Mostyn. His disposition was the reverse of mine. The more strongly he felt, the more grave and silent he became. This it was which aroused my suspicions. I knew that did he love, it would be with all the secret intensity of a studious, rather morbid, mind, which had the habit of brooding—brooding over joys as well as griefs. I was aware, also, that jealousy formed a strong portion of my brother's character.

All absorbed in my love for Cicely, it was not at once that

I suspected our being rivals; then, as I pondered upon the probability, the idea flashed across my brain.

Did Uncle Jaffery know of our cousin's surpassing beauty? Had he, in his dislike to his brother's children, planned this month's compulsory residence together, in hopes that enmity might spring from it? Had he not hated women? Was it not said a woman had been the cause of that duel in the plantation —the wound received in which Uncle Jaffery had never forgiven?

I have stated I loved Oswald dearly; therefore, there may be some persons who, believing in the generosity of strong affection, were they writing this story as a novel, might make me, out of my feeling for my brother, seek to overcome my passion for Cicely. But *I* don't believe in love's generosity. When analysed it is, on the contrary, one of the most selfish passions in creation. It absorbs us entirely within its influence; and I would sooner have died than yield Cicely—even to Oswald.

Indeed, after the suspicion, I the more openly paid our cousin court, hoping, by being the first in the field, it would make the right mine to bid him withdraw. It may here be hinted that the lady herself was the fittest person to decide that matter. Well, I know it; and she had decided. Yes; though not a word had been spoken, though she mirthfully rather held me off when I sought to touch upon the subject, I felt instinctively Cicely returned my love.

Christmas at last arrived—the eventful Christmas. It had lost much interest to me; I seemed to care little whether I was left a full share or nothing of my uncle's wealth, so that I could call Cicely wife; and I resolved that on this night, which was to decide so much, this also should be decided.

According to Uncle Jaffery's singular will, invitations had been issued to all the neighbouring gentry, and the Holme ball-room was crowded, its old walls echoing to the spirit-inspiring sounds of music and women's silvery laughter. Every window was a blaze of light, and cast bright reflections on the snow laying thickly without, till, at a certain radius, the darkness and the pine-trees closed it in.

To look at the old place, which for a year and more had been so dull and tenantless, it reminded one of a desolate old

age being suddenly re-endowed with youthful vigour. The case-
ments winked from beneath their heavy ivy brows; mirth
floated on the night air; all seemed happiness. It was to be a
merry Christmas, indeed.

Even Oswald appeared affected by the general good fellow-
ship the season ever brings. For the few days previously he had
kept much to his own room, had been silent and thoughtful in
company, and on being addressed, returned but short replies,
especially when I was the interlocutor. On being questioned,
he gave as the reason that his mind was engaged by a difficult
brief, containing a point of old law, which, could he fully
master, would not only win his cause, but make him a high
name in his profession.

This day, however, his bearing was totally changed. He
laughed and jested with the best, though in an excited way;
he hung about Cicely's skirts wherever she went.

'Confound him! would he have her all to himself?' I mentally exclaimed, in some annoyance. Then added, compassion-
ately, 'Poor fellow, does he not also love her—and he,
hopelessly? Poor Oswald! for—as surely as if her own sweet
lips had uttered it—I know Cicely is mine!'

Nevertheless, however certain of his mistress's favour, a
lover does not like to see his rival, though unsuccessful, en-
grossing all her attention; and I rejoiced at my determination to
speak that night; for, on our engagement being *un fait accompli*,
none could dispute with me the place by her side. The evening
was at its merriest, when I led Cicely from the ball-room, for
the ostensible purpose of showing her the northern lights,
which were flashing brilliantly. As we passed through an
ante-room, I wrapped a huge, thick plaid about her, and insisted
on her putting her little feet in a pair of snow boots.

Then, opening the glass doors, we stood on the terrace
together, watching the dancers. I cannot say I saw them
much; for my heart was beating right up in my throat, my
brain felt confused, and my usual easy flow of speech was
wanting. I yet feared to begin my confession, lest I might be
interrupted—for the servants were passing to and fro in the
inner room; so, declaring we should see the aurora borealis far
better from the rising ground at the other side of the plantation,

I drew her small hand through my arm, and led her down to the path, which had been well swept from snow. I do not in the least imagine she believed anything about the better view. I think she divined my purpose; for she could no longer meet my glance. She trembled, just a little, and I own her few sentences were not uttered with much wisdom.

At the other side of the plantation, we stopped and regarded the moving columns of light, as we had intended; but Cicely's little head now nestled confidingly close to my shoulder, and my arm encircled her waist. She looked at the heavens; I preferred to see their reflection in her eyes. The avowal had been made under the pine-trees—and I was not rejected. At that moment, Cicely and I were the happiest beings in all creation.

I don't know whether it is the same with every one as with myself; but I never feel my face near a pretty woman's, but some magnetic influence attracts my lips to hers. The law of adhesion, I suppose. In my betrothed's case, I saw no reason to suppress the impulse; so stooped just a little, and the deed was done.

She instantly broke away, her dimpled face suffused with mirth and blushes.

'For shame, sir!' she exclaimed; 'for such rudeness, you must do penance. So stay here, while I return to the Grange; I would not be seen entering the house with such a monster for worlds. Now, mind, do not move for five minutes, at least.'

She shook her pretty finger authoritatively, bent her dark eyes, radiant with love, upon me, then the tree-trunks closed about her graceful figure.

I never again saw Cicely Mostyn alive!

Determined to obey her, to prove how I heeded her every word—I waited, literally not stirring from the spot. As strictly as a devotee, I took out my watch to count the minutes. What a fund of exquisite happiness was centred in my being; my veins were dancing; my temples throbbing with it. I dreamed of seeing Cicely speedily in the ball-room; of beholding the conscious blush dye her cheek when our eyes met, and she recalled the stolen kiss.

The imaginary meeting made me forget our present separation. My eyes were still fixed on the watch, its hands having

moved over ten minutes unnoticed—for the sweet face floated between me and it—when the stillness of the Christmas night was broken by a fearful shriek.

Oh, heavens! I recognized it as Cicely's. In an instant, I was dashing in the direction. It did not come from the path we had traversed, but deeper among the trees. She had, no doubt, in her flight, taken the wrong way.

'Cicely! Cicely!' I shouted, as I ran; but no answer came. I searched the paths, the bushes; I called again and again— not a trace, not a sound. Could I have been deceived? I had begun to imagine so, when I reached a small, open space, where, upon the white snow, which had been scattered as by restlessly-moving feet, I saw—a dark, red stain! It was blood!

My brain reeled; my heart grew sick with a dread I dared not trust myself to analyse. I sought for other marks. Heaven help me! I found them. Found to lose, to find them again, till I emerged upon the broad expanse of snow before the front of the Holme. Here they were more distinct; but I needed them no longer as a guide.

An object extended on the white ground, just within the brilliant light from the ball-room windows, at once attracted my attention. With a heart as chill as the icicles on the trees about me, I sprang forward; then, with a great cry, sank on my knees by it.

It was Cicely Mostyn—my beloved—my darling—*dead*! She laid her face and bosom on the snow; one fair arm extended to the house, as if she had fallen in the very act of summoning aid. The dark, red stain was all about her now; and, as with passionate words, lifting her, I turned her towards me, the plaid falling away, I beheld the crimson life-stream welling forth from a ghastly wound that disfigured her soft, white neck.

Again I shrieked for help, and this time so loudly, that no music could drown my voice. But, impatient in my frenzy, starting up, with my clenched hands I dashed in the panes of the glass doors upon the startled guests.

I need not enter fully into the scene which ensued, the mirth that had so rapidly been turned to mourning. Rapidly I recounted what had transpired; aid was summoned, and the

awe-struck guests, all in their bright, festive attire, grouped around, waiting it. A change had come over me. I no longer raved. I did not even speak. A dumb, stony expression of horror on my face—I stood, with folded arms, mutely gazing at the beautiful corpse at my feet. The night was about us; the dark pine-trees shut us in like a pall. Light was nowhere but in the holly-decorated ball-room, which, in yellow rays, streamed forth on the dead, on me, upon the guests, and the aghast servants huddled at one side, with the old housekeeper in the front.

They had once attempted to move the body, but, with a ferocity that alarmed them, I had bade them desist. Medical help was coming, but I knew my darling had been dead, even before I reached her.

Suddenly I looked up, not noticing how all shrunk away from my wild, haggard countenance.

'My brother,' I said, hoarsely, for my lips felt glued together. 'Where is Oswald?'

There was a pause, then I saw one of the servants, a groom, whispering to the other.

'Stand forth!' I exclaimed, in a tone he dared not disobey. 'Tell me—where is Oswald Tregethan?'

They now guessed what I had known from the first—that my brother was the murderer!

In evident trepidation the groom complied, but hesitated to speak. Striding forward, I seized him by the throat. In my fury at his silence, I could have killed him.

'Speak, hound!' I cried, 'or, by heaven, this night shall witness two murders instead of one!'

Terrified for his own safety he spoke; and I learned that, about a quarter of an hour previously, Oswald, with a scared, ashen face, had dashed into the stables, ordered a horse to be saddled, and at a break-neck pace, had plunged through the darkness towards the hills.

What had taken place between him and Cicely, I never knew; but I suppose he must have met her, and avowed his passion, when, finding its fruitlessness—that I was the successful suitor—he, in the moment of jealous, disappointed passion, must have dealt her that death-blow.

My lips compressed more and more, as I listened, but on the man's ending, I said, quietly releasing him, 'Go, instantly, and saddle the fleetest horse for me.'

He rose to obey, and I was about to follow, when the old housekeeper, dropping on the snow, and clinging to my knees, cried, 'No, no, Master Frank; there is that on your face fearful to look upon. This must not be—it must not—there has been blood enough shed this night. It was destiny, you nor he could not have prevented it. Remember, the Weird Woman of Tregethan! Wait!—wait, at least, till morning!'

I did not stay to answer. Flinging her aside, I hurried to the stables. At the housekeeper's entreaty, some of the guests sought to stay me; but the expression of the features I turned upon them, startled them back.

Aiding in the saddling of the horse, I led him out. Taking a stable lantern, I tracked the feet of Oswald's horse to the road. As the groom had stated, he had gone towards the hills. Throwing down the lantern, I leaped into my saddle, and plunging my spurs deep in the animal's side, pursued. It was a blind—a fearful ride; but I never hesitated. I blessed the moon for rising. I cursed the dark, floating clouds she brought with her. I cursed the snow, which hindered my hearing Oswald in advance.

An hour, and I was still riding on, now among the hills. I never thought whether I might be wrong—I *knew* I was right! Strange, too, but the country I was traversing—even the occurrence seemed as one acted long, long before, in that past which appears to have been another life in another world before our birth; and this was but the mechanical repetition of it? What was that? That sound amid the silence? His horse's feet? No; it was but the dashing of water. I was approaching some cataract or fall among the hills; there were many such. It was distant yet; but I was nearing it. Was I ever to overtake him?

Yes.

Even as I mentally put the question, the clouds abruptly drifted from the moon, and fifty paces before me, on the same road, was Oswald.

Uttering a cry of joy which was fiendish in its rapture,

I urged my horse to greater speed. My brother heard me—
looked once behind—then also increased his pace; but I shudder
now at the satisfaction I then experienced when I noticed his
horse flagged, and, indeed, was already dead beat, I *must* reach
him—nothing could prevent me!

The road, too, was a steep incline; its course being over a
hill; consequently I gained rapidly on Oswald. The dash of
waters sounded to me now very close, but I did not heed them.
'Where he goes,' I thought, 'I can follow!' Though each second
I shortened the distance between us, yet he was far enough
in advance to reach before me the crest of the hill, over which
he disappeared.

This drove me to frenzy. When I could not see him, I
dreaded his escaping. And I also rapidly reached the top.
Oswald was not twenty yards off. I shouted with triumphant
exultation, and spurred on.

The way, bordered by stunted bushes, was now level, and
within forty paces ended in a rustic bridge, spanning the water-
fall I had heard, and which I now remembered dashed down
from a great height between two hills, its bed being composed of rugged boulders and huge masses of rock.

A new fear seized me. I was aware how fragile were these
country bridges, and I thought if Oswald were to reach the
other side and swing it from its hold, further pursuit would
be impossible.

Encouraging my horse by whip, word, and hand, I resolved
to prevent his doing this. A moment longer, and I was close
upon him—so close that he must have heard my breathing,
as I heard his. He looked quickly back. Heaven, forgive me!
but if I live a hundred years, I shall never forget that white,
ghastly, affrighted face. At the instant, I felt no pity.

'Murderer!' I cried—'assassin!'

Then the old, old love rushed upon me—the love of our
boyhood and youth, when we had been all in all to each other;
and wildly I shouted, 'Oswald! brother! come back!'

Why was this sudden revulsion of feeling? I will explain.
As I had uttered the accusatory words, Oswald, with a cry had,
by a rapid pressure of his knees, caused his jaded beast to
spring forward beyond my reach on to the bridge. The frail,

rude construction trembled under the sudden shock; but there might have been no danger, had not the over-ridden brute, stumbling, fallen with all its weight against the sapling which served for a hand-rail. I saw it bend—snap—and horse and rider hung helpless above the abyss!

There was a fearful moment, that seemed like whole years of compressed agony, when Oswald, perceiving his danger, struggled manfully against it; but even as I bounded forward to lend my aid, the bridge fell, and I beheld my brother's form, blended in a confused mass with the horse, plunge down into the tumbling waters. He flung wide his arms, but yet uttered no sound. The shriek that echoed among the hills was from my lips. *My* shriek mingled with *another's*. Yes; in the air above came that sad, moaning, yet exultant, cry I had heard on the first night of my arrival at The Grange. My blood chilled to stagnation. I looked up as I reared my horse on its haunches, to save myself from Oswald's fate; and there, floating over us and the waters, was the Weird Woman with the Dead Eyes.

Her frightfully dilated pupils were fixed on me. The bony arm and hand were stretched down towards where my brother had disappeared. Then I knew where I had seen all this before. It had been the subject of my dream.

I remembered no more. Two hours after, I was found in a fainting fit, which ended in brain fever, by my horse's side, and in dangerous proximity to the edge of the water-fall; only by a miracle I had escaped death. My poor brother's body, and his horse's were found lifeless among the rocks.